DEATH IN THE PICTURE

A Cyrus Finnegan Mystery

DEATH IN THE PICTURE

MONCRIEFF WILLIAMSON

BEAUFORT BOOKS, INC.
New York/Toronto

No character in this book is intended to
represent any actual person; all incidents of the
story are entirely fictional in nature.

Library of Congress Cataloging in Publication Data
Williamson, Moncrieff.
Death in the picture.
I. Title.
PR9199.3.W493D4   1982   813'.54   82-4318
ISBN 0-8253-0104-1   AACR2

Published in the United States by Beaufort Books, Inc.,
New York. Published simultaneously in Canada by
General Publishing Co. Ltd.

Printed in the U.S.A.
First Edition
10 9 8 7 6 5 4 3 2 1
Designed by Ellen LoGiudice

For Eve, Michael, Carolyn, and Susan

Cuilibet in arte sua credendum est
Every person is to be trusted in his own art

Prologue

Mary half opened her eyes. She watched the figure tiptoe through the cottage bedroom. She knew perfectly well it was Anthony, her crazy husband, prowling in on her like this. He was becoming odder every day.

"Tony?"

"Sorry, pet. Tried not to wake you."

"What's the time?"

"Half past one."

"You bastard! Switch on the light. You get later and later."

"Sorry, old dear. Bus broke down. Go back to sleep."

"How the hell can I? Bastard. That's what you are. A middle-aged bastard." She disliked swearing like this. Went against her scruples, her childhood training by strict Methodist parents. "Why won't you tell me what you're up to? What new crazy scheme is taking priority over our marriage?"

9

"All in good time, pet. You'll see. I won't let you down again. This time we'll be in at the kill. Everything I do is for you. You know that."

"But the excuses! Your bus is always breaking down. The company should take it off the road."

"Just be patient. And don't be so damned nosy, you bitch. Now go to sleep."

Tony Kershaw switched off the light and climbed into bed. Why the hell did I marry such a timid mouse, he asked himself.

As for Mary, she was long past tears. Her husband scared her. He really did, though she didn't believe he would actually do her bodily harm. Yet one was so often reading about devoted husbands who suddenly cut loose and killed. So now she prepared herself for another wakeful night. Tony had dropped off already, as though the simple act of climbing into bed were a powerful sleeping potion in itself. What might happen if he were awake while she slept? Childish of her to be so mistrustful. If you couldn't trust your husband, whom could you trust? But wasn't Tony himself being childish? He seemed to be losing touch with day-to-day reality. Five years ago when she had stood at his side in the chapel listening to her father pronounce them man and wife, their world of love and security had seemed unlimited. But now Tony was becoming more eccentric daily. His grand dreams of fortune-making just never worked out. He became despondent and neglected his duties as a schoolmaster. At least his free-lance articles seemed to be paying off and there was no shortage of cash. And there was that book on botany for painters he'd edited. Perhaps he was a victim of moon madness?

I wish he'd never given up painting, Mary said to herself. Before he became an art master, he had been a full-time artist, and a good one. Though Tony was not a nice man, she loved him. She felt that if he started to paint again, whatever was wrong with their marriage would disappear.

Pity about Dad's paintings, thought young Stella Graham. A shame he hasn't more time for his hobby. Seems that the higher up the scale they go the busier policemen become, when it should be the other way. Seniority should mean more leisure. Let the juniors do the boring bits. A bit of cheek really, asking Mr. Finnegan to give Dad some tips about art appreciation. Not that there is very much to appreciate, these days. Mostly junk.

Still, Mr. Finnegan didn't seem to mind her taking the liberty of asking. He likes Dad, and as Dad would say, you never know what you can do till you try your hand at it. Said that about the O levels. Cyrus Finnegan is awfully nice. A real whizzo! Bit of a stuffed shirt at times, Mum thinks. I wouldn't have dared suggest the bit about art appreciation if Dad weren't so bonkers about learning to paint.

Peter Knowles liked to hedge his bets. There was quite enough risk as it was. That is why he did what he always had. Took the train from New Britain, Connecticut, where he lived, and checked in for the night in a Lexington Avenue hotel. Manhattan had a generous range of inexpensive hotels, and Peter Knowles liked to bank his money, not squander it. Hotels might change, but he always used the name John Brown. Easy to remember. Got the signature down pat, too.

He wasn't too worried. This was the fourth time they'd done it, but never for such high stakes. Risky as hell. Although she was dumb about some things, he trusted her when it came to being downright crafty and ruthless. Not that he'd keep her after the caper was over. Their quickie roadside-chapel marriage could be changed just as easily to a quickie divorce.

11

He'd given her an escape, just in case their plans went sour. He might still be able to salvage everything for himself. Better that way, than sharing. When one had a partner it was necessary to prepare a cover and pull out.

Peter Knowles lay in his comfortable bed and had comfortable thoughts about his future. There was still time to decide about the boy. Meanwhile, in London, because of the time change, the early risers would have finished breakfast and be on their way to work. All he had to do now was wait.

Palpitations indeed!

Mrs. Winterhalter popped a *marron glacé* into her porcine mouth and swilled it down with hot chocolate. Her pudgy fingers reached for another exotic sweet, which followed its predecessors into her capacious bowels.

Palpitations! Heart flurries! True, she was overweight, but so what? As a firm believer in home cures, for ham and everything else, she subscribed to several health-food journals, had read every diet book as soon as it was published, had joined weight-watching classes, and had come to the conclusion that she was one hundred percent normal. Fatness was good. Her statuesque, titanic bearing signified good health. What she knew she lacked was a sufficiency of sugar to absorb the body's liquids. It takes a strong, healthy person to carry weight. Weaklings collapse under the strain. What a lark life is when one knows that there is nothing wrong!

The pill Peter had given her was for emergency use, the last gasp! Not that she intended to swallow it. No sir! Peter had told her how he had obtained the pills. He'd been in charge of "special" stores in some intelligence field unit during the war. He had issued pills to agents. At least, that was what the records showed. Clever? A real smart guy was Peter. Who could every know whether the pills had worked?

Mrs. Winterhalter knew that sometimes people might think her a silly woman. A hypochondriac, perhaps? Obviously Peter had forgotten that he had once told her about the cyanide pills he'd pilfered, otherwise why had he pretended these pills were a new type of nitroglycerine compound, good for heart murmurs and palpitations. Or was it he who was now being stupid, pretending they were not lethal? Not that she cared, for there would be too much at stake. Not because of the present caper, no sir! She was confident that this time it wouldn't be necessary to kill anybody. But helping Peter dispose of his first wife was utter stupidity on her part, allowing Peter to con her into becoming an accessory, even though she had been spaced out on drugs at the time. No judge would accept that. She'd rather kill herself than go to jail or betray Peter.

It had been a most satisfying morning. The hired Rolls, with its cockney chauffeur, had given her much pleasure. It was a suitable vehicle for the occasion. She had particularly enjoyed the food counters at Fortnum and Mason. It was there that she had purchased the sugar-glazed chestnuts. She would have one more, then mix herself a very dry martini. The Rolls would be waiting for her outside the hotel at three o'clock. This gave her ample time for a leisurely lunch.

Doctor Edinburgh walked through his apartment, having taken care to avoid the caretaker's wife, Mrs. Gordon, a harridan of insatiable curiosity. No detail escaped him, from paperweight and paper knife on the Sheraton-style writing desk to empty wastepaper basket. Only the smell troubled him.

He sniffed again and frowned. Artists, he knew from his professional experience and exposure to their foibles, were slaphappy where details, especially financial, were concerned. Also, it would seem they were slaphappy when complying with his specific instructions. Boys will be boys, and so, apparently, will artists be artists. Doctor Edinburgh sighed, then sniffed again. Something would have to be done about that!

Superintendent John Graham snored contentedly. It was his first undisturbed night for some weeks. Mrs. Graham, comfortable from the warmth of his buttocks against her back, sighed and turned a page of the thriller she was reading. She never tired of rereading Edgar Wallace. Stella, like her dad, snored, though lightly, as befitted her virgin status.

The boy lay on his iron cot and looked at the night sky through his barred window. A light frost had been forecast for low-lying areas. He would give himself another hour. Simple plans get swift results, he recalled his father's saying to Mr. Grossmith. They had been talking about photography—the best, most economical layout for a darkroom. Processing color film was their most expensive commitment. It was better to do one's own developing. Couldn't trust anybody nowadays. Even one's father! Going off like that, and not a word from him since. Yet there was always that feeling, a sensing that Dad was there, in the background.

Bit of luck, really, landing the gardening job. Just as well he didn't mind hard work. And as Mr. Kershaw had said, even without your O and A levels, with a bit of agricultural gardening you could get a job anywhere, provided you were willing to work. Could even get a job as a grave digger; but for that you'd have to join a union.

Mr. Kershaw had taught him several other things. How to make stretchers and cut canvas. By keeping in the background with his ears open and pretending he was too dumb to understand, the boy had picked up a little knowledge. A

14

little knowledge about greed, for one thing. It took guts to do what he was doing. He'd be glad when it was over and he was back in the country, no longer having to sneak in and out of London. He loved the countryside, the flowers and fields, the tree-shaded river, and the clean air.

Cock-a-doodle-doo! Although people in cities did not hear them, all over England roosters were greeting the dawn.

Not only was this new day Friday the thirteenth, it was his sixteenth birthday. He must not forget to visit the hothouse before he left for London.

1

The two men left the restaurant and walked north toward Piccadilly and Old Bond Street. Friday the thirteenth was a day of glorious sunshine.

Superintendent John Graham, tall and spare, was dressed in well-cut city clothes complete with rolled umbrella, kid gloves, and bowler. A military moustache and regimental tie belied his true profession, a senior police officer and his avocation, an amateur artist. John Graham, fifty-seven and due for early retirement, liked to be well tailored.

The second man was Cyrus Finnegan. Tall, slightly round-shouldered, fairly overweight for a man of fifty-three, and downright untidy. Or careless. Though well polished, his brown shoes were ancient friends, slightly cracked. While he might never be mistaken for a tramp, one would never guess that he had a substantial private income enabling him to travel and visit art collections from

17

Melbourne to Moscow. By profession he was an art historian, a profession greatly helped by personal wealth and opportunities for leisurely study. For diversion he wrote scholarly articles and also provided columns on art criticism, journalistic reviews, for the London press.

Cyrus Finnegan was a mystery to even his closest friends, with the exception of Superintendent John Graham. All of them knew by now that he had served with the intelligence corps, MI-6, the British secret service. Not that anybody had many secrets these days, when born-again spooks like Malcolm Muggeridge (or perhaps it was Cyrus himself?) estimated that at any given moment of hostilities MI-6 must have had a total enrollment of at least 120,000 operatives. That one seldom met anyone who admitted to having associated with a clandestine group was due to simple statistics: the casualty rate was eight out of ten in the field because of general screw-ups at London H.Q. The twenty percent that survived had been ungainfully employed, mainly with office duties and spying on each other.

Cyrus seldom talked about this dark period in his life. When he did so, it was with considerable incredulity on his part. What he recalled sounded so improbable that he had come to regard his own participation in such foolhardy exploits with marked skepticism. When he had nightmares he would wake up with the icy sweats. All this, of course, merely titillated or bewildered the curious when they heard about it, for they preferred their friends packaged like deep-frozen haddock and chips.

Cyrus Finnegan was no haddock. He was upper-middle-class British, which in itself was a mark against him. His appearance was governed by a seemingly calculated slovenliness, a not-give-a-damn about clothes except on those infrequent and splendid occasions when he was obligated

18

to dress for official functions. Then, complete with decorations, he was transmogrified. Women were either instinctively repulsed sexually or openly attracted by the realization that the fingers now so gently caressing them had known powers of strangulation, karate, and other indelicacies of mayhem.

Those outside his immediate circle assumed from what he had done that he must be in his fifties. Actually, he was fifty-three but inwardly felt as youthful as when, in his early twenties, he had been living in the United States and had volunteered his services at the outbreak of war. The fact that Helga, his Norwegian housekeeper and companion, looked every day of her fifty-six years merely underscored his youthful mannerisms. What was important was that Cyrus Finnegan, perpetually young at heart, had a solid reputation as art historian and critic. Although on first acquaintance one might sense a degree of aloofness in his manner, the exact opposite was true. He loved life, respected his peers, loved God and mankind in equal measure, knowing that each was dependent upon the good graces of the other, and was a seeker after truth. He was willing to learn, even from those brazen sycophants who plague the art world like pig swill.

As a boy, Cyrus had wondered about his own name. He has asked his grandmother about it, as she was the person who apparently loved him best—because she harbored secret desires to turn him into a saint who, like herself, would not drink, smoke, or fornicate. He didn't know this about her, of course, but as he saw so little of his parents he had no other choice. The stupidity of his parents in choosing the name Cyrus was confirmed by a cross-referenced scrutiny, conducted by his grandmother, through the Old Testament books of Ezra, Chronicles, Isaiah, and Jeremiah. Cyrus was not only "the annointed one" and subduer of nations, he was also a friend of the Jews. Finnegan was more ordinary, being the name of an Ulster family that had crossed the Irish sea to settle and prosper in Scotland.

Because of his height, Cyrus Finnegan had a habit of bending over when talking to other people, even with Superintendent Graham, who was within half an inch the same height as himself. By and large, his was a forgettable face and figure that could pass unnoticed in a crowd; otherwise MI-6 would have had no wish to employ him. If he had a distinguishing characteristic it was his absentmindedness, not inappropriate for an art historian. Nothing serious, just a penchant for wearing unmatched socks, throwing towels instead of facecloths into the bathtub, or carefully scouring out empty soup cans before disposing of them in the garbage. He was also addicted to standing in elevators forgetting to press the "up" or "down" buttons. Once he had even climbed into the backseat of his car, waiting for a nonexistent chauffeur to drive him to his destination.

A childhood reading of books by Edgar Wallace, "Sapper," Baroness Emmuska Orczy, Erskine Childers, and Anthony Hope plus the complete works of John Buchan, Conan Doyle, and other masters of hunt and chase literature had whetted his developing appetite for the bizarre. Later, experiences in intelligence had polished his powers of deduction and observation into a disciplined force that became the terror of His, and later Her, Majesty's enemies. Above all, and this Superintendent Graham found to be particularly irritating, Cyrus relied on personal intuition. Intuition, the super felt, should be the jealously guarded preserve of the police.

"It seems to be," Cyrus had once commented, "the perfect crimes solve themselves through their very complications. It is the imperfect, flawed crime, premeditated or not, that gives one trouble."

"Humph!" the super grunted in his noncommittal way, not wishing to admit bafflement at such a seemingly ingenious observation. It was always better to wait and analyze Finnegan's remarks later, and in solitude. Cyrus had that irritating trait of often being right.

Cyrus Finnegan and John Graham saw each other frequently, whenever the former wasn't travelling around. The Superintendent had learned through close association that while Cyrus might occasionally say words backwards or run sentences inside out, the meaning still held true.

During the war, as a Special Branch officer from Scotland Yard, John Graham had been put in charge of recruitment and security for two Special Intelligence units formed to undertake a critical and dangerous dual function. Once in the field overseas, these establishments of carefully selected personnel would set up in the vicinity of brigade H.Q., the active command post close to the battlefront. Outwardly, they had the appearance of regular army units, drawing rations from the Navy, Army, and Air Force Institutes, but otherwise there was absolutely no contact between themselves and the surrounding troops. A miscellany of officers, apparently seconded from a variety of regiments and corps, seemed to be continually on the move. While the unit members' shoulder and arm patches were as varied and colorful as jelly babies, all ranks, regardless of headgear, wore an identical cap badge, to cover their true identities.

Responsible for infiltrating enemy-held territory with foreign agents and their own operatives, the units established safe houses, and acted as clearance points for returning agents and, once in a while, an escaped prisoner of war. Jointly directed by MI-6 and the Special Operation Executive irregulars of Baker Street, their duty was to deceive not only the enemy but their own countrymen and allies as well, thus protecting the greatest secret of them all, the

21

operational effectiveness of ULTRA, the German cipher machine whose prototype had been brought to England in 1939 by a patriotic Pole.

Given army ranks and uniforms, cover stories, and identities, these intelligence spearheads moved through Italy and across Europe; men and women, First Aid Nursing Yeomanry mostly, able to verify on the spot and update the ULTRA information transmitted through their receivers. The fact that this ultra-secret information was being put to use on the battle field confused the enemy, saved lives, and brought satisfaction to those who decoded every enemy message within a matter of hours.

Even under wartime pressures, security clearances for such personnel might take months or years. It was John Graham's task to interview and screen those whose names had been given to Winnie Churchill himself or a member of the Cabinet or Joint Chiefs of Staff and finally filtered back to him via the Deputy Director of Intelligence. Cyrus Finnegan had entered the Firm that way, having been recruited during one of Captain Graham's brief visits to the intelligence corps depot at Wentworth Woodhouse in Yorkshire.

Graham's presence at the depot was easily accounted for. Officially he was seeking volunteers to join the propaganda and psychological warfare outposts in the Balkans. Unofficially he was recruiting dependable ranks for MI-6. He arranged for Private Finnegan's immediate promotion to lance corporal and issued him a railway pass to London for that very afternoon. After swearing to conform to the provisions of the Official Secrets Act (signing the form for the third time since his employment in Washington, D.C., on the local staff of the British Passport Control in 1940), Cyrus climbed into the rear of a utility van, its canvas tied down to prevent him from seeing where he was being taken to, and was speedily transported to an intelligence training school "somewhere in England." As Graham was to confide to him many years later, the rapidity of his recruitment was made possible by his security clearance in Washington. Also—the super rubbed it in—Cyrus Finnegan's outward appearance after having endured twelve weeks of intelligence corps depot and courses for Organization and Administration in Derbyshire was that of total idiocy. He seemed to be barely capable of answering the simplest questions put to him with a plain yes or no. It was as if he felt he had been tricked and was immediately suspicious even when asked whether he thought it might rain.

Somehow, the survival of military training, plus weeks of intensive intellectual concentration, and the gradual wearing down of spontaneous reactions, to be replaced with a more cautious disciplined attitude, meant that one soon recovered from the petty indignities of what soldiers call "boot camp."

In recent years Finnegan and the super had seen each other often. Cyrus, after graduation from Oxford, was becoming known as a writer and art historian, while Graham was moving speedily upwards in rank and responsibility at Scotland Yard.

But it was their shared military experiences which so greatly added to their friendship. And, because both men had been trained, as it were, to think and, often, act deviously in spy catching, or "running" agents, they frequently joined forces, as it were, and applied such deviousness in the calling of criminal bluff.

"There'll come a time," the super said ruefully one day, "when the new generation will take over; men and women who know nothing about what went on, or how we were trained to develop our hunches, using a sort of second sight. By that time, I'll have been put out to grass."

"Oh, I don't know," Cyrus answered brightly. "I'm not so pessimistic. We weren't always infallible. Nobody is.

True, we had certain advantages as regards past experience, but I think the new lot on the way up will probably do much better. The world you and I shared still goes on. The only difference is that the police, the criminals, and the intelligence services are more sophisticated, computerized on both sides."

In recent years Finnegan and the super had seen each other often. The super played cricket on weekends during the summer, or else he took his daughter, Stella, to matches at London's two great cricket grounds, the Oval in Kennington or Lords, which was just across the street from their house in St. John's Wood. A couple of winters ago he had been wounded in a shoot-out while intercepting an armed robber in London's Notting Hill. During his convalescence he developed a fondness for painting with acrylics, finding watercolors too messy and difficult. Now he was trying his hand at oils. Because Stella knew her father always read the articles by his friend Cyrus Finnegan and was much better tempered after putting in a few hours at his hobby, she had arranged for Cyrus to take him around the art galleries from time to time.

Superintendent Graham, who had earned the rank of Major the same year Cyrus was promoted to staff sergeant, had never in his life been given to sentimental reflections. Even his marriage had been delightfully free of intimacy. As far as he was concerned his bride, though he liked her—indeed, he declared that he loved her—brought to their marriage an essential provision of common sense and stability. If love entered into their honeymoon, then he had left the love and sentimentalizing bit to her. So long as she could cook, darn, and carry on a conversation and wasn't too greedy in bed, what more could one ask for? If there was an answer to that one, he certainly didn't know it. Nor could he understand why his darling daughter, Stella, sometimes referred to him as a male chauvinist piggery, smells and all.

The super and his wife had been married now for thirty-five years. In three more years he was due for pension and early retirement. This meant that they would be moving to the cottage they had bought on the Dorset coast. He would miss London. He would find it rather dull, especially when it meant not being able to find excuses for inviting Cyrus to share some of the more tricky cases. After all that training, Cyrus could hardly be regarded as an amateur. They made a good team, just as they had done in Germany while waiting for their demob papers, infiltrating the Soviet Zone, warding off the tedium between operations by getting merrily drunk on *Steinhäger*. The only sentimental chink in Graham's armor was his affection for old comrades.

Superintendent Graham marveled at the tortuous mental paths traveled by Cyrus to point an accusing finger at the guilty. There were now half a dozen lifers behind bars who were still wondering what had gone wrong. As Cyrus Finnegan was never called upon to appear in court and give evidence, none of the guilty knew his name. If they had been told, they probably wouldn't have believed it.

Having negotiated Piccadilly and Albemarle Street, Cyrus pointed at the double windows and rear entrance to Messrs. Thomas Agnew and Sons, dealers in fine art to a succession of royals.

"After we've done a quick run-through at Sotheby's, we'll pop along to the newly-opened Princess Gallery. Not too far from here. You're not getting bored are you?"

"Of course not," growled the super. "Why d'you supposed I'm egging you on? This is Stella's idea, as you well know. Thinks me an uncultured boob. Left my art education too late, though I'll do my best. Might learn something after all."

Superintendent John Graham concluded his statement with a grin.

"Trust you're being discreet, Cyrus? Not a word about these art-appreciation courses to anyone! Hate to think what the assistant commissioner would say if he heard about them."

"What if I tell him that once in a while you consult me about some of your more difficult cases?"

"I'd call that bloody blackmail!"

They both laughed. It had been like this when they were in the army; always joking about the top brass.

After leaving Sotheby's auction showrooms they turned right from New Bond Street and cut east through a short lane that backed on the corner shop of Perry's, the crown jewelers.

"Bond Street. High class shops and tarts," observed the super. "Did six months here on foot. Cork and Burlington streets, then over to Soho. Always at night. I'd just graduated from policeman's training at Peel House and was scared some pimp would cut my throat. Gather present-day tarts are not up to prewar standards. They put out less and cost more."

"Everybody's cutting corners these days," Cyrus said regretfully. "The art world's no exception. Too much money chasing too few objects. England still sets the pace and standards, still the hub. Paris, New York, South America, Japan, West Germany, Switzerland. They're all trying." Cyrus had recently published a short monograph about the Swiss artist Paul Klee.

"Switzerland is a good clearing house for art. Watches, electronics, laundered money. Some of the best works of art pass through Switzerland sooner or later, usually on their way to the United States via London. Lichtenstein and Monaco also clear goodies from time to time. Some of it laundered art!"

"And what about crooks?" the super cut in. "Fakers and forgers! We hold our own there, I bet. Can't beat the Brits for skulduggery! How do the buggers dispose of their loot? Interpol works overtime mailing photographs of stolen works, but it's seldom we hear of anything being recovered. Unless there's a tip-off to an insurance company, it's vamoose to the majority of them. That Dutch affair. You remember the Rembrandt stolen from Everdingen Castle Museum near Haarlem? The Everdingen Rembrandt it's known as; they were lucky to get it back!"

"Took long enough," Cyrus reminded him. "Two years. Most museums and private collectors can't afford the insurance premiums for Rembrandts. In that one instance there probably weren't any complications about having to refund paid-out insurance. Another racket, by the way. Some insurance companies expect you to refund them at current market values. Brokers may have paid out two hundred pounds, but they'll ask you for three hundred and fifty quid if there's been an increase in value in the interval between theft and recovery."

"A bit unfair and unethical isn't it?" the super said disapprovingly. "Just like in any other line. There are good guys and bad guys. You have your share of bad ones in the art world. These days the papers are full of it. Art crooks going international, no less. I blame air travel."

"How right you are," said Cyrus, coming to a stop at a pedestrian crossing. "Newton Street is around the next corner. Let's hope the Princess Gallery isn't one of the places where crooks hang out. Not yet anyway. Hasn't been open long enough."

Cyrus Finnegan took an assortment of invitation cards from his pocket. He selected the most garish, a three-color job vulgarly embossed with the artist's signature. Charles. No surname. He handed the card to Graham.

"The Princess Gallery has been open only a few months.

Bit swanky in such a place as that street. However, it is close to Bond Street, and that's what matters. For the snobs anyway. Charles is a discovery by the way. Edinburgh told me when I wrote a piece on the gallery that Charles has great promise.

"So had Harry the painter," the super reminded him.

"But he was a house painter!" Cyrus exclaimed. "I remember his case. Ten years for grand larceny wasn't it?"

"Exactly." The super was amused. "Fulfilled his promise, too. Dabbles in silk-screens. Jails these days are packed with artsy-craftsy do-gooders. Idiotic belief, in certain high quarters, that art is good for crooks. Easy to rehabilitate through art and poetry readings. Remember Smiley Jones? Dead keen on lithography. And Razor Jack? Six years for attempted slashing and rape. He's got the edge on them too," the super punned. "He's in a prison without bars, and sculpts. A real dandy. Better, I suppose, than carving up tarts."

"Is that why you yourself have taken up painting, super? To deaden your baser instincts?" smirked Cyrus.

"I paint because I'm bored with the telly," Graham answered snappishly. "Besides, learning to draw and see colors in relationship to other colors . . . well, I find it most satisfying. Wish I were better at it, that's all. Which is why I'm hanging on to your every word, trying to keep an open mind. Always have done, I suppose, otherwise I wouldn't be up for promotion once in a while. Not that I go for that long-haired abstract stuff you fellows write about. Nothing in it, far as I can judge."

"You'll be surprised how absorbingly interesting it can be once you get the hang of it," Cyrus admonished his friend lightly. "Blobs and squiggles and blotches are what a layman sees. There's a great deal to good abstract and nonobjective art forms. You'll learn."

"Just another bloody art racket, if you ask me," the super

countered. "Like dope and football pools. Suckers can't spot when they're hooked. Nuts! Stella was telling the missus and me about some chap who sold his entire exhibition for twenty thousand pounds. Didn't even sign his pictures. Had his dealer do it for him. Know what he said when he was asked why? Said he couldn't read nor write! How's that for making fools of the public."

"But he could paint!" Cyrus pointed out. "Artists don't necessarily need the three R's. I know painters who never open a book!"

"I bet they know addition and multiplication. Can add up the profits all the way to the bank. Right?"

Cyrus and the super continued along the narrow pavement deep in discussion, barely noticing the general shabbiness of what had once been a fashionable street. Pleasantly old-fashioned cobbles and lamp posts were reminders of a past never to be entirely obliterated. The shells of the surviving buildings had been modernized. Glib store fronts were imposed upon Victorian brickwork, an incongruous juxtaposition of masonry and synthetics. Apparently the few other pedestrians were also heading towards the Princess at number sixteen.

At one end of the street, coal was being unloaded, sack by sack, from one of the remaining horse-drawn delivery carts. Three or four manholes on both pavements lay open. When the coals had been tipped from sack to cellar the coalman replaced the covers. It was a leisurely midafternoon scene. The horse was totally preoccupied with the oats in its fodder bag.

"Before we go inside," said the super, stopping near the window in which one of the Charles's paintings was displayed on a miniscule easel, "tell me what to expect. How does the Princess Gallery rate?"

"As a newcomer in a highly competitive field? About three quarters up, I'd say. Too early to judge. I know nothing about its financing, whether it's Doctor Edinburgh or his wife who has the capital. Possibly they have a backer. Haven't inquired. They'll need lots and lots of capital to purchase and hang onto the goodies till they can sell at a handsome profit. The secret of being able to run a sound business in the art world is to be able to hold on to stock and watch its value climb. Fashions change, but more important, fashions repeat in cycles every twenty years or so."

"Another racket, eh? Just as I suspected. All this modern rubbish is just a cover for the real valuables stored in the back room." The super seemed well pleased with his ruminations. "And Edinburgh? What sort of specimen is he? Bit of a charmer, I expect. Have to be if he's going to catch himself a few well-oiled clients. And I don't just mean Arabs!"

"Edinburgh is Viennese, came here in the thirties and changed his name. Following a Jewish custom he took the name of a town or city as a surname. Sometimes they chose a country. In his case he just liked the sound of it. Edinburgh was one of his favorite cities."

"Could just as easily have called himself Aberdeen or Melrose?"

"Of course. An oddball, but I like him. He's not only a doctor of medicine. He's also a fully qualified psychiatrist. Studied clinical psychology. Worked with Freud and Jung and in nineteen forty-seven had himself attached to one of the state mental hospitals in the United States."

"Got himself a good consultancy practice here?" the superintendent asked.

"Very extensive. Specializes in artists. Performing artists also, but he's especially interested in painters, sculptors, their likes and dislikes. Told me once that to really come to grips with the meaning of art, one must read Tolstoy's *Insanity*. Do you know what I find most fascinating about him? His war record," said Cyrus.

30

"Though you were going to say he gives cut-rates to art critics suffering from advanced schizophrenia. I'd go along with him there! So what's so special about Edinburgh's record?"

"He joined the Pioneer Corps. In the ranks."

"Wasting professional knowledge, wasn't he?"

"The War Office apparently had to drag it out of him. Forced him to show a bit of responsibility. Reminded him of the Hippocratic oath he'd sworn when he graduated from medical school. Having been forced to take a commission in the Royal Army Medical Corps, so to speak, he then volunteered for special duties. Had himself attached to a commando group."

"A commando-trained psychiatrist!" Superintendent Graham threw up hands in horror. "Logical I suppose. I mean, his becoming an art dealer. Takes all kinds."

Finnegan and Superintendent Graham prepared to enter the gallery, above whose door was suspended a small golden crown. At that moment their attention was diverted by the arrival of a taxi. Apart from the coal cart and a Rolls parked further along the street, it was the only vehicle in sight.

The young blonde who stepped hurriedly from the taxi thrust some banknotes into the cabby's outstretched hand and, with lowered head, pushed her way past the two men and ran into the gallery.

"Well, I'll be darned!" said Graham explosively. Believing in old-world courtesies, he had been about to tip his bowler. "What very strange behavior. Smart little number, but rude for all that."

"And deathly pale," Cyrus noted. "Frankly, I thought she was going to throw up! She looked sick."

Another taxi arrived. Its four occupants descended with more dignity. Finnegan and Graham took up the rear, and all six entered the Princess Gallery as one group.

"Let's hope Mr. Charles or whatever he's called isn't superstitious," the super murmured. "For a private viewing, Friday the thirteenth could spell trouble. Not that I swallow old wives' tales."

"Probably had the date picked out by his astrologist," Cyrus reassured him. "When all else fails, artists usually turn to astrology. On the other hand, this may have been the only date Edinburgh had available."

It was not Charles who welcomed them but Doctor Hans Edinburgh himself.

"Welcome," he greeted Cyrus effusively. "Good of you to come. This will mean we can count on at least one good review! And who is your friend?"

"Old army chum, Hans. Meet John Graham. Not a collector yet, but on the verge of being interested." Cyrus watched them shake hands. "That's Mrs. Edinburgh, Maria, over there talking with those very distinguished people we followed into the gallery. But beware, John, don't let Maria or Hans chisel you out of your life savings, though they'll try their damnedest."

"Always the joker, yes!" Doctor Edinburgh smiled broadly, offering them cigarettes before lighting his own. "I must hurry along and speak with the others, if you'll excuse me. But take your time looking around, Mr. Graham. If you've any questions, ask me or my wife. Not my bored-looking stepson, lolling at the table over there. Don't expect any information from him unless it's about cars. He's just helping us with the catalogues for the afternoon. Maria and I don't have any extra staff. We're short-handed, so we have to rely on family."

"Is Charles here?" Cyrus asked.

"Not yet." Hans Edinburgh seemed put out by the question, but only for a second. "Didn't turn up for the special

32

luncheon Maria and I had arranged in his honor. He's very young. Rather hates meeting strangers. Not at all brash like so many young people nowadays. It wouldn't surprise us if he's a no-show."

Superintendent Graham appreciated Doctor Edinburgh's easy command of the English language. Just a mere trace of accent. This was not so with Maria, who now moved to greet them. Hers was a high, throaty Italian voice. A singer? Could well be. After introductions, Maria Edinburgh joined her husabnd in apologizing for the absence of the artist.

"After the majority of guests have gone," she informed Cyrus before trotting off to talk to a rather blousy, statuesque, and formidable woman who had just that moment seated herself on one of the few available chairs, "we'll be having champagne cocktails downstairs in the lower gallery, for very special guests like yourselves. It'll be in about half an hour, if you can wait that long. I expect Charles will at least join us for drinks."

Cyrus gave her one of his warmer smiles. He preferred Maria to the doctor, who always appeared to be acting in a surrealistic play.

"Thank you, Maria. I suppose we can endure another thirty minutes of abstinence! Come along, John, let's admire the pretty pictures. Let's start with that flower study over what was once a fireplace. The painting looks well above that marble mantelpiece."

"Flowers?" the super sounded incredulous. "I can't see any flowers. Just blobs of color. Stella could have painted that in her pram!"

"My dear super." Cyrus propelled his friend toward the mantelpiece. "Take a good look. And please note that I'm not the only one who likes it. That little red seal on the frame indicates that it's been sold."

"Good God!" the superintendent muttered. "Some people have the rottenest taste! Don't they? Give me Whistler's mum any day."

And thinking of taste, Superintendent Graham said to himself, Edinburgh takes first prize for tailor's dummyship. That dreadful suit with pockets trimmed with gold thread. A lightweight tropical material, but at least well fitted to the doctor's thick, muscular body. And the shoes! Black and white with points! A style much favored by the Tottenham Court Road underworld. As though to outdo the rest of his raiment, the doctor's breast pocket sported a scarlet handkerchief, matched to his tie. Quite impossible, of course, to accept the esthetic judgments of a man who dressed so loudly! What a contrast to Maria Edinburgh, whose matronly spread was elegantly concealed by a simple black dress, with matching Gucci shoes and handbag.

"Where's our blonde got to?" asked the super.

"Not a sign. Must be downstairs. Daresay we'll see her later on. At the happy hour."

But it is damned odd, Cyrus was thinking. Rushing into an art gallery during a crowded private viewing and doing the vanishing trick.

Outwardly, it was your usual crowd of smartly turned-out middle class. More women than men, yet considering the time of day, when most men and women would be at work, the guests were average. Fifty-to-sixty age group? The few scruffy guests, bony-armed women sporting handcrafted bracelets and dressed is the style of prewar Balkan peasants, accompanied by equally conformist companions —bearded, bifocaled and denim-jeaned—undoubtedly were part of the Princess Gallery's "stable."

Superintendent Graham had parked his bowler and umbrella on a table near the door, which had been placed there as a temporary cloakroom. He was only half listening to Finnegan's earnest explanations of color balances, tonal

retardation, recession of diagonal planes, and other sub-
tleties apparently used by painters such as Charles to con-
fuse the public. The super would wait till he could read
Cyrus's Sunday column. Like so many critics, Cyrus was
more in command of the written word than the spoken.
Meanwhile, the super allowed his thoughts to settle more
comfortably, speculating on the manner and *raison d'être*
of private viewings. Were they all part of one mammoth con
game? The superintendent felt, as he often did these days,
not only piqued but tricked.

Cyrus Finnegan was not in the least surprised that the
super's attention had wandered off. It merely reaffirmed an
opinion he had held since they were first together in the
army: that Superintendent Graham was a highly bright,
intelligent individual. Not for a second had he been de-
ceived by the nonsensical art terms, some of which Cyrus
had fabricated for his own amusement. It was funny and
surprising how often artists seemed incapable of writing
simple, straight prose, resorting instead to pseudo-intel-
lectual bunkum. What was even worse, it had become
common practice to reprint such meaningless verbiage
later in magazines devoted to highbrow junketings, well
padded with photographs of the artist in his or her studio.
Surely works of art were their own best ambassadors? So
why all the flotsam?

Superintendent Graham looked thoughtfully at Doctor
and Mrs. Edinburgh. He could see they were troubled.
Fellow seemed likable enough. Something odd about his
eyes, though. Pair of blue icebergs, as good a description as
any. And set in such an ordinary face, too! Grayish, sallow
complexion. Thinning gray hair on top. Broad forehead,
small ears. The super mentally tabulated characteristics for
identification. It was an annoying habit of which he couldn't
rid himself. Useful, though. As for Maria Edinburgh? A
diva! Undoubtedly! Something about her eyes he hadn't

noticed till now. Pill popper! That was her weakness. Uppers and downers! What horrible expressions Americans used, yet how descriptive.

"How out of place Edinburgh's stepson looks," commented the super.

"He's a racing driver," Cyrus informed him. "Name of Giuseppe Dagerra. His father, Maria's ex, is a Milanese car manufacturer. Gives Gee, that's his pet name, a handsome allowance. Looks exactly like his mother, don't you think? Mona-Lisa-ish face, alabaster complexion. Never think of him in the racing pits, would you? Yet look at his hands! Spatulate fingers, broad hairy wrists. Maria once told me that Signor Dagerra is a redhead. Genes play the darnedest tricks!"

"What's he doing here in England?"

"Racing. Brands Hatch and Silverstone racetracks have competitions coming up. There's also test driving in Yorkshire later this week. He lives part of the year in London, anyway. Studying to be an engineer. Second year university."

The two men had completed their tour of the exhibition and now exchanged pleasantries with Maria, who came to introduce them to an imposing lady who had determinedly planted her broad base on one of the delicate Regency chairs. Maria made the introductions.

"Mrs. Winterhalter is a New Yorker," she said gushingly. "And our first patron this afternoon! She has just bought that beautiful study of a gloxinia that you see above the mantelpiece. Isn't it a lovely painting, both of you?"

"Spirited," Cyrus answered politely. Although he liked the painting, "spirited" was an adjective he employed regularly when he was at a loss for words, or was not ready to commit himself.

"I bet you that little item set you back a bit," the super quipped overfamiliarly.

36

"Fifteen hundred." Mrs. Winterhalter quoted the price as though discussing a box of peanut brittle.

"Pounds? I say!" The super was flabbergasted.

"Dollars," Maria Edinburgh corrected him casually. "As you can see it's quite a large canvas. It's also a sound investment. Believe me!"

"I just couldn't resist such a bargain. One would pay more in Manhattan!" Mrs. Winterhalter purred. "Gloxinia is one of my favorite plants. Just right for the temperature in my apartment too. Anything less than seventy degrees and the leaves fall off. Did you notice how very, very clever the Edinburghs have been? Or don't you spot what I see?"

Superintendent Graham looked vaguely in different directions. Cyrus jerked his sleeve.

"Look over there, John. That plant on the table. It's a gloxinia. What a nice touch!"

"Hans's idea," Maria said, almost too apologetically. "I had nothing to do with it." Jealousy? Cyrus asked himself. Or just plain sulks?

"Well, anyway, I think it was cute of him," Mrs. Winterhalter beamed. "Are you sure you won't mind having it delivered to the Savoy? I know it isn't usually permitted to remove paintings till the close of an exhibition. But this time the situation is a bit different. I'm sailing to New York next week and want no complications with the New York customs! Isn't it just too bad Charles himself has missed his own private viewing! Do tell him how so sorry I am not to have met him. Tell him I do so hope he makes lots and lots of sales."

"I will!" answered Maria Edinburgh. "We'll have the painting sent round to your hotel first thing tomorrow morning. Charles is at the threshold of a promising future. You can see five more red seals already."

"I guess his works will increase by leaps and bounds? In value I mean."

"No doubt whatsoever," Maria assured her. "Hans, over there, is talking to dear Miss Gammel. She's just bought two of Charles's watercolors. You'll see them later when you join us for champagne cocktails in the lower gallery."

"Oh! No thanks," Mrs. Winterhalter protested, thinking she'd prefer a very dry martini any day. "But I will, I will, though! Champagne is good for the heart, people tell me. Not that there's anything wrong with mine! My very first husband said I kept my heart in my pocketbook. Wasn't that a beastly thing to say?"

Cyrus and John Graham freed themselves from Mrs. Winterhalter's overbearing company and moved to a less crowded part of the room. Both wished they'd soon be summoned downstairs for drinks.

Explaining that he must put "sold" seals on her pictures, Dr. Hans Edinburgh left Miss Gammel, rather impolitely, she thought, and rushed downstairs. Miss Gammel was as unobtrusive as the underside of a sofa. Uncared for in clothes and person, she carried a string bag stuffed with old newspapers, though dealers guessed the bag was stuffed with banknotes as well. Having been so impolitely deserted in the middle of the conversation, her lips made a soundless circle, then clamped shut.

"Rich and eccentric," Cyrus said about her. "Always buys a minimum of one work from different exhibitions she visits. Has dozens and dozens of paintings stored, either in galleries from which they were purchased or in several houses she owns. Plans to give them to the nation. Poor nation!"

Odd, Superintendent Graham was thinking. Not odd Miss Gammel. Odd, that as soon as Maria Edinburgh saw her husband going downstairs, presumably to his office, she half ran across the gallery and snatched the old-style replica telephone off its cradle. She was eavesdropping. No doubt at all that this was an extension to the office phone.

She listened for only a few seconds, then replaced the receiver. Her expression showed relief. Reassured, perhaps, that she had not heard what she did not wish to hear. Was the good doctor a philanderer, the super asked himself? Most unlikely. The psychiatrists of his acquaintance were home-loving, domesticated cowards; too disenchanted with the human condition to seek entanglements of their own. Just like detectives. Ah well! Doctor Edinburgh was back upstairs. He'd even waved cheerfully to his wife. So that's that then, thought the super. But of course it wasn't.

The scream was piercingly shrill. It came from the lower gallery. Not once but twice. It brought the majestic Mrs. Winterhalter from her chair like a spring. Cyrus, who had been talking to some acquaintances, glanced anxiously at the super, who in turn shook his head in disbelief. Racing up the stairs at full trot was the blonde young woman whom they had seen emerge earlier, with no less speed, from the taxi.

She kept her head lowered and, before she could be stopped, was out into the street, running as fast as her pretty legs could move. Legs as shapely as a chorus girl's, Superintendent Graham noted. It was one of his professional accomplishments to note details in times of crisis, while other were confused and panicking.

Preposterous! The young man Gee Dagerra fled in wild pursuit through the door and in his violent haste knocked sideways the table upon which rested the super's hat and umbrella. In seconds Cyrus and he exchanged looks again, Cyrus as if saying, sorry, super, for getting you into this. Everybody moved toward the stairwell to confront the cause of the scream. It was Maria who reached the top of the staircase ahead of the others. White with shock she gripped the parapet and Edinburgh rushed to comfort her. But someone else pushed him roughly aside, the super

39

observed, as though the doctor had no business to touch his wife. Their interloper had been introduced to Superintendent Graham as Tony Kershaw, schoolmaster and freelance art critic for the *Daily Post*. A rather unkempt, country type, the super remembered noting.

The momentary tableau dissolved, to be replaced by movement and hushed voices. Those who had courage enough to peer over the stairwell parapet, as Maria had done, saw Cyrus Finnegan crouched over the body of a very young man, not more than a boy, really, lying flat on his back with his feet on the bottom stair. They couldn't see the expression on the boy's face, thank heaven, for it was not a pleasant sight, the neck having been wrenched and twisted sideways, like a cork unwilling to part from its bottle. Another twist such as this, Cyrus was thinking, and the young man's head would have detached itself. At least it was a clean death, with only a trickle of blood coming from the left side of the mouth.

Upstairs, people were beginning to move toward the door. Maria Edinburgh was now sitting at the table on Gee's vacated chair. Mrs. Winterhalter, Kershaw, and Miss Gammel were animatedly discussing the situation with a couple who, along with another latecomer, had entered the Princess Gallery a few minutes earlier. Bugger it! Hell and damnation! The superintendent cursed silently, scooping his bowler off the carpet. My afternoon off!

Being a no-nonsense man of action, he gave peremptory instructions to a responsible-looking young man standing nearest to the door that nobody should leave the gallery until the police arrived. He commanded Doctor Edinburgh to telephone the police and inform them that both ambulance and doctor would be needed. The superintendent knew that in times of crisis, a majority of persons were only too relieved when somebody took charge, even in their own homes. Which made it understandable why

Edinburgh himself was willingly dialing the emergency number. The super was now asking himself why Edinburgh was still in the upper gallery? Surely, as proprietor of the establishment, one would have expected him to be downstairs with Cyrus Finnegan and what was so obviously and unpleasantly a corpse.

From his vantage point at the top of the staircase, Superintendent Graham could now confirm for himself that this was no accident. Where he was standing, the lighting showed clearly two parallel lines in the thick ply, heel tracks where a body had been dragged by its shoulders across the luxurious carpet.

2

The body had been quickly identified by Kershaw as that of Charles. Charles, the artist without a surname.

It took less than five minutes for the arrival of an ambulance and police car from Savile Row Station. Detective Sergeant Purvis, an unshakable and unshockable person of much ambition, was not in the least disconcerted to find Superintendent John Graham of the Yard there, though his presence in such offbeat company was surprising. Until now, he had favorably regarded the super as a philistine, like himself, though a fleeting recollection of a large still life signed "J. Graham" in the last annual Police Art Society show flashed to mind. He himself had visited the art show only because his fiancée, a policewoman in L Division, made batiks and tie-dye fabrics and was not only an exhibitor but a prize winner.

Purvis was six feet of solid, athletic bulk. He was clean shaven, green-eyed, and, although in his early thirties, sufficiently old-fashioned-conventional to keep his jet-black hair not merely close-cut but cropped. His tolerance foundered at the sight of the younger unkempt, shaggy riffraff who were his juniors. As far as he was concerned, they could remain his juniors forever, that is, until they came to their senses and looked less like the Danish army. As for the juniors themselves, those who were his colleagues felt that Purvis could do no wrong.

He could be gruff and rude, but he was fair. Always. And when it came to criminal investigations, there were those in higher places, such as Superintendent Graham, for example, who recognized Detective Sergeant Purvis as being especially gifted, in his unsubtle way, at solving the seemingly unsolvable.

"For your information, Purvis," said the super with the friendliest of smiles, "it's all yours. I'm off duty and I don't want my weekend messed up. Not on your life!" Graham grinned at the sergeant. "Besides, I doubt if you'll have to bother the Yard. Should be able to tidy it all away by tomorrow. Just an unfortunate accident."

"An accident, sir?"

"Wouldn't you say so, Purvis?"

"If this is an accident then pigs have wings. I'd better send for the lab boys. Cameras. Better post a copper in the street to control the curious. Would you mind calling in for me, sir?"

"Gladly. Meanwhile, Cyrus here will tell you what happened. That is, not what happened, but what he and I saw. You remember Mr. Finnegan don't you? We worked together on the case of the missing stump."

"Pleased to meet you again, Mr. Finnegan." Purvis nodded offhandedly at Cyrus. "Now tell me what the hell's been going on."

The three of them were standing to one side while the police surgeon examined the body. When the rest of the

43

team arrived Purvis and the super went upstairs and began the labor of taking names and addresses and statements. Purvis had learned never to break routine procedure. The dross would rise to the surface quickly enough through the sieve of cross-examination. But it would be good to have the knowledgeable Superintendent Graham help him all the same.

"Can't I persuade you to return on duty, sir," Purvis pleaded when the super rejoined them. "Of course I'll have to question you and Mr. Finnegan like everyone else, but I'd really appreciate your help, sir. Especially at this stage."

Accident or murder, steps have to be taken.

"Wonder if you'd mind concentrating on the lower gallery, sir?" Purvis asked the super. "I'll stay up here and take names and addresses. No point in keeping these people hanging around. Mr. Finnegan can be of great assistance in helping me sort out who's who."

It didn't take long. Purvis, seated at the catalogue table, had the guests come up and give names, addresses, and telephone numbers. They were then allowed to leave. Dr. and Mrs. Edinburgh gave their address as 3 Belsize Pound, Haverstock Hill.

"Pound?"

"It's a cul-de-sac. Six blocks up from Chalk Farm Station." Doctor Edinburgh was still considerably shaken. His voice quivered. "If you will excuse me, sergeant, I'd like to take Mrs. Edinburgh home. I could send her back in a taxi on her own, but I don't think it wise. It's been a dreadful shock for both of us."

"By all means, sir. It'll be some time before we're through. Perhaps you'd leave us the door key. I'll see that everything's securely locked when we leave. No sign of your stepson, sir? Or the young lady who fled in such panic?"

"He may have gone to his flat." Hans and Marie exchanged anxious looks, warning signals. As though the doctor had not intended to mention the flat.

"Flat?" Cyrus, like Purvis had never heard of its existence.

"It's my flat, really," Hans Edinburgh said, almost too casually. "I let him live there during term time, or when he comes to England for race fixtures. It's off Harley Street and I use it as a consulting room in addition to my own office and consulting room in our house. I use my Harley Street flat for very special consultations with patients who are well-known public figures who don't wish to be spotted by some snooping newspaperman." Edinburgh paused and dabbed at his nose with his scarlet handkerchief. "Of course, when such an appointment is made, Gee keeps out of the way. Takes himself to the cinema or whatever. Always most cooperative."

"Well, sir," Purvis said reassuringly, "at this stage we'll just center our activities in the gallery. If you give me your door key now, then you can take Mrs. Edinburgh home. We will want to see you again, of course. Tomorrow morning."

"How about making it ten o'clock at the gallery?" Hans said quickly. "I've got to come to fetch Mrs. Winterhalter's picture and take it to her hotel. I promised her it would be delivered Saturday morning."

"As you wish, sir." Purvis escorted the Edinburghs to the door.

"Ten o'clock. And if you can come up with any ideas or remember something that could be of assistance in my inquiries, please phone. I'll be either at Savile Row or at home. Here's my telephone number on this card."

45

When he had locked the door, Purvis returned to the desk where Cyrus was idly flipping through the pages of *Artnews*. From the stairwell they could hear Superintendent Graham's voice as he talked with the police surgeon.

"We'll go downstairs in a couple of minutes," Purvis said, taking out his cigarette case. "Tell me, Finnegan. What's so bloody private about a private viewing? Strikes me 'public viewing' is a more apt description of this mob."

"No, Purvis, this is a modest, very modest gathering. If you want mob scenes, go to an opening at the Tate. Nothing like the crowd scenes at Canadian and U.S. galleries I've seen, I assure you."

"What's behind it, anyway?" Purvis seemed genuinely interested.

"Partly snob, I suppose. Though even that's unfair. Some people, particularly collectors, like to have first peek at what's going on. The dealers also go along with the 'favored client' principle. And artists like to have their friends and other artists get together. Also, many private galleries have the artist foot the bill for hospitality. It's for the artist to invite whom he or she wishes. The gallery invites the purchaser."

"Champagne cocktails!" Purvis interrupted him. "That young man lying downstairs doesn't look as though he could have paid for a pint of wallop, let alone host a cocktail bash like this. Poor fellow. In every sense poor, if appearances mean much these days."

"In this instance," Cyrus said positively, "we must assume that the Princess Gallery is picking up the tab. Which means there must be something very special going on, if, as you've often remarked, appearances count, even though deceptive. Private views, incidentally," Cyrus continued informatively, "are an offshoot of the earlier custom of academicians inviting friends and patrons to studio at-homes, usually on the Sunday afternoon immediately preceding sending-in day for the Royal Academy show. Same custom in France for the Salon. And of course, younger artists, even students in the Paris ateliers, would get together to compare their proclaimed masterpieces. All jolly good fun, but also serious. And for the nouveaux riches, to be invited to an academician's at home was next best to a royal command. Royals attended these functions. Still do. Did you know Queen Victoria was an insatiable admirer of art and had painters bring their works to Windsor Castle for her to see?"

"Well, blow me down," said Purvis, almost agreeably. "Takes all kinds. It might even account for what you and the super were up to. You, I can understand. It's your racket! But Superintendent John Graham? Now, Mr. Finnegan, tell me once again everything you can recall about this afternoon's events. Start with your arrival at Newton Street."

Cyrus was not in the least intimidated by this sudden reintroduction of formality. When he had finished speaking and Purvis was rechecking his notes they turned to the list of names.

"Somewhere in this lot, Mr. Finnegan, is a murderer. Plain, simple fact. Now it's up to us to clear the innocent. Obviously there are the outsiders, whom we can forget, unless events prove differently, and the insiders." Purvis lit another cigarette. "It's my experience that in any group or gathering there are insiders, those who really are in the know. Close friends. Relations. In on the track and not mere interlopers. Please look through this list, Mr. Finnegan, and put a mark against the names you think are insiders. Close to the Edinburghs. When you've finished, we'll join the super. If I know anything about John Graham's methods, he'll want us to go through the gallery like a laser through steel. He'll be right on target!"

It occurred to Cyrus Finnegan that with the exception of

47

Doctor and Mrs. Edinburgh and Gee Dagerra, there were only five names that tentatively fit with Purvis's notions of an inner circle. Thee were the two dealers, Messrs. Grossmith and Wurlitzer, who were well established in the art trade. Then there was the elderly Miss Gammel, potty as a flowerpot—yet what was known about her, aside from her immense wealth and her pack-rat approach to collecting? Anthony Kershaw described himself as art critic (Cyrus had misgivings about the title), painter, botanist, art teacher. Surprising how little one knew about people one met on a regular basis. Fellow might be a chemist, for that matter. Eccentric? Perhaps. He'd heard about Kershaw's being a painter but had not seen examples of his work. Must be something there, to justify his position as part-time art critic on the influential *Daily Post*. Although Cyrus didn't like Kershaw's style, he felt the man knew his field and came across with authority.

Perhaps the remarkable Mrs. Winterhalter could be added to the list of insiders, now that she had purchased a painting by Charles. Who else? The blonde? Nobody, not even the Edinburghs, claimed to know her identity. Or was there a bit of evasiveness? Covering up for Gee, who had rushed after her like a hound.

Purvis looked disappointed. "Are these the only names you can give me?"

"Have a heart, Purvis. I've seen a lot of these people at different openings and I don't know them any more than they know me. Faces. Possibly one or two of them know my name and connect it with my face, because I appear on television once in a while. But that's all."

"Is there a missing link?" Purvis asked.

"You mean somebody who's not here, in person? Could be. Yes, could be."

Very peculiar, thought Purvis. Nonsense, that bit about young Gee going to Doctor Edinburgh's Harley Street flat.

48

Why hadn't he come back to the Princess Gallery? He'd probably caught up to the blonde and they'd gone into hiding.

For the first time Sergeant Purvis noticed the elegance of the gallery's interior decoration. Sand-colored walls, discreet lighting, Empire-style furniture, a suspended off-white ceiling, and thick taupe-gray carpet. Really swank, with nothing to distract attention from the pictures.

Downstairs in the lower gallery the color scheme was similar, Purvis noted as he and Cyrus rejoined Superintendent Graham. A bit cramped for space, which obviously was why only two walls were used for hanging. The east wall was built of imitation glass bricks through which one could see the blurred outlines of a desk, two chairs, and a filing cabinet. Its open entrance was an invitation to potential customers. Call oneself a dealer with a gallery, but one was really a shopkeeper with a shop: to do business one had to be accessible. Purvis saw a narrow door partly hidden by a bookcase in the far corner of the south wall. The door led to a largish room, a converted cellar with whitewashed walls partly filled with storage racks. The room must have been excavated under Newton Street, for above his head Purvis could see the pavement manhole, closed with an inside bar. What really held the sergeant's puzzled attention was a heap of coal, not more than half a sack, on the linoleum floor.

Purvis heard the sound of a toilet flushing and Superintendent John Graham reentered the lower gallery through a door in the west wall. Cyrus Finnegan was standing in front of an old-fashioned studio easel, peering through his pocket magnifying glass at a detail of a painting that Purvis instinctively tagged as an Old Master. Like the coal in the storage room, it looked out of place.

"Seascape by van de Velde," Cyrus said. "A real beauty.

It's what I mentioned earlier as we were walking along Ryder Street. Edinburgh makes his money with paintings like this. Couldn't make a go of it by sticking to contemporary art. This is where capital is invested. All spare profits from his consulting practice would be ploughed into this sort of thing. Superb!"

"Would he really have enough capital?" asked the super.

"We'll have to ask him if he's got a backer," Cyrus said slowly. "Of course, Grossmith and Wurlitzer could be in on a deal like this. The painting could well be theirs, here on consignment. In which case Edinburgh would perhaps get only a ten or twenty percent cut. Mind you, with van de Velde that wouldn't be chicken feed."

The corpse had been removed. The police team had completed their duties. Graham, Purvis, and Finnegan were alone in the gallery. Their expressions were grim. Even the van de Velde, a seascape with lowering sky and storm-tossed fishing boats, seemed to match their solemnity. Half a dozen bottles of Dom Pérignon and plates of untouched canapés had never seemed less wanted. They rebuked by their presence. *O tempora! O mores!* That time and manners of private viewings could suddenly turn so unseemly!

It was well past six o'clock. The three men so poised for action were incapable of deciding what to do next. A pub? A pint of bitter or something more heady? The telephone on the office desk broke their reverie. It was Purvis who lifted the receiver.

"Princess Gallery." He listened. "No, madam, you've nothing to concern yourself about. The painting will be delivered as promised. Good night." He replaced the receiver. "That was Mrs. Winterhalter. In a dither. Worried that she mightn't get her picture delivered to the hotel. That we might hold it as evidence, of all silly notions!"

It was a relief to laugh.

"Well, sir, if it's all right with you, I'll pop along back to my office and put on my thinking cap." Sergeant Purvis switched off the lights in the lower gallery and led the way upstairs. When the upper gallery was also in darkness, he carefully locked the main door behind them. In the street it was still an early evening of sunshine and warmth. Seen through the window, the small painting by Charles, supported on its easel, somehow managed to make the deserted interior of the gallery ominously dark.

"Off with you, then," said the super, remembering that he had not replied to the sergeant's request. "We'll meet here in the morning. Ten sharp. No, better make it nine. That will give us an hour before Edinburgh gets here. Perhaps by then we'll have a better idea of what this is about."

"Would you like a ride, sir?" Purvis held open the door of the police car that had been waiting for him.

"No thanks. I'm going to ask Cyrus Finnegan to invite me to his flat for a noggin. I could do with one. Even two or three. Hang it, this is supposed to be my day off, what's left of it."

"Be my guest," said Cyrus, only too glad to have the super visit. "I'll have Helga conjure up a bite to eat."

3

"Well, my darlings," Helga exclaimed. "You have the air of troubled peoples!" Her Norwegian accent held warmth.

Helga was Cyrus Finnegan's housekeeper. She presided as châtelaine of his top-floor flat in Queen's Court South, an older apartment house close to Chelsea Town Hall. Cyrus tolerated its smallish rooms and tiny kitchen and bathroom because the view from the corner windows in the living room commanded one of the most spectacular panoramas of West London. To John Graham, a regular visitor of whom Helga totally approved, it was not only a room with a view, it was a hideout. He envied Cyrus his privacy. His own world offered no such sanctuary.

"Drink, Helga, and food. Lots of food," Cyrus teased her. "Thought requires food and thirst requires two huge gin and tonics."

"Make mine vodka, please," said the super. "And troubled peoples we are indeed."

"Another murder, John?" Helga was on first-name basis with all of Finnegan's friends, who were carefully chosen and therefore few in number.

"Afraid so. Haven't got our teeth into it yet, eh, Cyrus?"

"I regard my part as that of an interloper," Cyrus said firmly.

"Then thank goodness for Purvis!" Graham chuckled. "It's his baby, this one."

Helga, a stocky, middle-aged, woman, listened intently and smiled. Her flaxen hair was neatly braided in a circle above her high forehead. She wore a short, sleeveless embroidered jacket of red and gold, which complimented perfectly the Norwegian dress of light-blue cotton. Her starched white apron somehow brought out her sharp, observant blue eyes.

The super had never pressed Cyrus for a full account on how he had "acquired," or, more precisely, "rescued," Helga during the war from somewhere north of Trondheim in the course of an abortive British invasion. Along with several other patriots, she had been in imminent danger of extermination by the occupying Nazis. Her husband, her two small children, and her parents had been executed, and Helga was hiding in the forest behind their burned-out cottage when Cyrus found her. She herself had later returned to Norway on three occasions, descending by parachute and attending personally to the gory revenge for her kin. Nowadays her only interests were cooking, sewing, and collecting photographs of the British and Norwegian royal families. On the kitchen dresser were autographed photographs of King George VI and King Haakon, who had stood for Norwegian patriotism while in wartime exile in England. The fact that King Haakon of Norway had been honorary colonel of the Green Howards at the Richmond depot where Cyrus had done his basic infantry training

53

kept things nicely in the family, as it were. Bit by bit the super had gained Helga's confidence and worried from her a more passionate and understandable explanation for her enduring devotion to his friend.

On that darkening winter afternoon when Cyrus Finnegan had come across her hiding place in an abandoned quarry in the forest about six miles from what until that morning had been her home, she was suffering such emotions of terror and of total loss of such hysterical immensity that she had virtually thrown herself on his mercy.

She had heard the rustling sounds of his approach and thought he must be one of the German soldiers who had fired as she fled the scene of flames and execution. She knew they would keep looking for her. In panic she had crawled into a shrubbery thicket that hid her yet enabled her eyes to follow each cautious movement as Cyrus crept along the narrow track between upright pine and spruce trees. The shrubbery wasn't much protection. What if he spotted her? She knew what to expect. Rape, then a bullet. Or perhaps death first and rape afterwards. Nazis were not fastidious.

With thankfulness in her pounding heart she realized that this rather unkempt young soldier in khaki, adorned with an automatic weapon she couldn't identify, two looted German potato-masher hand grenades dangling from his belt, a rifle slung over one shoulder, and a monstrous revolver peeking from its holster might indeed be a killer— but he would not be hunting her.

"Gute Gott I was frightened, John," Helga recalled, with only the faintest of smiles at this grim memory of her life. "I though I was seeing a Negro! I'd only seen pictures of black men. I had heard they boiled missionaries for supper. It wasn't till after Cyrus brought me back to England for training with the Secret Service that I learned how soldiers

54

sometimes blacken their faces with shoe polish so that their white skins can't be spotted by the enemy."

"Did he spot you?"

"He didn't. No! I was trembling so much it was a wonder the bush didn't shake as well. At least I knew he wasn't a kraut, though I couldn't guess what else he was. You must realize, John, I'd never been more than a few miles to visit neighboring farms or the village. Hadn't even been to a cinema. A real country lass, ja! So I kept hiding till he had gone a few yards away, when I scrambled out after him. I had decided he must be Swedish. Although they were neutral, there were some brave Swedes who had been helping our underground."

"Then what happened?"

"I called to him in Swedish, Help me, Sir! I was in a panic because he had disappeared round the next corner. Or else I'd scared him too! So I stood perfectly still, afraid to breathe, when suddenly there he was standing behind me, telling me in Norwegian to put my hands up. I'd scared him, too, he told me afterwards. All I could see were those white teeth grinning through his black face. What happened next I am ashamed to talk about."

"What?"

"I lost control of my bladder. Then I collapsed into his arms. I knew I was safe."

Cyrus and Helga took ten days to rendezvous with some Royal Marine commandos who were waiting to be picked up by the navy.

"I never knew Norway has so many fjords," Helga said. "Marshlands, bogs, and so many difficult mountain ridges. When I thought it would be safe I would get us food from different places. And we made love."

"Do you mean that Cyrus seduced you?" John Graham didn't like to think about sex outside marriage.

"Goodness no! I seduced him!" Helga wondered why John Graham looked so shocked, then remembered Cyrus's telling her that the super was very conventional. Seen too much of the seamy side.

"You must understand that I had lost everything. Everything I cared for, and when one is filled with tragedy, with a terrible sadness that seems it will never go away and the world seems to have stopped, then the making of love can be passionate and violent. Ja, I know it is to escape that one plunges, trying to grasp one's life again before it is too late. The first night Cyrus gathered branches and made a shelter for us at the edge of one of the flatlands and we huddled—"

"Cuddled?"

"That is so. We cuddled together for warmth and then a great passion took over my body while I wept for my dear husband and little ones and all that we in Norway were suffering from, that monstrous devil, Hitler. But when we were back in England it was over for us. The sex part."

"Why didn't you go back to Norway when the war ended?"

"But what for? By then I had done my killing revenges. One dead kraut for each of my loved ones, including my parents. Five in all. Then I was at peace with myself. Because I loved the British for giving me sanctuary, and because Cyrus was now my only family, I offered to housekeep. He gives me pocket money. After the war I got hold of my father's small savings. And there was government compensation for our farm. I am well provided for."

"Never considered remarrying?"

"What for? Cyrus Finnegan and I, we live together as what you British call consenting adults."

"Which means something else again," John Graham corrected her. "To us British, that is. Common law, I think, is better."

56

"To us it means living as friends, as adult persons. We have risked our lives for each other, so why spoil things by getting married when we are so happy in our own style? It would be insincere."

"This all seems most illogical of you," observed Superintendent John Graham when he reported Helga's remarks to Cyrus. "And you, my dear Cyrus, are a most logical person. About everything except in your views on modern art, that is. I'd have thought you'd have married Helga. I think you owe it to her."

"Go carve yourself a pair of marble balls, super. If Michelangelo were still around I'd have him carve you a pair for Christmas."

"Well, well, touchy aren't we," said the super, not in the least put out. "And by the way, old chap. Do you know that you've got your top button in the wrong buttonhole. Meant to mention it earlier. At the private viewing."

"Wish to hell you'd told me at the time." Cyrus adjusted the buttons, silently pledging to take greater trouble over his appearance in future.

"This must be quite the friendliest room in Chelsea, even in London," the super rambled on. He said this nearly every visit. The walls were almost totally concealed from floor to ceiling by pictures. He'd been told the names of the many artists represented but had forgotten all of them, a fact that had much annoyed his daughter, Stella. And there were books on shelves, tables, chairs, and even the floor. It was a miracle, he thought, how Helga managed to control such chaos, adding her own touch with daily bunches of fresh flowers, seeing that Finnegan's cigarette boxes, a dozen or so, were kept stocked with Egyptian, Turkish, American, and English tobacco, and that there was always a well-stocked bar for crisis situations such as this.

Drinks in hand and with background sounds of pans and

dishes banging in the kitchen, Cyrus Finnegan and Superintendent Graham reviewed the problems that Sergeant Purvis would be grappling with.

"Point in question," said the super. "If young Gee chased after that blonde young lady when she fled from the gallery, what did he do when she came running into the gallery? He must have known her. Did he just sit lolling and looking bored?"

"We were outside in Newton Street," Cyrus reminded him. "She'd vanished when we followed those four people inside."

"That's what I'm getting at! Why didn't young Gee follow her downstairs?"

"She probably signaled to him to stay where he was."

"Humph. Damned queer behavior, however one looks at it. I'm not satisfied."

There was a short silence, both men half noting the brilliant sunset beyond the bulky silhouette of Earl's Court Stadium.

"We were very observant, were we? Really bright ones! Tell me, Cyrus, about those two dealers who arrived just before the body was discovered. Forget their names."

"Grossmith and Wurlitzer."

"Sound like a couple of Hollywood comics," snorted the super. "Now give it to me straight, O.K.?"

"Their Ring's been operating for years, but I've never got the hang of it," John Graham admitted.

"Simple, really," said Cyrus. "Even describing it makes me boil when I think of how the innocent owners of goods being auctioned, quite legally, stand to get ripped off. Say youyou've put a drawing up for auction, John. The auctioneersand a couple of your knowledgeable friends say it should fetch between fifty and a hundred quid. Well along comes the Ring. There are usually not more than six. They've appointed a ringleader for the sale. They take it in turns to be the bidder. They know your drawing has a reserve bid of fifty pounds, and that the auctioneer will probably start calling at five pounds. They know also that, handled properly, a dealer can eventually probably sell the drawing for a good mark up. So, they all hold back and the ringleader bids and the item has been sold for sixty-five pounds. After the sale, probably in the nearest pub, they all gather and hold another auction. The one who bids the highest pays off the others. For example, if Wurlitzer bids up to ninety, he'll collect the difference in cash, twenty five quid. That is, sixty-five from ninety. Get it? And so on. The man who's bid the highest gets the drawing, pays off everybody and adds what he's paid the others to his total mark-up. Meanwhile the poor owner just gets his sixty-five pounds less 10% commission for the auctioneer, sometimes higher, plus tax."

"And the auctioneer doesn't know this is happening?"

"Not necessarily. Or, if he does, nothing can be done. The mock-auction is a private sale between friends, and not a chargeable offence that can be proven."

"Are Wurlitzer and Grossmith ringleaders?" inquired the super, "or just participants who never turn down the opportunity to make some extra loot that can be kept hidden from the tax men!"

"Can't answer that one," Cyrus said emphatically. "But I can tell you this. I've purchased one or two things from them, and they've always been most fair and aboveboard. Got that Derain from their gallery in Wigmore Street. Also that Matisse graphite sketch in the corridor, next to the kitchen. No, they have to be aboveboard on occasion, but it's also a fact that at other times they are very much "belowboard" when it comes to rigged bids. But to say so is to risk landing oneself with an action for libel."

"What else do you know about them, Cyrus? Why would the Edinburghs appear to be on such friendly terms with them? You saw how Doctor Edinburgh welcomed them this afternoon?"

"They do his photography. Those top-quality black-and-whites that all dealers need. When I last visited their place, they were setting up a color lab as well."

"Anything else?"

"I'm taking it for granted they take half shares in paintings, such as that Dutch canvas now at the Princess. Have them dotted around in different galleries on consignments. I mean, Italians or Germans, say, will have works on consignment with their British or French Counterparts. Markups are considerable because sometimes it will take two or three years, even more, before a work is sold. And there is also the increasingly risky matter of currency. Pounds up, dollars down, Swiss francs and Japanese yen up. Yet paintings and other works of art, even taking markups into account, are still sound trading commodity staples. Almost as good as gold!"

"Anything else about their operation?" The superintendent seemed genuinely astonished by Cyrus's insight.

"Not really." Cyrus paused as though remembering something. "A while back, three or four years ago, I think, they ran a small restoration business. Didn't make a go of it, though. Employed an art restorer called Peter Knowles. Bad lot, I'm told. Could take a wreck of a canvas and make it look like new. And charge for it. That's when Grossmith and Wurlitzer had their disagreement with him. If he happened to be alone in their shop—it can hardly be called a gallery, even now—he'd add a few quid—a couple of pounds here and there—for himself on anything he sold. He was also a suspected fence. Something happened. I don't know exactly what, for I'm not particularly intimate with the circles Knowles moved in. Anyway, he vanished."

"Dead?"

"Just packed it in. I've heard rumors that he lives in Italy.

60

That he has a villa in the south of France. That he's moved to Wellington, New Zealand. To the States. Anyway, he's no longer around."

Helga now returned with a tureen of spinach soup, Norwegian style, mugs of coffee and Norwegian spice cake, baked that afternoon.

"Bon appétit, my darlings," she said, placing her tray on the low table between their chairs. "Help yourselves and eat hearty. Myself, I go off to bed."

"Thank you," said Superintendent Graham. "You are perfection, Helga. No wonder Cyrus looks well padded! And speaking of Cyrus. Tomorrow, when the reporters learn that Cyrus Finnegan was at the Princess Gallery at the time of the murder, you can expect lots of telephone calls. Daresay even one or two snoopy visitors knocking at the door. I think it would be best if you just say that Mr. Finnegan has gone away for the weekend. He's going to be troubled enough as it is."

"Why?" asked Cyrus, speaking for both Helga and himself.

"Because this is a murder right in the heart of fashionable art galleries and shady dealings and so forth, Purvis is going to keep picking your brains, Cyrus, till you're dizzy! And so will I. Protect him, Helga. See that he has peace of mind and time to contemplate." Superintendent Graham sounded suddenly quite serious. "From what you've been telling me, Cyrus, dealers must be pretty brainy and crafty people if they're to make ends meet."

"As a collector and art historian," Cyrus replied, "I'd say that dealers have enough collective brainpower between them to run the world. I've got the greatest respect for them. And as for the boys and girls in the major auction houses, you should find out for yourself the type of high-grade qualifications they require to keep abreast." Cyrus smiled disarmingly at both Helga and the superintendent.

61

"Of course, they're not a patch as brainy as you coppers at the Yard."

"I know that," Superintendent Graham agreed modestly.

Sergeant Purvis was seldom totally at ease with his fiancée. He was surprised to have such an attractive young lady in love with him. His colleagues, if he only knew, referred to her as Purvis's sex symbol. Not disparagingly, of course, because policewomen, especially pretty ones, added a universal cachet to the force. If you wanted to land yourself in trouble, just say one word against them! But Purvis, a shy man in her presence, felt that asking her to give up their Friday evening at the flicks, as he had done earlier, was a personal imposition. Every married policeman was always having to put duty ahead of home life, which could be sheer hell. And here they were at it already! Cooped up in the station instead of the movies.

Purvis had only to look across the cafeteria table and reflect for a moment on the sheer adoration in Helen's eyes to see that she was thrilled not only at being with him but at being taken into his confidence. Although she was not yet off duty and out of uniform, she was only too happy to spend the evening listening to him describe the setting where a young artist had been brutally dispatched. Between mouthfuls of a second helping of peas, French fries, and corned-beef patties he played down the gory details and managed to introduce some sideswipes at artists in general, and Charles in particular, for spoiling his weekend.

"Tell me, sweetheart," said Purvis, polishing off his third cup of tea, "what the devil's a collage? Though at first it was college, spelled wrong."

"It's a mixture of textures, pasted on a support. Canvas or wood. That's the general idea."

"You mean a mess?"

"Can be, when not done properly," said Helen, amused. "Nails, paper, string, bits of cloth. Composed into a picture. Sometimes a sculpture."

"Serious?"

"Definitely. Tried it myself a couple of times. It's also a good cover-up if you can't draw. Done properly, it looks nice. Even the very best painters, men like Picasso and Braque, have done collages.

"Young Charles had a couple of them listed in his catalogue. Rest of his stuff were paintings. Oils and watercolors. Cyrus Finnegan showed me which was which. I quite liked the watercolors," Sergeant Purvis admitted. "They were understandable. Fields and trees, mostly."

"They're called landscapes," said Helen, placing her hand lightly on his big fist, suddenly worried that she had sounded patronizing. But Sergeant Purvis had not taken her remark as anything but a clear statement of fact.

"Beats me, sweetheart," he said, "where you get so much knowledge to put into your pretty head. O and A levels and a bit more than that, if you ask me. Why, I'll bet you'll be the first lady commissioner while I'm still a downtrodden sergeant. Mark my words!"

Back in his office, with Helen seated at his side, Detective Sergeant Purvis reapplied himself to the worrisome problems of willful murder and the search for facts leading to conviction. Premeditated? Spur of the moment? Accidental? He would ask himself those basic questions over and over again. Who? Why? As for when, that question had been partly answered already. Or had it?

Facts! Purvis repeated the word to himself. After a succession of experiences in police court, as a magistrate and in other judicial capacities—when he had been metaphorically speaking, bloodied, to use a most appropriate foxhunting term—Purvis knew that he must have facts and that it would do no harm to have additional background, supplementary information in order to outfox a policeman's bête noire, lawyers.

The courts were aswarm with self-confident, opinionated whippersnappers who had somehow managed to make their way through law school firmly convinced that they were the hidden pearl in every legal oyster. Early in his career Purvis had been ensnared. It wasn't until Superintendent Graham had taught him how to assemble evidence that he regained his shattered confidence. Proud, self-adulatory, pontificating, pompous pricks was how the super's erudition had classified the entire legal profession for the sergeant's amusement and benefit. Purvis knew that the super had several close friends who were lawyers and one cousin who was a judge in high court. But for men like Sergeant Purvis, who depended on native intelligence and common sense, it was a reassuring opinion.

"What does he mean by 'impasto'?" asked Purvis, who had been silently ruminating and making notes for the past half hour.

"It means painting with knobs on," Helen replied laughingly. "Not really. It's a common way of describing thickly applied paint. Loaded on with brush or palette knife. Will that do, or shall I be more technical and tell you about glazes. That sort of thing."

"I thought it was a type of pasta. Spaghetti or noodles."

"What on earth are you reading?" Helen asked him.

"Introduction to the young man's catalogue. Here. See if you can make head or tail of it. Written by Anthony Kershaw. He was there this afternoon. One of the witnesses. Know anything about him?"

"No. But hand over Who's Who in Art. I'll look him up."

While they had been at supper, one of the police clerks had gone to the central library at the St. James's Park headquarters and obtained a variety of reference books,

64

ranging from *Whittaker's Almanac* to *Pear's Encyclopedia.*
"Doesn't say much," Helen commented when she found the reference. "Anthony Kershaw, painter, writer, schoolteacher. Married to Mary Jane. Exhibited usual places. Edited a book, *Plants for Painters.* Textbook obviously. And another, *History of Botanical Drawing.* Lives at Dower Cottage, High Wycombe. That's all."

"Sounds a bit mixed up, if you ask me," said Purvis. "I mean painting, writing, editing, schoolmastering. Wonder what else he does. Judging from the flower paintings that Charles was exhibiting, I'd say he hadn't been reading Kershaw's books. Mr. Finnegan was trying to explain them to the super. You should have heard him! Nobody in his right mind can explain that nonsense. Just done to fool people!"

Sergeant Purvis suddenly seemed to look straight at his fiancée as though he didn't see her. She knew the signs. He'd thought of something, but wasn't sure how to express it. She waited patiently till he spoke.

"Funny about Miss Gammel," he said. He'd already described the eccentric lady collector during supper.

"In what way?"

"Well. You'd think that with all that money she'd have bought the flower painting that was bought by that American. It was the biggest and, according to Finnegan, the best piece in the show."

"You said Miss Gammel bought two of the watercolor landscapes in the lower gallery. What's odd about that? Perhaps they were more to her taste, as they were to yours."

"Maybe," Detective Sergeant Purvis concurred. "It's just a thought."

After a further interval of silence, during which Purvis wondered whether the super and Finnegan had come up with anything he'd overlooked, he once again ran his finger down the names of those who had attended the private viewing.

"Perhaps Miss Gammel was steered away from that particular painting," he suggested.

"Isn't that being a bit devious?" inquired Helen. "I mean, after all, why be so complicated? Perhaps it was far more simple. That the American lady, Mrs. Winterhalter, happened to get to the Princess Gallery first. First come, first served."

"Possibly," Purvis reluctantly agreed. "Come along, sweetheart. Let's pack it in. Half past ten and I'm beginning to think in riddles. I'll drive you home."

After he had escorted Helen to the house in Cadogan Square where several policewomen shared flats and had opened the door for her, Purvis suddenly gripped her by the arm.

"Your day off tomorrow?" he asked her, knowing the answer.

"Yes. And Sunday, thank goodness. It's been a long, boring week."

"Then will you do me a favor? Come to the Princess Gallery soon after nine. Superintendent Graham and Finnegan are meeting me there."

"Won't I be in the way?"

"Not a bit. I want you to look at the paintings. Those upstairs and the water colors in the lower gallery. You have an eye for art. I want to know what you think."

"I'm not an expert like Cyrus Finnegan. You should be asking him, not me."

"I don't want what you call an expert opinion. I just want your impressions of the gallery and the exhibition. Anything that strikes you. And I'll be particularly interested in your reactions to Doctor Hans Edinburgh, who'll be joining us later. I want to know if you will agree with me that he is one big phony!"

4

It was fortunate that Peter Knowles had not heard Cyrus Finnegan citing London as the center of the art world. As an adoptive New Yorker, one who commuted irregularly from Connecticut when business required, New York was indeed the Big Apple. The apple of the eye of Mammon, to put it crudely. Manhattan was the fleshpot in the world art markets. With it as a base, one could move things anywhere. On mornings such as this one, with Saturday crowds jostling along Fifth Avenue, sun-warmed shoppers intent on pleasure, as was he himself, New York was as stimulating a city as any of the several in which he had resided. He felt happy, and thus saw only happiness in the faces of strangers. Even the store mannequins seemed wildly sophisticated and sexy, as though dummies were not to be left out of man's delight.

The cablegram had been delivered, first verbally over the telephone, then in a telex copy waiting for him at the hotel reception desk. Naturally, it had been addressed to Mr. John Brown. SIGNAL RECOGNIZED STOP GOODS PROMISED. The sign-off "Melita," which was none other than Mrs. Winterhalter's given name, was a code indicating that there was a slight problem, but no cause to worry.

Peter Knowles spent half an hour watching the animals in Central Park Zoo. He purchased food for those he was permitted to feed, silently commiserating with them because of the bars on their cages, which reminded him of places he preferred to forget, then took the pathway leading to the Metropolitan Museum. Privately, he preferred smaller institutions of more manageable accessibility, such as London's Wallace Collection. The Metropolitan Museum was just too damned big. Peter Knowles remembered his own panic and confusion during his first visit to the Metropolitan, when he had gotten lost and never had found what he was looking for. Then, as now, he was interested in the Rembrandts.

Nobody had ever satisfactorily explained to him the reason why Rembrandt was so popular. Same with Leonardo da Vinci. One would be hard put to find a more boring picture than *La Giaconda*, otherwise known as the *Mona Lisa*. As for Rembrandt, he suspected his paintings were popular because they cost so much. You could stand in front of the Met's masterpieces and be mesmerized at the thought of piles of golden dollars. He had read with considerable interest and amusement the newspaper accounts of the missing Rembrandt, so recently returned to the Everdingen Castle Museum near Haarlam in Holland, from which it had been stolen. But why the fuss! Peter Knowles had been studying the works of Rembrandt for years and might be regarded as quite an authority on that painter. Yet there *was* an attraction. He felt it in himself. Not just the money, but the legend.

68

As he climbed the steps leading into the galleries that house, along with other popular treasures, Rembrandt's *Aristotle Contemplating the Bust of Homer* (what a half-assed title for a picture!), Peter Knowles felt a thrill passing through his body, a tremor like a rippling tide. The tide of fortune? Anticipation of what he would shortly see, or what he knew he would see again?

It was always a little unwise to let oneself leap ahead in anticipation. Tempting fate, really. But without the instincts of a gambler, what would be the point of living? As for the international time zones, they merely added to the excitement when so much was at stake. God bless the Wright brothers. Even Leonardo had appreciated the advantages of air travel.

Peter Knowles was self-interested and calculating and would not flinch, were a death convenient to his plans. If people wanted that painter of dark-brown moods, Rembrandt, then he would find ways to satisfy their demand. Not for him the highlights of Rembrandt's chiaroscuro, his flickering nuances enriching landscapes and portraits with golden glow. Bugger Rembrandt! Bugger everyone! Like so many visionaries working for their own purposes, Knowles was impatient to get going.

Although the summer day and early evening had been pleasantly warm, during the night a strong wind rose and blew violently at the trees surrounding the Kershaw's cottage. Accustomed to such sudden changes in weather, those who reside in the country grow used to nature's variety. After all, that is half the enjoyment of country life. For those who live near the sea, weather carries an extra bonus.

Mary wished that she and Tony lived near the sea. She found the Thames Valley dank and dreary with its fogs and river mist. Still, she enjoyed the summer days when she could spend timeless hours gardening. She knew from experience that the wind that now slammed against the roof, rattling tiles and windows, would be short-lived. The BBC had forecast a clear, sunny Saturday like yesterday. She would pick some tomatoes, tie the broadbeans more firmly to their stakes, and mow the front lawn.

It was already two o'clock in the morning, and she was unable to sleep. Her bedside light flickered when a branch touched the power line outside. Not that she was afraid. The howling wind was really quite companionable! She disliked being on her own in the cottage, and with windows latched and front and back doors locked she knew that she was physically safe from harm. What kept her from sleep were her nagging thoughts about Tony's behavior. He was a completely different person from the man she had married. Ridiculous, really, because she was sure she was not alone in observing the change. Perhaps she was being too dramatic. Possibly there was a simple explanation that accounted for his long periods of silence. Evening after evening he would come home, usually after midnight, without telling her where he'd been, or what he'd been doing. Well, one of these days she'd follow him, if possible, and find out what he was up to. Treating her more like a stranger or a child than the wife who loved him dearly and would forgive him anything. Anything! After five years of marriage she was only now becoming aware, and most reluctantly at that, how marriages such as theirs could easily be tipped into disaster. Without mutual confidence even the best would founder. Instinctively she felt she had been caught up in something beyond her control, something she didn't understand.

What had she done wrong? Nothing. Her conscience was clear, but was his? Had he fallen in love with some passing fancy? Mary realized from what she'd read in novels and women's magazines that temporary infatuations could become permanent unless the other partner did something about it! She had no way of judging such matters, having been a virgin herself when they had married, but she felt privately that sexually Tony was pretty cold. Even frigid. It seemed most unlikely that he would get entangled with another woman for the sake of extra sex. She knew that some women were predatory bitches determined to ensnare another's husband. Veritable barracudas. No, she didn't think her Tony would fall for one of those.

Mentally she itemized their former daily pattern. A good breakfast at seven. Preparation of sandwiches and thermos, but only on days when he said he would not be lunching at school. Mondays, Tuesdays, and Fridays he took the eight A.M. bus to Marlow. From Marlow he took another bus to Twyford Junction and walked the half mile to school. Usually home by six. Being an art teacher, he had no schoolwork to correct. Tuesdays and Thursdays he went to London to visit galleries, sometimes taking her with him, though she disliked all big cities with their crowded streets. She preferred walking in the beech woods near their cottage. On weekends he liked to go sketching. Most evenings he would write for a couple of hours. Articles, then his book. He was always there. Some wives might have found their life together extremely dull. But she had been happy enough until the change.

It was on sleepless nights like this, when she lay waiting to hear him open the front door and comes upstairs, that their former life seemed a century ago. And the lies! Well, he didn't tell her lies. He just brushed aside her inquiries. He had told her he'd given up painting altogether, even sketching on the weekends. Yet she could still smell paint and turpentine when he crossed the room or when he bent to kiss her. Not a strong smell, but there all the same. She

71

pretended not to notice. At least it was better than sniffing some nameless, exotic perfume or discovering lipstick on his shirt collar! There was none of that, thank goodness.

It was just that he didn't confide in her when it was obvious that he was very worried about something. And there was another change. He was no longer tight-fisted about money. He bought her surprise presents unexpectedly, not just on birthdays and at Christmas. Bought some nice furniture, too. He had talked about buying a car. No more busing to school. Told her the editors were paying more for his articles and that his books were selling well! Sheer nonsense. It just wasn't true. She'd made inquiries. Damn it all! She was going to find out! He wasn't going to get away with it any longer!

That night, Tony Kershaw didn't come home. Mary was forcing herself to swallow some breakfast toast and coffee when she saw him open the garden gate. She could see from his expression that something horrible had occurred, some disaster.

For a brief second she reflected what to do. Was her imagination playing tricks again? If she hadn't known him so well, or thought she did, she could well have interpreted his appearance as a threat to her own safety. He looked angry enough to slit her throat! Instead, he came towards her and hesitatingly embraced her, as though wishing to comfort her, his kisses the merest touch on either cheek. Her moment of fear passed, sensing that he was glad to be with her, seeking sanctuary perhaps.

God! How much she wished he had confided in her these past months. She had never seen him looking so distraught. Or was this more play-acting on his part, a continued evasion of truth, some new deception ready to engulf her?

"Tony!" she found herself shouting. "You look ghastly! Tell me what on earth's happened?"

"I forgot that it's too early for you to have seen the

72

papers. Read this." He handed her a copy of the *Daily Telegraph*. "It's about Charles. He's dead. Murdered. Looked like an accident."

"Oh no!" Mary let the newpaper fall to the floor unopened. "When? It just can't be!"

"Yesterday afternoon at the Princess Gallery. I was there. It was the private viewing of his first exhibition. I'd gone there especially to review it. Of course, you weren't to know he had become an artist. That I'd been giving him special lessons."

Mary realized that she was sounding hysterical, that she would start swearing at him again.

"My nephew gets killed and you don't bother to at least telephone!" The impact of Tony's words was striking home. "But this is unthinkable, Charles's being a painter, maybe so, but why the secrecy? His exhibition, you say? Just too farfetched."

"He asked me not to tell you," Tony said meekly, following her into the living room. "Afraid he'd flunk it, as he flunked school. Didn't want to disappoint you. So now you know the reason why I've been keeping such strange hours. I've been staying late to teach him. It was I who arranged with the Edinburghs to give him this show."

"No way am I going to swallow that one," Mary caught herself shouting at him, so lowered her voice. "A sixteen-year-old who is still learning to paint, having a one-man exhibition in a swank West End gallery. That's preposterous!" She paused, then continued impatiently. "And why be so secretive. Why in heaven's name didn't you tell me. I was beginning to think you'd been tom-catting around with another woman!"

"It's too complicated to explain. Especially now, when we're both upset," Kershaw snapped back at her. "Christ! If it had been as simple! I never expected this, though. It changes everything."

73

"Everything? What do you mean by that? Or am I left out of the picture, as usual?" Mary picked up her half-finished cup of coffee, then put it down again. She was trying desperately to gather her thoughts.

"I suppose you've cabled?" she asked him.

"No. I've just been wandering about London half the night. Missed the last train and had to wait for the milk-run. Besides, I didn't know what to write. Cables are so impersonal.

"It means we'll be responsible for the funeral, I suppose?" Mary felt tears welling up; in another minute she would lose control and slap him across the face for being such a weak, ineffectual ninny.

"Naturally we'll have to pay, but not till after the inquest. I understand it will be held this coming Tuesday." He paused, avoiding her eyes. "The autopsy is being carried out this morning. We won't hear the results, of course. We'll have to wait."

"Do you think he'll come over for the funeral?" Mary asked.

"Not the way things are now. The whole business gone wrong. He won't like it. Not one bit."

"I don't understand. What do you mean? What business has gone wrong? What are you suggesting? Isn't Charles's death enough, or is there something else you're hiding from me? Wouldn't put it past you."

"Nothing that affects you," he answered curtly. "I'm so bloody exhausted I must get some rest. I'll go upstairs and lie down for a couple of hours."

"And the cable?" Mary reminded him. "Are you going to shirk that? Or do you want me to send it?"

"That can wait. Whether he gets it now or tomorrow, nothing will make any difference. I'm as upset as you are about Charles. Bloody terrible end, no doubt about that. I'll just have to do some rethinking, that's all."

"Another of your rotten schemes backfired, is that it?"
Mary said viciously. "I should have known!"

Mr. Spokes, the school's head gardener, entered his hot-house shortly before eight-thirty on that glorious Saturday morning, the day after the murder he'd just been readng about. In a few hours the flower show would be opened to the public. Judging would begin at nine-thirty, which meant he still had an hour to go. Judging usually ended promptly at eleven, when the judges, including himself, retired conveniently to the nearest pub. There, he and his colleagues would debate, over numerous pints of beer, the subtle grading of awards, honorable mentions, entries of distinction, third, second, and first prizes. Though he always tactfully withdrew when his own specialty of flowering plants was being scrutinized, year after year Mr. Spokes had the satisfaction of winning such awards as the county silver cup and the *House and Garden* Gold Medal.

He moved slowly along the narrow aisle between the crowded shelves until he reached the special table reserved for the plants and vegetables he would enter. This year, in his opinion, while several of the entries would do well, none would do better than the majestic pink and red gloxinia (*Sinningia speciosa*), which he had personally nourished and nursed with those special plant foods that produced such miracles of horticulture.

Superintendent Graham, with his delight in puns, might have described Mr. Spokes as being a very down-to-earth person. Like the majority of professional gardeners, he was a calm, patient, soil-cultivating man who liked nothing better than to be left alone to talk with plants and vegetables. Having done his bit as a soldier during two world wars he kept very much to himself, as if day-to-day communication with the human race would be a waste of time more profitably used for the benefit of flowers.

75

Stooped, gray-haired, with a crippled leg and other wounds not visible when he was dressed, Mr. Spokes was a model of patience. Nobody had ever heard him swear. But if someone had been with him that morning and seen his astonishment being replaced by panic, he would have heard cursing and swearing in a variety of oaths, until Mr. Spokes regained his usual calm. Obviously, there was a mistake. The gloxinia, complete with pot, was missing. He could see the empty space where it had stood. But then, who would steal a plant, early on a Saturday morning, unless for a practical joke? One of the boys was playing tricks!

He remembered telling young Knowles, who helped him with various chores such as watering, not to load the van for the flower show till he was instructed to do so. Mr. Spokes himself would load the gloxinia. He'd been explicit, and young Knowles was a quick learner and quick on the uptake. He would make a good gardener one of these days. Had green fingers. Knew almost as much about the care of plants as he did himself. It would be one of the other kids up to pranks. He would go and find Knowles, because he should have been here with the van. Theft? It was downright vandalism. He trusted that no harm had befallen the plant. If it didn't turn up, then he'd have to substitute the African violet, *Saintpaulia ionantha*.

Mr. Spokes went in search of the matron.

"Where's young Knowles?" he asked when he found her coming out of the dining hall.

"He's hopped it," the matron informed him.

"Hopped it? What d'you mean? He should be helping me with entries for the flower show."

"Well, he's gone, that's the long and short. Bed was slept in but he was missing at Friday's roll call and breakfast. Vanished without telling anyone what he's up to."

Mr. Spokes made his way back to the hothouse. He was

76

baffled but was no longer worrying about the safety of his plant. What had got into the lad? He was a quiet, likable young man and had been as excited as a bee about the flower show. It would be unnatural for him to steal. Nor would he be likely to get into mischief like some of the other lads. He was a quiet, country-loving lad who would make a good gardener. From Mr. Spokes, if he had been asked for his opinion, there could be no better character reference than that.

5

On such a sunny summer's morning as this, London, like New York, sparkled.

Cyrus Finnegan, having tossed and turned most of the night, read the morning newspapers with only a modicum of attention. As usual, too many generalizations. Too many reports of occurrences of which one would only read the beginning. Meaningless tidbits filed from overseas agencies with a fat chance of one's ever learning the outcome. Cyrus preferred specifics. For example, the *Mirror* now informed him that the Italian racing driver Giuseppe Dagerra, stepson of Doctor Edinburgh, was engaged to Trudi Harwick, now appearing in *Pop Goes the Easel*, a hot-rock adaptation of *La Bohème*.

Helga, whom Cyrus had expected to show at least some interest in this information, merely shrugged her shoulders and went out to the kitchen to make him a second batch of pancakes.

The telephone cut through the silence.

"Purvis here, sir," said the sergeant, temporarily forgetting yesterday's informalities. "Will you be free to come with me to the Castle Theatre before we go to the Princess Gallery, sir?"

"Won't that be a bit early, old chap? We've a nine o'clock rendezvous, with the super, and Edinburgh's joining us at ten."

"Won't take half a jiffy, Mr. Finnegan. I've already spoken to the stage manager. He's waiting for us now."

"On a lovely summer Saturday morning like this! He'll bless you for that! Theater people like to sleep late, rain or shine."

"They've a rehearsal set for later. Something to do with this afternoon's matinée. Trudi Harwick played hookey for both performances yesterday. Her replacement has to rehearse a couple of routines. I'll send a car for you, Mr. Finnegan. In fact, it is probably outside your building right now."

"Crafty bugger, aren't you! Why don't you put me into uniform and turn me into a dick!"

"We appreciate your spirit of cooperation, sir." The telephone clicked.

Mr. Hy Silver, stage manager, greeted them without much enthusiasm. He was a young man in his late twenties, with an expression on his shallow face indicating that he was totally resigned to the twists of fate and that nothing he saw or heard could shake a phlegmatic indifference to matters not directly related to his job. His eyes reflected wariness, his mouth was set with cynicism. And anger also, Cyrus noted.

"Just what is this?" he asked impatiently. "First it's reporters and now police. Reporter from the *Mirror* was camped outside the stage door waiting for me when I

79

arrived. Maria Edinburgh had let her see the list of those who'd been invited. Trudi's name caught her eye. She'd done a piece on her when the show went into rehearsal. I'd told her all I knew after last night's show. Apparently that wasn't enough for Miss Eager Beaver. Expected me to know everything about what the girls do with their spare time."

"What exactly do you know?" Purvis asked him politely. Mr. Silver glanced at his clipboard.

"I can give you her physical description, is that it? Five feet seven, I reckon. Bit tall for a chorus line but our director likes them that way. Rockettes in minis. Good leg show that can be seen and gawked at, no matter where your seat is. Brunette. Hazel eyes."

"You're sure we're talking about the same girl? The Miss Harwick I'm looking for is a blonde."

"Wigs!" Mr. Hy Silver unbent enough for a brief chuckle. "She's a brown hair, believe me. I've done three shows with her, in addition to this one. One notices. Not that I'm all that stuck on girls. Just see them as props, get me? Lot of legs and arms waving about. Some fair, some dark, a couple of redheads. Must have good legs and snappy figure, plenty of oomph in the round, get me?"

"We get you," Purvis observed. "Is she better than the others?"

"Yes, you could say so, I'd go along with that."

"Yet you're replacing her after only missing two performances? Suppose she's ill?"

"Then she'd have her landlady phone in. Skip a rehearsal or performance, boy, and that's it. With half the kids in London "resting," and most of them willing to sell their mums for even a walk-on! I tell you, discipline and promptness, they're what count. Tough, I know, but in theater we'd collapse without discipline and a sense of responsibility. Takes dedication."

"I'd like to have a word with some of the other girls. Or is it too early in the day?"

Mr. Hy Silver once again looked at his clipboard.

"There's a photo call set for ten-thirty. Then afterwards some of them go right into rehearsal with Trudi's replacement. Doubt if you'd get much out of the company. Doubt if any of them could tell you the color of her nail polish. Trudi kept very much to herself. Bit standoffish."

"Then we won't take up any more of your time," said Purvis. "It may be necessary for us to send an officer round later on to ask some questions. But only if we have to. Did she give a telephone number?"

"Yes. It says messages can be left at six-six-one, ninety-nine eighty-six."

"That's Hampstead, surely," Cyrus Finnegan cut in. He flipped rapidly through a pocket diary. "Thought so. Doctor Edinburgh's number: Haverstock Hill. Not true. Hampstead, but people living there like to pretend it's more classy."

"Well I'll be damned!" Sergeant Purvis grinned happily. "How's that for starters, Finnegan! It's a ruddy marvel the way clues pop up when least expected. So now we'll let you get on with your work, Mr. Silver. Thank you for your help. I hope we won't need to trouble you further. Just one last request. Do you mind if Mr. Finnegan here dials that number?"

"Go ahead, please." He pointed at a wall telephone.

While Cyrus Finnegan waited for somebody to answer his call, Purvis made one or two entries in his notebook.

"You told us a few minutes ago that Trudi Harwick was a bit standoffish. What do you mean by that?"

"Difficult to answer that one," said Mr. Silver. "Just seems that recently she's been a bit less friendly. Used to be quite a chatterbox. I could see for myself—from a distance, as I said before, I don't pay much attention to girls.

81

Nowadays when she's not on stage she's off reading in a corner by herself. Racing magazines. Motoring, that sort of stuff."

"Only natural if she's engaged to be married to a racing driver, wouldn't you say?"

"How were we to know about that? Hadn't heard of this Daggers, or whatever you call him, till that reporter told us. She got that gossipy tidbit from Maria, I daresay." Mr. Silver paused for a moment's reflection. "Besides, what is it she's been up to? Surely you don't suspect her of murder. Doesn't mention anything in the newspaper about her actually being at the Princess Gallery when that bloke was killed, does it?"

"No, it doesn't. Why should it? Nor does it mention that Giuseppe Dagerra was there, either." Purvis saw Cyrus replace the telephone. "No reply, Mr. Finnegan? Well then, let's get along to the gallery. On with the show."

"You're so right," said Mr. Silver, but to himself.

"Unlike the super to be late," Purvis said when they arrived at the gallery. He unlocked the door, after picking up a couple of newspapers that had been propped against it.

"Give him five minutes, shall we?" Cyrus Finnegan seated himself at the catalogue table.

"Well, what do you make of it, Mr. Finnegan? Bit of a rum one, wouldn't you say? I've asked Policewoman Maitland to join me here later. She's bang on when it comes to art."

"At least the papers report it as accidental death," Cyrus said. "Murder's not hinted at. How's this for a caption? 'Boy genius takes secret with him.' And here's another. 'Nameless young artist steps from picture.' Damned bad taste I'd say!"

"Any ideas, Finnegan? The super once said the first rule

is to observe the obvious. A second tip is to ask oneself whether the impossible is possible."

"What's obvious?" queried Cyrus. "I'd say that obviously Charles didn't paint these pictures. The paintings downstairs, the watercolor drawings, are completely different in style as well as media used. I find it difficult to believe the same artist painted the ones downstairs and also these in the upper gallery. Secondly, did you notice how Kershaw seemed to take over? Pushing Edinburgh aside, trying to comfort Maria. She went to Kershaw first. Not to her husband."

"Nothing strange in that! Kershaw was nearest to her, that's all. People react instinctively when they're shocked. But where the devil is the super? Edinburgh will be here shortly. Try his home will you? Ask when he left."

It was Stella who answered.

"Mr. Finnegan! I was just looking up the Princess Gallery in the phone book. I tried to get you at your flat, but Helga said you'd gone to Dublin! Dad told me to try the gallery because he didn't want to ring his office. He's had an accident!" Stella's voice sounded just like her mother's.

"What's happened?"

"Nothing serious. One of those silly, stupid things. Could happen to any of us. He slipped on the stairs."

"The super's slipped on his staircase," Cyrus informed Purvis while listening to what Stella reported.

"Early this morning, round about six. Told Mum that he couldn't sleep because he was worrying about a murder and that he had tried to prove something, something to do with the way a person might trip. He's not badly hurt, thank goodness. Doctor has already been and told Dad to stay in bed for the weekend and rest his back. He's also wrenched his shoulder."

"Tell him that I'll drop in to see him later this morning,"

83

said Cyrus. "Sorry and all that, but it was silly of him all the same, fooling around on the staircase. He might have broken his neck."

"He did ask me to ask you to tell Sergeant Purvis one word. Impossible."

"Impossible. Thanks, Stella. See you later. Tell your Dad message received, loud and clear."

"Daft bugger," was the sergeant's only comment.

Perhaps he would have said more, but at that moment Doctor Edinburgh entered the gallery. In one hand he carried a small wreath. He paid no attention to Purvis and Finnegan. Removing Mrs. Winterhalter's painting, he placed the wreath on the mantelpiece.

"In memoriam," Doctor Edinburgh said quietly. "I thought it appropriate. To have a sign of respect for the dead. When we open again on Monday, people are bound to be curious. I've placed notices in the *Times* and *Telegraph* calling it a memorial exhibition."

"You don't waste time, do you doctor!" Purvis said sarcastically. "Putting his prices up, too?"

"Your remarks are quite uncalled for, sergeant."

"They were meant to be," said Purvis, getting ready for battle. Sanctimonious runt, he thought privately.

"I ordered Maria to remain at home," Edinburgh said, ignoring the sergeant's rudeness. "Bed rest. Gave her a sleeping draft last night. She also has some tranquilizers if she needs. A member of my profession has to be particularly wary when prescribing for his own family."

"Risk of the enthusiastic overdose, eh?" said Cyrus. "After a row, nothing simpler, I suppose. Yet you and Maria appeared to be on best of terms when we saw you together yesterday. You always are."

"Oh yes, we are," Edinburgh said, almost too enthusiastically.

"And your daughter? Does she get along with both of

84

you?" Purvis put the question abruptly, indulging in shock tactics.

"Yes, indeed." Edinburgh was not a person to be caught off guard. "But how did you learn about her? I was going to tell you this morning. Yesterday, everything was so muddled, it just didn't occur to either of us that you'd want to question Trudi Harwick. That's the stage name she uses."

Sergeant Purvis wouldn't let himself be sidetracked. "That she was the young lady who discovered the body and screamed like a banshee? You let her run from the gallery, chased by your son-in-law, pretending all the time that she was a stranger? Come on, doctor, act your age. Why didn't you tell us her identity? Or did you expect to get away with it?"

"You didn't ask," Doctor Edinburgh began, then changed his tactic. "No, that won't do, will it? I left it to Kershaw to tell you. He seemed to have taken over. To be in control."

"Mr. Kershaw seemed to be more concerned about Mrs. Edinburgh than your daughter, doctor," Purvis said bluntly.

Edinburgh brought another chair nearer to the table and sat down. This morning he was wearing a dark suit, white shirt, and black tie and shoes. He seemed to have shrunk a little during the night. Perhaps the act of mourning made him appear shorter, as bodies shrink for coffins.

"Then let's start at the beginning, doctor. Trudi Harwick. That's her stage name, so what's her real name?"

"Trudi Hertz. She retains our family name. I changed my name from Hertz to Edinburgh soon after I came to England. Trudi didn't join me till after the war. After her mother had been taken to Buchenwald, she lived with relations in Poland and then in Czechoslovakia. The United Nations relief people reunited us. I'd never given up hope that she would be traced."

"And the present Mrs. Edinburgh?"

"Maria and I married six months before Trudi was found. Not that it would have made any difference."

"Did you meet Mrs. Edinburgh in London?" This time it was Cyrus who spoke. He felt that Purvis would not object if he cut in.

"I met her in Yugoslavia. She was singing in the Dubrovnik Music Festival. Young Gee was with her. She'd already separated from her husband. With us, it was love at first sight." Doctor Edinburgh blushed unexpectedly. "Sounds silly, I know, but it's true all the same. I followed her from concert to concert. Italy, Spain, Paris, and Brussels. We were married eventually in Holland."

"That must have been a busy year for you, doctor," Purvis said. "Rough on your practice. What happened to your patients?"

"Oh, it wasn't a lightning courtship," Edinburgh reassured him. "It was a good three years from when we first met till we got married. Then six months later my darling Trudi arrived in London. The Red Cross flew her to Amsterdam, and I fetched her from there."

"So, where is she this morning, doctor?" Cyrus Finnegan and Sergeant Purvis watched Edinburgh closely.

"That I can't tell you," he replied. "Your guess is as good as mine."

"Except that you have an advantage over us," said Purvis smoothly. "You can tell us more about your stepson and the flat you let him use when he's in England. No, she's not there." Purvis raised his hand, for Doctor Edinburgh was about to interrupt him.

"We had the flat checked last night. I'm going round there again myself after we're through here. Explain, if you will, sir, these special patients who prefer not to come to your home. Why do you need two surgeries? What with gadding about Europe, having a nice home in Hampstead and a posh consulting room-cum-flat off Wimpole Street, though our men tell me it's nearer to Marble Arch, there can't be much shortage of what some of the rest of us find difficult to lay our hands on. Cash!"

"You're leaving out the Princess Gallery as another of the doctor's assets," Cyrus reminded him. "Or am I exaggerating? What about Tony Kershaw and our old friends, Grossmith and Wurlitzer? What's the setup there, doctor?"

"And what about Charles," Purvis added, as though in afterthought. "It's beginning to look murky, doctor. We need some answers."

Doctor Edinburgh appeared to absorb this barrage of questions with equanimity.

"Shall I deal with the patients first? There aren't many of them, but they are well known and influential. It would be a disaster for them publicly if their illnesses were generally known. Some have already spent time in hospitals or clinics. Drugs. Alcoholism. Self-destructiveness. Retrogressive depressives. And a high proportion of schizophrenics. The art and theater worlds are crammed with such unfortunates."

"And the world of music?" Cyrus knew the super suspected that Maria was taking uppers and downers. Or something harder.

"Surprisingly, not to the same extent," Edinburgh said quietly. "It could well be something to do with rigid discipline required, if one is to endure the monotonously long hours of daily practice. It is my theory that the act of handling a musical instrument leads to sublimation of self: transference of repressions, so that the violin, piano, or voice, even, becomes the id." Edinburgh's voice sounded soothingly professional.

"That might also apply to writers," Cyrus commented smiling. "Though in my case, hours spent at my typewriter have done nothing to get rid of my anxieties. My typewriter has a fat chance of becoming my id. I'm even uncertain

87

whether my typewriter is friend or foe. And what about Charles? Was he one of your specials? The police are trying to trace his parents, which is difficult as we don't know his surname."

"Haven't got a line on his parents yet," said Purvis. "But we'll have something on the lad by this evening. No secrets hidden from our computer, where crime's concerned, though so far it would seem the only crime the lad commited was to paint those horrible pictures."

The brief silence which followed upon the sergeant's weighty prophecy was broken abruptly by Doctor Edinburgh.

"I'll save you all trouble, sergeant. Charles's name is Knowles. You remember Knowles, don't you Finnegan? Saw quite a bit of him at one time in the London Galleries, didn't we? Particularly Tony Kershaw. He married Knowles's sister. The lad's mother was one of my patients. She did away with herself, poor dear. Father deserted him, too. Without the Kershaws' taking an interest in him, the lad might just as well have been an orphan."

"If you don't mind, Mr. Finnegan," said Sergeant Purvis, once he had recovered from Edinburgh's surprising statements, "I wonder if you'd be good enough to pop along and have a word with the super? You'd better take a taxi as I'll be wanting my car later. I'll stay here with Doctor Edinburgh. We've quite a bit to talk about, haven't we, doctor?"

"I'm sure about that," Cyrus heard Edinburgh say as he left to find a taxi. He'd probably get one outside the Westbury.

He would have liked to stay and hear what approach Sergeant Purvis would follow. Having provided such valuable information in such a dramatic manner, it would now seem that Edinburgh would retire and make Purvis dig hard before he would tell him more. Edinburgh had turned defensive. Unfortunately Sergeant Purvis was inclined to be aggressive when handling those who had the misfortune to be foreign-born.

Even driving the circular route via Regents Park the journey by taxi took nearly thirty minutes. The traffic was not particularly heavy for a Saturday, but the driver stuck strictly to speed limits, timed his arrival at each traffic light as it turned to red, and quite correctly, if overzealously, thought Cyrus, gave priority to prams and dawdling children at every pedestrian crossing.

Cyrus Finnegan, comfortably enclosed behind the glass partition, let his thoughts roam with barely subconscious guidance on his part. He was glad to have this thirty minutes to himself. The more he reviewed the sequence of events, went over again in his mind the statements made and subsequent comments and observations on the part of Superintendent Graham and Sergeant Purvis, each issue became clouded. Somewhere, he realized, there lay buried a pattern of circumstance. Cause leading to implementation. A series of events, over how many years? In which countries?

This morning had been established the family link among Edinburgh, Trudi, Maria, and Giuseppe Dagerra. Now there was a further link from Knowles, to Charles, to Mary Kershaw and Kershaw himself, a partner in the Princess Gallery. A partner without financial investment, Edinburgh said. This in turn reintroduced Grossmith and Wurlitzer, who at one time had employed Peter Knowles, Charles's father.

Considering the situation in its widest, geographical sense, obviously the first country was England. Edinburgh and Maria had settled there with Trudi—his daughter, her stepdaughter. Gee Dagerra, Maria's son and Hans Edinburgh's stepson, were engaged. Nothing improper there. Quite legal for them to get married eventually. Gee himself

89

was domiciled in Italy and only lived in London during term time or on visits for racing.

Grossmith and Wurlitzer would travel to the Continent, mostly to Paris, Zurich, and Rome. They had told Cyrus this when he asked them once whether they ever visited large art exhibitions in West Germany. He himself had just come back from visiting the huge Dokumenta Art Fair at Düsseldorf.

Peter Knowles? Cyrus remembered him as a good-looking, well-dressed man who would now be in his middle forties. Reddish hair. Well proportioned. Trim. Quite a salesman, with a flair for making unusual "finds," the Haarlem Miniatures, for example. Knowles had sold them to a museum in Latin America. Cyrus didn't remember which country. Knowles had even published a paper on Haarlem Miniaturists, a forgotten group of seventeenth-century Dutch painters. Before he became a dealer, Peter Knowles had read for a degree in art history and followed with one year's postgraduate work at the Courtauld Institute. A convenient shortcut, to crime apparently.

That would have been about sixteen or seventeen years ago. Peter Knowles had already been on the make while Cyrus Finnegan, who had just completed his war service, was still a student. He had been arrested for suspected fraud. The Haarlem Miniaturists were his own invention. But the crown prosecutor had been unable to prove that Knowles had actually forged the works himself. Because the third parties lived in Damascus and Latin America the case was eventually dropped. Shortly afterwards Knowles vanished, only to reappear some months later in Cape Town. His imaginative application of art scholarship left his dealer colleagues agog with unexpressed admiration. And he had left behind him a son. And a sister. And a young woman who chose to escape from life. And a brother-in-law. Murky, thought Cyrus, agreeing with Purvis. At least Knowles was far away now. On the other side of the Atlantic? Perhaps. Nobody had seen him in London for years.

While Cyrus ruminated on this and other points that were still, at this stage, undecipherable, he decided that after he had finished his visit with Superintendent Graham, he would take an afternoon train to High Wycombe and drop in on the Kershaws. Somehow, he felt it would be timely to do so. Purvis would have to get along without him.

Mrs. Graham opened the door. In the background Cyrus saw Stella, as pale and shaken-looking as her mother. She had Mrs. Graham's coloring, blue eyes and auburn hair, but otherwise her looks were those of the super. And she had his mannerisms.

"Gosh, we got such a scare," Mrs. Graham said excitedly. "Five hours since it happened, and he's still sore."

"The doctor said there's no need for us to worry, Mum," Stella said comfortingly. Cyrus suspected she must have said so a hundred times already.

"Will you take a spot of lunch with us, Mr. Finnegan? I'll fetch a tray up to Dad's room. Just soup and salad."

"That will do me nicely, Stella, thank you."

Cyrus had always liked the Grahams. Stella was now sixteen. Same age as Charles Knowles. He thought sadly about their different backgrounds. Charles, with parents who had abandoned him. Stella quietly secure in the villa close by the Lords Cricket Ground. The super kept a powerful pair of binoculars in the master bedroom so that he could watch the matches. He had a season pass to the grounds, duly paid for annually, but that was kept for the national and international matches. As Cyrus followed Mrs. Graham up the narrow stairs, Stella blew him a kiss and grinned. She had once told Cyrus she wished he were her godfather, so that he'd have to take her to zoos and pantomimes and Madame Tussaud's.

"Here's our invalid," said Mrs. Graham.

From a large double bed cluttered with newspapers and notebooks, the super grinned back at him, like an older, mischievous impersonation of his daughter.

"Damned experiment didn't work," he said. "That's one way of looking at it, I suppose. On the other hand it did work all right. Proved that young fellow could only have dislocated his shoulder, at worst. Just as I did. The police surgeon said nothing about dislocations, did he? Fill me in on what Purvis is up to. Good lad, but inclined to bully."

Cyrus told him about their visit to the theater, about Trudi's being Edinburgh's daughter and no blonde.

"All in the family, Cyrus. Still think Edinburgh did it? Queer lot, I'd say. My hunch is that Edinburgh killed the lad."

"How could he? John, you and I saw he was only downstairs to telephone. Charles wasn't even in the gallery."

"But we don't know that Edinburgh telephoned. All we saw was Mrs. Edinburgh lift the extension receiver and listen. We didn't hear any sounds. Bells. Sometimes when one dials, the bell echoes faintly on the extension. What we saw was that Maria appeared to be satisfied. Not because of what she'd heard her husband saying over the phone that was different from what she imagined he might be saying. It was because she didn't hear anything. He wasn't on the phone at all!"

"Beats me, John, that with enough brainpower to unravel something as complicated as that, you hadn't enough common sense not to try some tom-fool experiment, like accidentally on purpose trying to break your thick neck without actually breaking it while falling down a stairway. I always thought you chaps at the Yard solved problems with slide rules, not sliding downstairs. Measure for measure. And a little bit of calculus thrown in, supported by photographs and those canny miracles of forensic analysis."

"Your words," the super replied, "make me wonder yet again how on earth Helga puts up with you. I was proving a point, as I trust our good sergeant is doing this very moment."

"I suspect he's already one clue ahead of his boss," Cyrus quipped. "Did you know he has a nice policewoman acting as your stand-in?"

"That will be his girlfriend, Policewoman Maitland." The super sounded pleased. "Jolly lass, that. Not in the least bit starry-eyed. By now she'll have her sergeant sticking pins into Edinburgh, as though he's mounting a butterfly. He'll manage without me. Won't have to bring the Yard into it. But he'll be counting on your support, Cyrus." Superintendent Graham turned sideways, his face twisting from pain and effort. "But I'll be lying here thinking. I'll come up with something."

"You'd better take it easy, John."

"The devil I will." The super's forehead was perspiring. "Last night you told me you didn't think that the paintings in the upper gallery were by the same person who did those downstairs. You said it was pretty obvious. Well, it wasn't obvious to me. Granted the ones upstairs might have been painted by a chimpanzee. But the watercolors downstairs . . . well, from my experience as an amateur, I'd only say they show promise."

"Funny you should remind me of that," Cyrus said. "I thought when I first saw them that somebody was being careless. Deliberately playing around when actually they could do better. Nice, pretty landscapes, but with inaccurate color tones."

"Pleasing enough for Miss Gammel to fall for two of them!" intoned the super.

"Which reminds me," said Cyrus. "Purvis told me he telephoned her yesterday evening. He was puzzled about what we had said about her looking so surprised when Edinburgh dashed downstairs so suddenly. It appears there's nothing to it. He'd just told her he'd already chosen two watercolors for her. He'd rushed down to put red seals on them before somebody else purchased them. Miss Gammel is quite used to that sort of thing. She's not really interested in seeing what she buys. Just interested in possession. Her expression was not of surprise. It was consternation. She was still not quite at home at the Princess Gallery. This was only her second visit. She was afraid Edinburgh might be taking advantage of her. At any rate, she told Purvis, she doesn't really like Doctor Edinburgh, nor his wife."

"Humph!" Superintendent Graham snorted in disbelief. "Fools are soon parted from their money, and that's a fact."

At that moment Stella appeared with a tray loaded with luncheon for two. Cyrus reminded himself to phone Helga and have her tell Sergeant Purvis that he was going to High Wycombe.

"Right now," he said to the super after Stella had left, "my money's on somebody else. One of five men. You follow?"

"What about women? Plenty of women artists in the world."

"Yes indeed, bless them. A few, only a few, mind, every bit as good as men, especially when it comes to sculpture. But we're dealing with paintings."

"Do you think Trudi Harwick murdered the lad?" asked the Superintendent.

"Certainly not. Even though she is an actress, small parts, chorus line and so forth, hers was no act. She was terrified. Also, she'd have to have a motive. Motive for

94

killing a boy of sixteen! That alone suggests something exceptional."

Cyrus adjusted the pillows so that the super could swallow his soup without spilling it from his mug. For a while both men ate in silence.

"Do something for us will you, Cyrus?" The superintendent pushed aside his unfinished salad. "When you get back from Wycombe, just write the answers to a few points that I find confusing. Any old order. Why do you think that young Charles Knowles didn't paint those pictures? Didn't or couldn't? Why all this private view business? Elitist. Champagne cocktails for the chosen? Why hold any exhibition when one is so young? And what about the Dutch painting on the easel? You said that when you and Purvis toured the gallery this morning it was still on the easel but that the easel had been put in the storage area. Criminals and motives, that's our theme song, isn't it? A mix of criminals and intelligentsia. One smartass outsmarting the others. Now you see it, now you don't, ladies and gents. It's staring you in the eyeballs." Superintendent Graham paused reflectively. "And another thought occurred to me during the night, Cyrus. With all the theft going on here and there; that Goya from the National Gallery, the Cézannes from Chicago, the San Francisco Rembrandts. The picture slashing. It is my understanding that all galleries are hooked up to some type of security. Like banks. Sonic detectors. Window and door foil. Signal mats. Yet when Edinburgh handed Purvis the key to the gallery door and we promised him that we'd lock up when we left the premises, do you recall him mentioning a security system? Even furriers and antique shops have electronic systems these days. Yet the Princess Gallery hadn't."

"No, he just told us to lock the door," Cyrus agreed.

"Which means that either there are no security devices

in the Princess Gallery as yet, or else Edinburgh doesn't think they're necessary. That he hasn't got anything there that's worth stealing."

"Or that one would notice," Cyrus said in afterthought.

"That Dutch painting in the lower gallery. What about that?" asked the super. "Something fishy about it, do you think?"

"Could be just a decoy." Cyrus paused thoughtfully. "Or a red herring," he added. "There's more to this man than meets the eye!"

"Wish I'd thought of that one," said the super delightedly. Then he became serious again. "The reality is murder," he said solemnly. "It's our duty to solve it. If possible, before Tuesday's inquest. Do you realise, Cyrus, we've wasted almost twenty-four hours since it happened! What's holding Purvis up, I wonder. He ought to have reported to me by now, even though, technically, I'm off duty. This new generation of coppers has no respect for authority. In a hundred years there won't be a copper around capable of finding a missing sand bucket, unless it's fed to him via a computer giving the total grains of sand. Bugger it, Cyrus. I feel like an old man. I'm tired."

6

"What did Doctor Edinburgh answer when you asked him about the exhibition?" Helen had been waiting for Purvis back at the office.

"Said it was Grossmith and Wurlitzer's idea. Something to do with that Dutch painting in the lower gallery. The three of them are going shares. Didn't mention Kershaw."

"But they haven't sold it, have they? Not yesterday afternoon?"

"How am I to know the answer to that?" Purvis remarked crossly. "From what I've heard, they should have tried Miss Gammel. Hell! the Doctor's lying his head off! I bet that when I question Grossmith, Wurlitzer, Kershaw, and who have you, they'll lie their bloody heads off also!"

Purvis and his girl were once again seated in the cafeteria. Normally, on Saturdays when they were both off duty, they would have a pub lunch. Both Purvis and Helen lived in lodgings where the facilities were inadequate for making anything beyond tea and toast and washing panty hose. They took all their meals out. That was another reason for getting married. As Purvis's parents lived in Liverpool and Helen's in Southend-on-Sea, both of them pined for home cooking.

How lovely she looks! Purvis allowed himself a few wallowing private thoughts admiring her appearance. A pretty rose-colored knitted jersey and brown trousers made of whipcord. Suit-pants, he conjectured, because there was a matching jacket. It never crossed his mind to tell her how lovely she looked. Too embarrassing. Like sorting out that business between pants and knickers and trousers. The Yanks didn't know how to treat the queen's English. What a daft name, pantsuits. For God's sake why not call them knicker-suits? Panty hose. Knicker hose didn't sound right. It was too bloody embarrassing!

"Why are you chuckling?" Helen asked him.

"Just thinking," Purvis answered, coloring slightly. "I see you're still wearing our engagement ring," he added by way of diversion, being at a loss for words, which under other circumstances might have panicked those serving under him. But Policewoman Maitland was already used to his ploys.

"When we marry, I'll expect you to wear a wedding band also, as the men do in North America! Separates the meek from the wolves."

It was well after two o'clock when they finished their steamed puddings with custard and seconds of nut-brown tea.

"I've got to check another lead," said Purvis. "Probably a dead end. Care to come along? Just routine. But it will help having you with me. You distract the eye."

"Thanks a lot," said Helen. "I'll come anyway! I like being an eye-catching decoy. Did I ever tell you what happened to me that night in Green Park?"

98

"Yes, what is it?" Mrs. Gordon opened the door of the caretaker's ground-floor flat, which she shared with her husband. As usual, Mr. Gordon would be at either the corner pub or the Saracen's Head in the next street. "If it's lodgings to let you're after, you've come to the wrong place. These flats is all spoken for, a long whiles back and far into the future."

Pity. They looked a nice young couple. He tall, broad-shouldered, not unlike Mr. Gordon when he was a young drayman, driving a delivery wagon for Watney's brewery—before he developed a slouch and went to pot. And what a pretty young thing with him. Nice rose-colored sweater and one of those fancy thingamajigs girls were wearing. Trying to pretend they were men, when with most of them it was only too obvious that they were girls, and not particularly clever at hiding same. Looked like rear-arsed freighters!

"We're not wanting to rent. We're looking for Signor Dagerra."

"Fifth floor back," said Mrs. Gordon, preparing to close the door.

"So the card beneath his bell showed us," Sergeant Purvis persisted. "We tried the doorbell, but it didn't work. That bell and letter-box combination seems to be on the blink."

"None o' the bleeders work," said Mrs. Gordon resignedly. "My old man's too bleedin' lazy to fix 'em. That's what. Letting the flats go all to buggery, 'e is. I expect the owners will have us slung out, if 'e don't mend 'is habits. Was Mr. Dagerra expectin' you. I could telephone up, if that would help."

"Would you, please?"

" 'alf a jiffy, then, lad," said Mrs. Gordon, firmly slamming the door. "I'll 'ave to check."

"I'd hate to live in a place with her for a caretaker," said Helen. "Doesn't appear to have washed for a week. And

99

that greasy dress and apron. Wonder the owners allow it!"

"Maybe the flats are O.K.," Purvis said optimistically. "Edinburgh implied it's a very good address."

The door was reopened. Mrs. Gordon seemed less confident.

"No luck," she said hesitatingly. "Do you know 'im well? The Italian gentleman, if 'e's the gentleman you're after."

"A friend of his asked us to call on him. To do with next week's motor races."

"You a bookie, are yer? So that's it. Thought at first you was coppers."

"You're perfectly correct, ma'am. I'm Detective Sergeant Purvis. This is Policewoman Maitland. And please don't slam the door again. We're just trying to get in touch with your tenant. No need to be alarmed."

"Well, I must say!" exclaimed Mrs. Gordon. "Don't surprise me, the way you coppers disguise yourselves these days. Didn't fool me for one minute! Nor does Signorey Dagerra. Queer fish that young man is, and that's no exaggeratin'. Always coming and going. Doesn't have any visitors, though 'e's got a bit of a blonde skirt tagging along 'im lately. No hanky-panky, mind you! We don't allow any carryings-on in these flats. Mind you, if she 'appened to nip upstairs when Mr. Gordon and me aren't noticing, then we wouldn't know, would we? A lark's a lark. Ain't it?"

"You're implying that he doesn't keep regular hours?"

"That's it. And there's somethin' else too. The flat is rented by a doctor. Edinburgh's 'is name. Got one of them rooms all fitted out like a swank consultin' room you see in the movies. But 'e's never 'ere. Never seen 'ide nor 'air of 'im since 'e moved in a couple o' years ago. Mr. Gordon says 'e's sublet to that young Italian, but I don't believe it. Fishy carryin's-on, mark my words. Visitors will call after dark. Just when you expect Signorey Dagerra to be bye-byes; more likely as not 'e's out walkin' the streets. Sometimes well after midnight before 'e turns in."

"How do you know all this?" asked Helen. "You must keep a very close watch on your tenants!"

"That's no untruth, young lady. I've eyes in me 'ead like anyone else. Only I believe in usin' 'em! Besides, if anything 'appened when Mr. Gordon's at the boozer, place'd go up in flames, like, I'd be the one what gets the blame. Mark me!"

"You mean to tell us that Doctor Edinburgh never has any patients call to consult him?"

"Not what these eyes 'ave spotted. Nor 'as Mr. Gordon seen 'im, or them. Queerly peculiar we think it is."

"What about letters or other messages?"

"Postie leaves letters for the Italian. Letter from Italy, mostly. 'E's a student at London University 'e told me once. Motor-races on the side, hobbylike, though to Mr. Gordon 'e says 'e's a pro and one day will be champion. Win the Grand Prix."

"You've never noticed any letters for Doctor Edinburgh?"

"No, sir, 'e pays in advance. Lights, rates, all paid by management. The telephone is in Dagerra's name. Postie 'ands us the letters to sort and put in their boxes."

"Well, then. I'm much obliged to you. You've been most helpful." Friendly and tactful was the routine. "Should you meet Signor Dagerra during the weekend, I wonder if you would be good enough to have him ring me, either at the office or at my home." Sergeant Purvis handed Mrs. Gordon his card. "Tell him I'd like a few words with him. Nothing to be alarmed over. Just a routine matter."

"I'll tell 'im if I see 'im," said Mrs. Gordon. "And if I don't see 'im, will you call back?"

"I'll even come back, ma'am," Purvis said suddenly. "Next time, I'll have a warrant to search the premises. But we hope to have heard from your tenant before that becomes necessary. I hate surprises."

They were about to take their leave when Purvis, as if suddenly alerted, swung again.

"A final point, Mrs. Gordon. This person, or persons, who came to the flat after dark. Ever caught a glimpse of them?"

"Mr. Gordon 'as. Just a man. 'E was too bloody sozzled to remember what 'e looked like. Caught 'im sneakin' in the back way from the alley. 'E'd a key, too. It weren't the doctor, though. 'E were positive about that. Only said it was a man."

"Nothing else?"

"Once or twice we've 'eard a couple o' men goin' up the stairs. They never use the lift. Could be anybody, couldn't it? Goin' to one o' the other flats. Nothin' unusual for tenants to use their back-door keys. Some of 'em park their cars at back. And these days, what with call girls and suchlike creatures carrying on, I mean, where is one, eh?"

Later while they were driving back to Savile Row, Purvis handed Helen his tobacco pouch and asked her to fill his pipe. Was he a chauvinist male pig like the super? It was too early to tell. She just loved filling the pipe. It was his.

"Routine duty for police wives," he informed her. "You'll get used to it! Don't pack it too firmly. You'll catch on. Just routine like everything else in a copper's life."

"I'll fill it this once, just to show willing. You won't turn me into your slave." She flashed a smile at him. "And how, might I be so bold as to ask, did his lordship know that Charles's mother's name was Grossmith?"

"Routine again: it was Edinburgh who told me. He's anxious about his stepson. Said he hadn't time to go and see him himself as he was delivering Mrs. Winterhalter's picture as soon as I'd finished questioning him. Wondered why we hadn't been to the flat already. I didn't tell Edinburgh we'd been keeping a watch on the flat all night. He's worried bald."

"As regards routine, you're a little off course, aren't you?"

102

"Perhaps, but if you don't follow routines, you risk confusing the issue."

Driving south through Hyde Park, Purvis stopped near the Serpentine and lit his pipe.

"Thanks," he said. "Not bad for a beginner. And now, young Helen, I'm going to drive you back to your digs. For myself, I'm going to drop in on the super. Warned him I wouldn't leave him alone. I'll phone you after supper unless something develops. We're waiting to hear about Finnegan's visit to High Wycombe. He's got his nose into something. Though I can't guess what."

"You know, darling," said Helen, leaning across and kissing him. "I really think you're terribly clever. And so does the super, letting you handle this case on your own. Not counting Finnegan, that is. You're probably the brainiest bloke in the force. Including the super!"

Edinburgh had good cause to worry.

Mrs. Winterhalter took the painting from him, offered him a martini, and asked him to stay to lunch. He refused both invitations. He explained that he'd undergone a most exhausting experience being "grilled" by Purvis. It was time for him to look after his wife. He had given her another sleeping draft before leaving for the Princess Gallery. He didn't like her being in the house without even Trudi to attend to her needs. He had already had to explain to Mrs. Winterhalter that Trudi was his daughter.

He took the underground, and during the journey that for once passed too quickly, wondered how successful he'd been in blinkering the police.

Doctor Edinburgh was not given to panic. He relied on his ability to organize others, freeing himself from possible incriminations later. Perhaps this time he had overextended himself? Beads of perspiration trickled across his brow; the sweatband inside his old-fashioned gray fedora hat felt as clammy as his hands.

He alighted at Chalk Farm station and took the passenger elevator to street level. Since it was Saturday afternoon, he found he had the lift to himself. With such turmoil in his mind, he had difficulty mustering the sequence of events. The beginning was the point at which all events were assembled. He always started from there, but now a black, gut-chilling sensation enveloped his body and spirals of fear arose up his spine like the flames of purgatory. It had finally started. After all these years he'd panicked. A few words spoken and he'd lost his head.

And there was the telephone call from Wurlitzer. Midnight. He supposed that Grossmith was probably standing at Wurlitzer's side, listening to what his partner was saying. They seemed inseparable, those two. Midnight. What a terrible hour! Kershaw had joined him shortly after eleven. They'd both looked in on Maria to make sure she was settled for the night. Kershaw hadn't said much, for he was as shocked as the rest of them that Charles should have died so violently. If only Kershaw hadn't left so abruptly. Had said something about needing to walk, to get some fresh air. If only he'd been there when Wurlitzer telephoned. They could have acted together. Done something. At least they would have talked, and Edinburgh, although he had overreached himself and gone beyond the permissible, could have justified what had happened.

As for Maria, Doctor Edinburgh was thinking as he let himself into the house, they had been mistaken. She ought never to have been taken into his confidence. That is to say, Kershaw's confidence, because he himself was not really involved. He'd merely provided the facilities, the operational headquarters, so to speak. That Maria had fallen for Kershaw had been an unforeseeable complication. Quite one-sided, unless Kershaw was bluffing. Edinburgh knew the range of her passion. Saw from the first that Maria was emotionally unbalanced, but who isn't where passion takes charge. And now she was prostrate with grief for a young artist whom she had never met, and only knew by reputation; a reputation wholly fabricated by Kershaw. Kershaw had acted as chicken-livered as himself.

Doctor Edinburgh felt his wife's pulse and was relieved to note that her appearance was normal, and her heartbeat steady and that, as far as he could judge, she was no longer running a temperature. Her breathing was slow and regular, her body enveloped in peaceful slumber. If only he were in her place! He was the one who was feverish now. Try as he would, his fear returned again and again.

Carefully he rinsed the two tumblers on the bedside table. He refilled the carafe with cold water. Carefully he covered her shoulders with a sheet and smoothed the blankets without waking her. Before coming upstairs he had fetched a decanter of brandy from the dining room. Now he partly filled the second tumbler and drained the brandy in one swallow. He poured some brandy for Maria and left the decanter on her table. Mixing drugs and alcohol was not always advisable. As a medical man he was fully aware of the dangers. He knew also that there was little or no risk of aftereffects, provided the dosages were taken in moderation.

It would soon be five o'clock. He would have liked to have telephoned Kershaw and arranged a meeting. But even that was too risky at this stage. Or what about Finnegan? He would like to tell Finnegan what had happened. But that would be asking for trouble as well, because Finnegan was friendly with the superintendent. It seemed more than coincidental that Cyrus had brought Graham to the private viewing. Stupid, of course, to have such foolish thoughts. It really was a coincidence! Nobody would have anticipated that Charles Knowles would be killed, within a few feet of the law! From now on, he would have to stick to intuition. Do what he could to stall, at least until he'd contacted Trudi and Gee. Wherever could they be hiding themselves? And why? Had Trudi really seen what had happened? Had she heard?

Well, first things first, thought Doctor Edinburgh, closing the door and setting off down the hill to the station. He must try and get into the flat without being observed. He'd given the back-door key to Gee, but no matter. The police would undoubtedly be watching the building. They would recognize him, for Purvis would have given them his description. But even this would make no difference. As owner of the flat he had every right to go there whenever he wished. And so, of course, had Gee or his friends.

What was important was to go there now. To find out whether what Charles had told him was true. To get there before the police. Or had he already wasted too much time fussing about Maria. She wasn't worth the effort!

Trudi and Giuseppe felt wretched.

The hot sunshine bathing the moors of West Yorkshire went unnoticed. From the members' enclosure, beside the pits, they watched the drivers adjusting goggles, adjusting straps and safety belts, tightening their headsets. Assistants were now locking the protective roofs over their drivers' heads. The driver of a turbo-engined Ferrari gave a thumbs-up signal, which Gee acknowledged. This was the final event of the day. After the winner had crossed the line, he and Trudi would be free to drive back to London. Meanwhile engines revved and roared and the crowd grew excited.

Trudi was calmer now, but at first he'd hardly known how to handle her. Forcing her to get into his car, they had driven to the flat against her protest. He couldn't think of where else to take her. Certainly not to Hampstead. And she'd been sick. Miserably sick and shivering, wrapped in a blanket and his overcoat, she'd sat on the sofa while he went into the bedroom and changed into clothes more appropriate for the next day's racing. He'd packed pyjamas, for both of them, two sweaters, and a change of shirts.

"Handy that you keep spare toilet things here," he reminded her. "Don't move. I'll pack them. Just you take another sip of Fernet Branca. I know it tastes foul, but for settling stomachs, it can't be beaten. It's Italy's antihangover elixir! Good antidote for poison!"

Trudi had swallowed a liqueur glass full of the evil-smelling concoction. It stayed down. Gee continued trying to be cheerful.

"We can't just run off like this!" Trudi appealed. "It's not right! We're being treated as decoys. We oughtn't to have run for it. The police will have it in for us."

"And why? You and I are married, aren't we? The police have nothing to go on. Mark me. That reporter girl from the *Mirror* who interviewed me about the Monte Carlo rally. Thank goodness I told her we are only engaged. She'll have no idea who you are, that you're Doctor Edinburgh's daughter. Nothing to connect you."

"But after what's happened! What I saw. If we do a bunk and disappear I'll be an accessory." Trudi had inherited her father's flair for languages. That, together with daily elocution lessons to begin with, and then constant exposure in drama and dance school, had enriched her vocabulary of slang.

"You need time, Trudi, dearest. Besides, if you stay, then I'll have to stay here with you and we'll miss tomorrow's trials. We've an experimental Ferrari in the lineup and I've got to report to the race committee on its performance. Twenty-four hours won't make all that much difference."

"It will, you know." At first Trudi was adamant, but in

the end they had left shortly after sunset. They stopped for a snack at Doncaster, and checked in at the Imperial Hotel in Darlington, Yorkshire, shortly after midnight.

Before turning in Trudi had telephoned home, but the line was busy. Instead of trying again later, she had a bath and climbed into bed. Gee was already asleep.

They had argued most of the morning. Trudi had refused breakfast and lunch, saying their snack the previous evening had brought back the sickness. It was that seafood casserole she'd eaten for lunch before going to the gallery the previous afternoon. No doubt about it. She had a bout of ptomaine poisoning. She ought to have gone to a hospital and taken an emetic. Gee had been about to say that she'd get good treatment in the prison sick ward, but checked himself in time. Black humor was not one of his gifts. His jokes fell flat.

This was the trouble. He didn't know whether she was really in trouble or not. What she had told him during their drive up north seemed so improbable that he just didn't believe her!

"I don't think we're acting like responsible adults," Trudi said, after the race had gone two laps. "You didn't see the body. I did. I felt it."

But Gee's attention was now concentrated on the Ferrari, which took the east turn in a three-quarter skid before correcting. Good driving! Good car!

"We'll go back to London immediately. I promise. Only twenty more laps. Be patient, darling. The world's not coming to an end."

As they neared Stamford, outside London, later that night, Trudi settled back in her seat, staring at the stars.

"That bit about the world not coming to an end," she said. "Perhaps it's awful of me, but I somehow feel it wouldn't matter, not that it's likely to. That would be the easy way out, for all of us."

108

"I don't follow."

"Don't you feel about your father the way I feel about mine? Isn't he a stranger? Doing what he wants. After my upbringing in strange homes, always with that uncertainty about the future, that I had no real identity of my own. Then suddenly, after moving from camp to camp, being told out of the blue, 'Trudi, you're going to join your father. He's living in England. You're going Home, Trudi.' Home with a capital H. Dammit, Gee, I was already an adult, nearly twenty-one. I spoke three languages and had my ambitions set on the stage. Then bang! You're dead! You're now Trudi Edinburgh, if you please. At least I kept my own name. Hertz, and Harwick as my stage name. I'll stick to that, even though legally now I'm Mrs. Signora Dagerra. How's that, now? We're legally man and wife!" Trudi was laughing.

"I don't get the business about our fathers?" Gee said, hoping that she wasn't becoming hysterical again. "I like my father. He's hardworking, conscientious and conventional. He's kind to me, always has been. If I'm spoiled rotten, I can blame him."

"Lucky you," Trudi said, not unkindly. "I wish I felt the same about my father. I've never really liked him. I think my Doctor Edinburgh is all pretense. I can almost feel his scheming. And you should see the miserable lot of patients he bosses with his phony psychiatry. Broken reeds and lame dogs, the British call them. What happened yesterday at the Princess Gallery only half surprises me. You see, I've no feeling for family. If he's punished, I'll not shed a tear."

"Stop baiting me, Trudi darling," Gee said endearingly as they turned off the motorway. "You didn't tell me what happened. What was it that you saw that makes you an accessory after the fact if you don't turn yourself in?"

"I saw Father kill Charles. That's what I saw. And heard. So now, let's get back to the flat and telephone the police."

109

7

Cyrus Finnegan wasn't sure how he was going to handle the situation. On one point he was confident. Kershaw would not be glad to see him. Cyrus had decided not to drive in his own car. Trains were frequent and he would have time to think.

That train journey, uneventful in itself, allowed Cyrus a period for meditation, for concentrated thought focused upon Doctor Edinburgh's disclosures. So now there was established a link among Peter Knowles, whereabouts unknown, his sister, Kershaw, Maria Edinburgh, and the doctor himself. As Knowles had at one time worked for Grossmith and Wurlitzer, there obviously must be a further link there, also. So what about Knowles's son, Charles? What had the boy known that had made his murder an unpleasant, though inevitable, outcome? Who among those so closely associated felt so threatened, so afraid, so terrified of the consequences of discovery, that it became necessary to kill a boy not yet out of his adolescence? When Cyrus reached the village where the Kershaws lived, he realized that Superintendent Graham, in sending him on this mission, had been merely reconfirming that Art with a capital A was the common link. That being an art historian and writer, Cyrus was the most likely person to recognize the exact nature of that link. But what, Cyrus asked himself, if there is some other factor? Something that has nothing to do with art at all?

There was a cricket match taking place on the common. It was a pleasant summer scene. The two teams, dressed in white, were set against the rich foliage of beech trees, with a blue, almost cloudless sky above. Cyrus joined the few spectators taking shelter in the shade of an enormous chestnut tree. Taking off his jacket and tie, he settled himself on the grass to watch a couple of plays. He needed these extra minutes of relaxation. Instinct warned him that if he was to be of real assistance to the super and Purvis, to find his way through a maze of apparent irrelevancies to the heart of the puzzle, there would be little time for rest from now on. There would be unpleasantness: there might also be some personal danger to himself.

On the far side of the common he could see Kershaw, in the background of his Elizabethan cottage, clipping his garden hedge. The snap of his heavy shears and the click of cricket bat and ball were the only sounds to be heard, other than the joyful noises that birds and children make on midsummer afternoons. At that moment one of the cricket wickets fell and a voice shouted, "How's that?" Even on a lovely summer day such as this, Cyrus thought ruefully, at this very instant somewhere a human life was being felled just as violently. Then it would be a policeman who would "How's that?" The beginning of a thousand questions, and so few answers.

At least I know the answer to one question, Cyrus

111

thought, as he walked towards the cottage. Edinburgh murdered Charles. Evidence to prove this would be forthcoming, of that he had no doubt. His job now was to keep this knowledge and suspicion to himself.

Kershaw was loading a wheelbarrow with clippings and therefore did not see Cyrus open the gate. When he did see him, his expression was a revelation of shock and amazement.

"Good God, Finnegan. You're the last person I expected to see." The words were unwelcoming. "I thought you'd be in London working with that detective bloke you chum around with."

"I ought to have telephoned you, I know," said Cyrus apologizing for this breach in manners. "But you know how it is. Lovely day. Just felt I had to get out of town. Get some good country air. Took a chance that you'd be at home. Thought I'd ask you some questions about the Norwich School and their influences upon the later watercolorists of the nineteen thirties. It's a period I know so little about, yet I have to—"

"Come off it, Finnegan!" Kershaw snapped, pulling at a large thistle that had become entangled in a clump of polyanthus. "Stop pretending! You make a bloody poor liar and I'm not taken in, not for one bloody second. Your policemen friends have sent you to ferret! What makes you imagine that I, or Mary, for that matter, will be involved?"

"Involved?" Cyrus said with concern. "But not at all. At least, as professional colleagues we are all involved, aren't we. We're friends of the Edinburghs. We were both at the Princess to lend support and write our articles. Mine won't be out till next Sunday, by the way. Did you get your piece written?"

"Certainly not. How could I? I mean, the lad's dead, and what the hell is there to say about him now? He's washed up before he'd started. Finished. But come round to the back.

112

Mary's weeding but I'll get her to make us some tea. It's such a lovely afternoon we'll have tea in the garden."

Kershaw tipped the contents of the wheelbarrow on his compost heap next to the rhubarb. Mary set aside her bucket filled with weeds and came to welcome her unexpected guest.

"How nice to see you again, Mr. Finnegan. It must be years since you last visited us."

"At least two," Cyrus agreed. "Tony and I see a great deal of each other, as you know, at openings. But he keeps his charming wife to himself."

Mary is truly a background wife, Cyrus thought to himself. Even Kershaw seldom mentions her name, he realized. But one could recognize for oneself that Mary had a personality that would not prevent her speaking her mind, despite her rather reserved manner. An enthusiastic gardener, he could see that. Wiry, rather than slight, but with little flair for dress and general appearance. One of the blue-denim crowd. Freckled and free of make-up, light brown hair rather dusty-looking, eyes hazel-green, sharp, and watchful. Watchful as though on guard. Against the world of nongardeners. Or against Kershaw. She's nice, thought Cyrus. We could be friends.

"You know, Mary," he said to her while Kershaw lit his pipe, "I've never noticed it before. Show's how unobservant even art critics can be. But you're remarkably like your brother."

Their expressions, as she and Kershaw exchanged glances, would remain etched in Finnegan's memory forever. His timing, quite accidental, had caught both of them unawares. Kershaw looked as if prepared to punch him in the jaw, restrained only because he could find no excuse to do so.

"And where did you learn that? Who told you?" he asked instead.

Cyrus was not sure whether this was the right moment, or not, to tell them what Edinburgh had said to Purvis in his presence. He decided to risk it.

"Hans Edinburgh. He told Purvis that the victim was Mary's nephew. Peter Knowles's boy." He let the words settle, then continued. "What Purvis is probably wondering at this moment is, why secrecy? What were both of you trying to hide, or weren't you? If you weren't then why this nonsense about a phony private viewing with phony paintings by an artist nobody would give a name to?"

"There was nothing at all phony with the pictures," Kershaw said quickly, and defensively. "The lad, Charles, was a genius."

"So therefore I ask you again, Tony and Mary, in that case why create a mystery to deceive the public? It doesn't make sense. All in all, you've quite a bit of explaining to do when Purvis or Superintendent Graham start fitting facts together. Right now, if there is something you would like me to say to them, or if I can be of help to both of you, tell me. I don't know either of you well. But acquaintances, like friends, can sometimes be handy when things have gone wrong. All I ask is that you tell the truth."

"Then for starters," said Kershaw, "you can leave Mary out of this. Do your damned snooping elsewhere. Keep the police away from the cottage. And if they want to question me further, though goodness knows why they should, then I'll come up to London. As a matter of fact I'm having supper at the Edinburgh's house tomorrow night. Sunday. Tell Purvis he can contact me there. But like everyone else who attended the private viewing I offered what little information I could, which in my case was damned all."

"But surely you ought to have told the police then that you knew Charles's identity."

"It was my first obligation to protect Mary. If I'd told them, and they'd got in touch with her without my warning

114

her of the situation, then matters would have been far worse. I needed to give her time to get over the shock. I knew the police would soon find out who Charles was. They always do find out."

Mary Kershaw, who had been listening to Kershaw as though she could hardly believe what he was saying, suddenly pointed at the garden gate.

"It seems our day for surprise guests," she said. "Who on earth can that be? What a grotesque-looking creature! Huge!"

"She's an American lady who bought one of your paintings," Cyrus informed her, noting that Kershaw had paled. The three of them watched the stately Mrs. Winterhalter walk awkwardly, in her high-heeled city shoes, along the crazy paving pathway, raising one pudgy hand to knock at the cottage door. Under one arm she carried a large, gift-wrapped box.

"Come back here, Mrs. Winterhalter," Kershaw called out to her. "We're by the summer house. You're just in time for tea."

Mary Kershaw, after the formal introductions to this grossly overweight lady, shyly accepted from her a large box of Benedict Liqueur chocolates, and fled to the kitchen. But Americans drink coffee, not tea. Or do they? I know what I'll do, she decided, I'll make both. She was used to talking to herself aloud.

She quite liked Finnegan, though privately she thought he might be standoffish. Not a real snob, but something there, all the same. Tony, she realized, obviously couldn't stand the man and was at no pains to hide his feelings. Which was stupid, really, because Finnegan had offered to help them. And if there was anything more certain than her nephew's death, Mary thought as she laid out the tea and coffee cups and sliced some fruitcake, it was the certainty that her husband was in over his head in trouble. She'd realized this for months, had worried herself sick, but she still didn't know to what extent. Surely he'd done nothing criminal! As Tony had told Cyrus Finnegan, she was certainly innocent. Stuck here at the cottage and alone most of the time, how could she become involved in anything.

Or not really so innocent, perhaps, when one considered the way she had neglected Peter's son. She'd never wanted anything to do with the lad when Tony brought him back from London over a year ago and told her that Charles was her brother's bastard. Was that so obviously a lie? She didn't doubt it. Well, that had been one way of describing the ungainly, pimple-faced boy whom she'd disliked on sight. An old-fashioned term in these days of permissive free-for-all, but she regarded herself as old-fashioned when that meant observing the niceties of life, being honest in one's relationships, and avoiding, whenever possible, the sordidness that cloaked the world like smog. So she'd told Tony to get rid of the boy and this he had done. At least, that is to say, they had gone off together the following afternoon and when Tony returned he was alone. Got the boy a job at the school. And now the boy had come back to haunt her. Dying, as the newspaper said, under mysterious circumstances!

"I am not the keeper of my brother's bastards," she had written Peter in a letter. Not very nice, nor Christian, she realized after she had mailed it to a general delivery in Toronto, where he was living. Perhaps if she'd had a child, even children, of her own, she might have accepted Charles into the brood. It was soon afterwards that Tony got a letter from Peter. One of those flimsy air-letter forms. After he had read it, he tore it into little bits and threw them into the kitchen fire.

"Peter sends you love and kisses," was all Tony said about the letter's contents. And it was soon afterwards that

Tony changed. Became withdrawn and uncommunicative. He still loved her, she knew that and could not believe his feelings might be otherwise; but she was no longer the center of his life.

Controlling herself, she carried the tray outside.

Kershaw, aware of the thinness of their canvas deck chairs, had provided Mrs. Winterhalter with a Windsor chair from his den. Over the hedge Mary saw several village children gawking appreciatively at Mrs. Winterhalter's Rolls, which was parked on the common, hopefully out of range of cricket balls.

"I'll just take a cup of tea out to your chauffeur," Mary said considerately.

"He'll do fine," said Mrs. Winterhalter. "No need to take him anything. He's paid by the hour. Expensive, but what are a few dollars if we don't enjoy them. If he wants tea he can drive to the nearest café. Nothing to stop him."

"I'll take him a cuppa just the same," said Mary, disliking Mrs. Winterhalter and all that her type represented.

"You were clever to find us," Kershaw observed.

"Not really," Mrs. Winterhalter purred, helping herself to a fourth spoonful of brown crystal sugar. "Hans Edinburgh told me where you lived. And what a picturesque cottage! Just like Ann Hathaway's. Have you been to Stratford-upon-Avon, Mr. Finnegan?"

"Never, I'm sorry to say."

"Then you're missing a treat. I do so adore Shakespeare, don't you, Mary? You don't mind me using your Christian name? Mine's Melita."

Mary, having returned from her errand, was sitting on an upturned log. Tony offered to pour her some tea and cut her some cake, but she refused. Mrs. Winterhalter took her third slice.

"Shakespeare bores me silly," Mary said rudely. "Now that you're here, Mrs. Winterhalter, er, Melita, I expect

117

you want to talk to my husband and Mr. Finnegan. If you'll excuse me, I'll carry on with the weeding. They seem to grow as fast as I can pick them."

"What a pretty young wife you have, Tony! Such freshness. Must be the country air." Mrs. Winterhalter beamed. "But now that she's gone, tell me what you know about this beastly murder. Are you sure it wasn't just an accident after all?"

"I know no more than you do, Mrs. Winterhalter. Finnegan here, he's the expert!"

"It is still far from clear what happened," said Cyrus, hastily improvising. "We know that the victim is the son of a dealer who left England a few years ago. Dealer is perhaps too general and vague a description. But that was his main interest. Name of Peter Knowles. The police don't know where to get hold of him. Rumor has him living in New York. Perhaps New England. F.B.I. are putting a trace on him. He may have changed his name."

For a second, only briefly, it seemed that a shadow crossed Mrs. Winterhalter's eyes. If she was confused she made a good job of concealing it. She had finished almost a plateful of buttered scones filled with Mary's home-made strawberry jam and now accepted a fifth slice of cake.

"Strikes me that name is familiar," Mrs. Winterhalter said unexpectedly. "Knowles? Don't you remember him, Tony? Surely you must. That guided-art tour you conducted. Low countries, West Germany, Luxembourg. That was when we first met, when I and some of the girls in my club joined your group in London. Two or three years ago. My, we all thought you so clever. Some of the girls must have had quite a crush on you, that's for sure."

And you also, you old bitch, Kershaw thought to himself, remembering the half dozen New England matrons who had been more interested in shopping than visiting art museums.

"No, can't say I recall anyone of that name," he answered untruthfully. "There have been so many tours. Not so many recently, now that I've got a good job teaching art at a school near here. Next summer, though, I hope to conduct a tour of Spain and Portugal for art lovers. You should try your hand at that, Finnegan. Can be quite stimulating."

"Are you certain the man you're thinking of was called Knowles?" Cyrus wondered whether she was talking quite innocently, or whether she already knew that Knowles was Kershaw's brother-in-law. She and Kershaw could well be conspirators. He would have to step warily.

"I guess I'm not so sure as all that. When one is a widow one goes on so many cruises and tours, it's sometimes quite difficult to remember where one has been, let alone whom one has met. So the poor creature was Charles Knowles was he. I'll have to write that name on the back of my picture, otherwise I'll forget. Will add something to its value, no doubt."

"Good idea," said Cyrus. "So you and Tony Kershaw are old friends are you? What a coincidence. But under what unpleasant circumstances you're meeting this time."

"They sure are. But at least this afternoon we can all relax in such beautiful surroundings and try to forget all about what happened yesterday. Isn't that correct, Mr. Finnegan? It was thoughtless of me to mention it. On all our minds undoubtedly. And now that I've finished that delicious coffee, and who said that the British don't know how to make coffee, I ask you, will you take me on a tour of your garden, Tony? I want to get back to London shortly, as I've got a ticket for this evening's show at your National Theatre. Can I give you a ride back to London, Mr. Finnegan, or are you staying here?"

"Just visiting," Cyrus informed her. "I'll accept your offer of a ride with pleasure. Tony and Mary will be glad to get rid of me, I assure you. Barging in uninvited like this."

119

"Just as I did, too," agreed Mrs. Winterhalter. "But then I always love it when people drop in on me when I'm at home." Like hell I do, she was thinking. She liked her privacy. At least Kershaw made no attempt to argue.

This will be a good time to leave the two of them alone, Cyrus decided, and walked over to where Mary was picking dwarf peas for supper. In the distance he saw Mrs. Winterhalter whisper in Kershaw's ear and at the same time give him something which he immediately put in a pocket. Cyrus felt more than satisfied to have his suspicions confirmed. This had been a prearranged rendezvous, though risky. He wondered if, like himself, Mary was also looked upon as an intruder. But it would have been difficult to have kept her out of it. After all, this was her own home.

"And what's that funny game those men are playing over there?" Mrs. Winterhalter asked, as Cyrus settled beside her in the backseat of her Rolls.

"Cricket."

"My, is it really! I thought for a moment it was some new type of softball. One learns so much when one travels." They were approaching the Beaconsfield bypass when suddenly Mrs. Winterhalter suffered a spasm of coughs. She was choking and clutched at her chest.

"Are you all right?" Cyrus gripped her arm. He told the chauffeur to slow down.

"I'm O.K.," she said, gasping. "Just tough to breathe sometimes. Heart flutters! Some type of allergy, I guess. Drive on, will you driver. I'm fine."

"And what happened during the drive?" Superintendent Graham asked, after Cyrus had described his visit to the Kershaws.

"Just an uneventful drive. We chatted about this and that. You know how it is. Although she asked dozens of questions, I don't think she paid any attention to my answers. Her thoughts were elsewhere."

"Notice anything about her driver?"

"Seemed like a nice chap. Well mannered. Middle-aged. Clean and smart-looking, which he'd have to be to drive for that high-class swanky hire firm. Probably has a couple of languages under his belt, just in case his passenger decides to take a last-minute trip to the Continent."

"Do you think she's likely to do that?"

"Why should she? She's booked to return to the States immediately after the inquest. She's promised to attend the inquest, so I doubt if she'd skip. She wouldn't miss the excitement. Something else to add to what she might look upon as knowledge gained through travel. You know, super, I don't trust her. I think she's more than a kindhearted patron of the arts."

"Takes all kinds," said the super, weighty with experience.

They were sitting in the super's bedroom. It was early Saturday evening. After Mrs. Winterhalter had dropped him off near Marble Arch, round about five o'clock, Cyrus had gone back to his flat, changed his shirt for something cooler, and then taken a taxi to St. John's Wood. He felt it important to review with the super all those little points that, taken by themselves, seemed not to matter. Reassembled professionally by Purvis and the super they would, he hoped, provide some form of coherence.

It was Helga's evening off. Not that she went "off" anywhere very much, except occasionally to a film at the Fulham Forum. But on Saturday evenings she didn't even leave a supper for Cyrus, knowing that there were enough tempting morsels in their well-stocked fridge. So tonight Cyrus had welcomed Stella's invitation over the telephone that he could join the Grahams for their Saturday night snack.

"What about the chocolates?" the super asked, after a few moments' contemplation of his notes. "Do you think they're poisoned?"

"Why on earth should they be?"

"It seems so strange to take a two-pound box of the most expensive liqueur chocolates on the market and give them to somebody one is meeting for the first time, even though she is your hostess at tea."

"If the Yanks have a fault, and they have many," Cyrus replied, "it is their tendency to err on the side of what someone once described as magnanimous generosity. Where an Englishman might pause before parting with three pence's worth of forget-me-nots, an American will buy three dozen roses."

"For strangers, especially," Cyrus affirmed. "I would suspect that Mrs. W. bought these chocolates for herself, to begin with. But the habit of giving generously when one is visiting probably overpowered her baser wish to hang on to them."

The super lapsed into silence once more.

"You won't have heard the result of the autopsy," he resumed.

"Yes. Purvis telephoned me when I was at home changing my shirt. Clean break separating the vertebrae, the larynx, snapping or twisting the *plexus brachialis*. Poor bugger." Cyrus found himself unable to suppress an involuntary shudder. "And a bruise on his right chest, from when he hit the stairs."

"Very doubtful, that bit," said the super. "As he was dragged, how could he have fallen against the stairs? But back to your lady in the Rolls. What is she doing this evening, for example?"

"She's going to see a performance at the National Theatre."

"Is she, indeed! Purvis made a note and told me that

when he was interviewing Doctor Edinburgh he was told she was spending the evening with him and Maria. All cozy, tête-á-tête-like."

"Sure it's not tomorrow night? Kershaw is dining with the Edinburghs himself tomorrow. At least that's what he told me just before I left High Wycombe. Perhaps he's dropping in on them uninvited. For that matter, why on earth would Mrs. Winterhalter pretend to be going to the theater?"

"I gather from some comments made to me by Sergeant Purvis," said the super, "Edinburgh and Kershaw had one hell of a row after he'd taken Maria back to the house from the gallery. Jealousy. Thinks Kershaw has been paying too much attention to Maria."

"It was certainly Kershaw who took charge yesterday after the body had been found. Maria turned to him for comfort and not to her husband. We both saw it."

"According to Purvis, there's been some sort of a to-do. Edinburgh was making no attempt to hide his feelings. But let us talk about your trip back to London with your pal from the United States."

"Not much to say, to tell the truth; she talked mostly about the difficulties of crossing the Atlantic by boat, which she prefers. Has a thing against flying. However, the *Q.E. II* sails from Southampton on Wednesday and she's managed to get a first-class berth. Wife of one of the Cunard directors was on an art tour with her, so she pulled strings."

"Thought she'd have talked more about the murder. You smell a rat?"

"I'm like the Pied Piper. I see and smell them everywhere. Being an art critic, I see them in various shades and hues, not just gray and brown. She was excited. Talked for the sake of talking. Quite exhausting to listen to so much idle chatter."

"Let's get back to the cottage, then," said the super,

ignoring Finnegan's sarcasm. "You've told me all you know about Kershaw. Teaches art. Writes articles on art. Has published a book. And now you learn for the first time that he sometimes conducts one of the culture tours that are becoming so popular since the jet age. All one needs is money and one can see the temples in Bangkok one day and visit Leningrad's Hermitage a couple of days later. Culture on the hop."

"One does indeed. Which reminds me, any trace of Knowles?"

"Not yet. Interpol and the F.B.I., we're giving him the works. As you know, if he hasn't a previous criminal record, we're stymied."

"So back to square Kershaw," said Cyrus. "Or not so square, when you take a good look at him. While he was showing Mrs. Winterhalter the garden and giving her a tour of the cottage, I helped Mary carry in the tea things and stack them for washing later. She also was inclined to be talkative."

"So?"

"I gather the rot's set in, though she can't quite see it. Not yet. Most apologetic, when I asked her about herself. Couldn't imagine why anyone would be interested in what she calls her humdrum existence. Thinks the trouble is that her hubby's a dreamer. To begin with he's a *peintre manqué* who's given up painting. She thinks he ought to be content to settle happily into life at the cottage with daily bus trips to the school he teaches at, somewhere near Reading. Incredible as it must seem, she doesn't even know what the school's called. And the weekends with nice walks in the country and sketching trips. Both of them together. Picnic lunches. She reading while he paints. Then a pub supper, then back to bed for a Saturday night chaser. She enjoyed that simple pattern. But that's all in the past, I gather."

124

"So?"

"So it was in the beginning. But recently, come Sunday afternoon he's impatient to get the weekend over with. Paces up and down, irritable. And worse to come. During the past few months he's been away from the cottage most evenings. Leaving her alone, coming back at all hours with not so much as an apology, let alone an excuse. I asked her what she would do if there was an emergency. Do you know what she answered?"

"What?"

"She said that in an emergency Tony was the last person she'd send for. She thinks he's yellow as chicken liver. Didn't give a reason. She also thinks he's having a nervous breakdown. Has been hospitalized twice before. Once just after their wedding. I asked her when she'd last heard from her brother. She was immediately on guard. Said she never hears from him. Though he occasionally writes to Tony, he never shows her the letters! She did make one observation—that at one time Kershaw and her brother saw a great deal of each other, when Knowles was working for Grossmith and Wurlitzer. It was Knowles who apparently got Kershaw interested in cleaning and restoring paintings, which is something I didn't know about him. Like the tours. Mary and Kershaw were introduced to each other at a party given by the Edinburghs, where she was employed as part-time secretary and receptionist. After their marriage, they rented their cottage at High Wycombe. She no longer has a job. Says they manage quite nicely, as Tony seems to have three sources of income. Teaching, journalism, and as tour master during school holidays. Once in a while he does a little picture cleaning, nothing complicated."

"Where's his studio?"

"Mary thinks it's at the school, that he has a room there, but she's not certain. I got the impression that while out-

125

wardly everything seems to be quite normal, beneath there is a strong undercurrent of mistrust. Even hate, perhaps. He's got a nasty temper. I hope for Mary's sake that he never loses control. Like Mrs. Winterhalter, he's in a highly excitable state. Resented my visit."

As it was a summer's evening, the bedroom window was wide open. Outside, the throb of traffic, the sound of voices and footsteps, and once in a while the sound of laughter provided an unobtrusive background to their conversation. From downstairs came the sound of Stella washing the supper dishes. Shortly afterwards Mrs. Graham could be heard playing the piano.

It was because of these sounds that neither Cyrus nor the super heard the telephone.

"It's Sergeant Purvis on the line, Dad," Stella called up from the hallway. "Says it's urgent, and that he'd like to talk with Mr. Finnegan if you can't come to the phone yourself."

"Tell him to hold on a jiffy," her father instructed her. "Here, Cyrus. Help me on with my dressing gown, will you. Nothing the matter with me. Just a bit stiff from lying in bed too long. Never did like lying in bed," the super grumbled as he limped towards the staircase. He could hardly stand upright.

When he returned, and obviously still in pain, Superintendent Graham crossed over to the wardrobe and removed a suit.

"Give me a couple of minutes while I dress, Cyrus. There's a car on its way. I'll join you downstairs."

"Crisis?"

"Damned right there's a crisis. Purvis was telephoning from Edinburgh's flat. Near Harley Street. Wants me there right away. You might as well come along too. Edinburgh's been murdered. Stabbed in the back."

8

Doctor Hans Edinburgh was very dead. The rococo hilt of the silver paper knife could not have been better placed between his shoulder blades. His head, turned away from the doorway, rested upon the Sheraton writing desk. His hands still appeared to grip the arms of his chair, his body was half bent, as though he were turning to see who it was who had crept up behind him. To Cyrus and the super it was immediately apparent when they entered the flat, that not only had the doctor been caught totally off guard but death had been swift, instantaneous, and executed with extreme efficiency.

Trudi and Gee, seated on the sofa, each of them pale and shocked, stared morosely almost as unseeing as the body at the table, while Purvis and Policewoman Maitland made a cursory inspection of the room. Purvis greeted the superintendent and acknowledged Cyrus with a nod.

"Glad you got here so quickly, sir. Sorry for getting you out of bed."

"What's the matter, Purvis? Letting matters get a bit out of hand, aren't you. Two corpses in two days! Whose body will you find tomorrow?"

"Seems that way, sir." Nobody paid any attention to the young couple. With the arrival of the police surgeon and the rest of the team from Savile Row, what was happening was like a rerun of the events of the previous afternoon. Because it was a Saturday evening, irritation at having their weekends interrupted was the mildest of their reactions.

As for Cyrus Finnegan, he felt sick to his stomach.

"What's that revolting smell?" asked Purvis.

"Turpentine and linseed oil," said Policewoman Maitland without hesitation.

"Christ! I'm allergic to turps," exclaimed Purvis. "You watch. Tomorrow I'll have red spots all over my face."

And while the flat was immaculately clean, with no sign of bottles containing either turpentine or linseed oil on the kitchen shelves, it was the unfortunate Purvis who found the discarded paint rag in a brown paper bag beneath the sink in the kitchen at the end of the corridor.

"This'll do me in good and proper!" he protested. "I can feel a rash on my skin already. Filthy stuff."

His fiancée took the bag from him and carried it into the living room to show the super.

"Know anything about this, young man?" Graham asked Dagerra.

"No. Never seen it before."

"Any idea who could have put it there?"

"No! Probably Doctor Edinburgh's friend. He used to borrow the flat for two or three evenings a week; usually left about eleven. One of the agreements we had was that I made myself scarce when Doctor Edinburgh wanted the flat for his friend. He would contact me and say when his friend wanted the flat. I had no alternative but to get out."

128

"Did the arrangement strike you as peculiar, to say the least?"

"Of course it did. But you try finding accommodation in London, rents being what they are. Especially when one is trying to save one's allowance for what is important, in my case racing. You'll agree to almost anything for a rent-free situation like this. My stepfather was good to me."

"You never saw this mysterious 'friend'?"

"Never. I just took it for granted he was an artist, because the last thing he'd do would be to open the windows before he left. Even so, one could still smell a trace of paint, or varnish and turpentine. And one night he'd left a saucepan of wax, at least it looked like beeswax, on the stove. I found it when I returned. Another thirty minutes and the pot would probably have burned and set the place on fire."

"Did he have an easel?" Cyrus Finnegan cut in. "Did you ever see any of his paintings?"

"Never." Giuseppe stroked Trudi's hand while he spoke.

"And what do you think of these?" Sergeant Purvis asked the super. "They were spread all over the desk, but I didn't touch them till the photographer had taken his shots of the body. Color transparencies, sir. Thirty-five millimeter."

There were sixteen of them. When the super had finished holding them up against the light, he handed them to Cyrus.

"Too bad we haven't a slide viewer. But we'll blow them up when we get back to the station. What do you think, Cyrus? Just a lot of colors to me. Nothing I recognize."

Cyrus looked at the slides, then returned them to Purvis.

"They mean nothing to me either. Looks as if somebody's been testing a camera."

"This all you found, Purvis?" asked the super.

"That's all. No camera, no paintings, nothing. Just this dirty paint rag. And the sooner the boys get it back to the lab, the happier I'll be. I'm beginning to itch already."

129

Finally, after what to Trudi and Gee seemed an endless purgatory, the superintendent turned his attention on them. He had waited till Edinburgh's body had been removed and only the fingerprint technician and his assistant were left. The surgeon and other members of the team had gone outside for a smoke, it being regarded as unseemly to light up when a corpse was still present.

Superintendent Graham pointed to a chair for Cyrus, then seated himself well clear of the writing desk.

"I've already taken statements from both Mr. Dagerra and Miss Harwick," Sergeant Purvis said, opening his note-book. "I'll put my jottings in order later on, sir. They got back to the flat round about six and found the body. They immediately telephoned me at the station, using that phone on the small table. Both swear they didn't leave the prem-ises. They waited in the bedroom, neither of them feeling too comfortable in the vicinity of the deceased. Constable Jones had a word with the caretaker's wife. A Mrs. Gordon. Mr. Gordon is still out. She thinks he'll be at the White City dog track, if he's not passed out in some boozer. She denies having seen any strangers in the vicinity of the building. She says she was keeping a special lookout because she was waiting for Mr. Gordon so that she could give him a piece of her mind. Mr. Dagerra and the young lady, whom he tells me is his fiancée, were in Yorkshire. West Yorks have been asked to verify this. And that's about all for now, sir."

"Splendid, Purvis. Thank you."

"Oh, I forgot to mention one slight point, sir. Doctor Edinburgh was holding one of the film slides in his left hand. Between thumb and forefinger. The other fingers were gripping the chair. The slide was pink. The first one you looked at. Just as meaningless as the others."

"Thanks, sergeant." Superintendent Graham smiled reassuringly at Trudi. "And now, young lady, tell me. Why were you in such a hurry to flee from the Princess Gallery

130

yesterday afternoon? Obviously, your screams indicated you'd had the shock of finding the body. You ran because of panic. Wrong, quite wrong of you to run like that, but in the circumstances forgivable. But why were you in such a hurry to enter the gallery? Mr. Finnegan, my friend here, and I were outside when your taxi arrived. You seemed all set for the Olympics."

"Because I needed to get to the bathroom. I knew I was going to vomit."

"An unladylike expression, Miss Harwick, but most descriptive. Do you know the cause?"

"Yes. It was a seafood casserole I'd had for lunch. I knew it was bad as soon as I tasted it. But I was ravenous. The second mouthful didn't seem as sour as the first. I'm sure it was ptomaine poisoning. Felt rotten after I'd thrown up. Splitting headache. It seemed I could still taste it when I woke up this morning. Even after a mouthwash. I'll never eat fish again."

"She was in terrible shape, sir," Gee said sympathetically.

"Perhaps, Mr. Dagerra, you'll tell us what the two of you did later on. Once you'd caught up with Miss Harwick outside in the street. But in the meantime, I'd like her to tell us again, in her own words, what happened downstairs."

Policewoman Helen Maitland stood discreetly in the background. She was accustomed to witnesses' breaking down or fainting. For this eventuality she always carried a small vial of smelling salts in her shoulder bag. Old-fashioned but effective. She was also a shrewd judge of character and knew that Trudi Harwick was not an hysterical type but rather a very together young woman. Therefore, Policewoman Maitland concluded, what Trudi saw yesterday afternoon in the Princess Gallery must have been dreadful indeed, if she was now able to take the discovery of a second murder so calmly.

To be outwardly calm did not mean that Trudi Harwick

was not inwardly frightened. She gripped the clasp of her handbag, opening and snapping it shut. Her cheeks were flushed, but otherwise her complexion was drained of color.

"You're feeling strong enough to answer my questions?" the super inquired. "I suspect you're still running a temperature, so if you feel you can't carry on, then we'll run through the questions another time. But first it is only fair to tell you that we know Doctor Edinburgh was your father."

"Oh God! When did you find out?"

"This morning. Your father told Sergeant Purvis and Mr. Finnegan. But having you for a daughter is no crime, surely?"

"But having him for a father? What about that, superintendent."

"I'd say that's quite irrelevant. Just as it's irrelevant that you and his stepson are engaged. Oh, I know. You haven't told me, but the newspapers did. Besides, I can see for myself you're both in love. Did you love your father?"

Trudi Harwick hesitated with her reply. Drawing in her breath sharply, she looked from the super to Purvis.

"No. How could I? He was a stranger to me. We've only known each other since I've been grown up. And now that I know he was a murderer, that he killed Charles, I hate him. I hate him even though he's been murdered himself!"

The super, Finnegan, Maitland were caught off guard. It was Gee Dagerra who spoke.

"She told me when we were in Yorkshire. That's why I insisted we return to London immediately. If she hadn't, could she have been charged with being an accessory after the fact, or whatever you English call it?"

"Until she tells us what she saw," said Superintendent Graham, "she's in a very vulnerable position. It will be for us to decide. At least you've saved us putting on a country-wide search for her."

132

"But I only saw what happened. I didn't kill that boy."
Trudi looked desperately at Gee, who put his arm round
her shoulder.

"We will still need proof that you are telling the truth,
miss," said Purvis, rather unnecessarily, thought Cyrus.

"Just take your time," said the super. "What you've just
told us . . . well, continue."

"Gee and I had lunch in a small restaurant, not far from
here, near Selfridge's department store. We had decided to
tell Doctor Edinburgh, my father, and Maria that we were
engaged and met to discuss the best time. We settled on
telling them immediately after the champagne reception.
We'd hoped they'd be feeling sufficiently merry not to be
upset. We both knew it was all right for us to marry.
Genetically, there was no blood relationship. And as far as
we know, it wouldn't be breaking any law, would it?"

"Stepbrother and stepsister."

"Sounds perfectly aboveboard to me," Cyrus observed.

"I could tell I was going to be sick as soon as we left the
restaurant. Gee was due at the gallery. He'd promised to
help with the private viewing. Answering the telephone.
Doling out catalogues. Pretty boring, really, as he's not in
the least interested in art except as a form of money."

"Money?" Cyrus exclaimed.

"I suppose it will come out into the open, anyway," Gee
said rather sheepishly. "Just a little arrangement between
my father and a couple of London dealers. You know them,
Mr. Finnegan. Grossmith and Wurlitzer. They were there
yesterday afternoon."

"What sort of arrangement?" asked Purvis.

"I take the odd picture to Italy once in a while. My father
has a nephew who is a dealer in Florence. He sells the
paintings, and then when either Mr. Grossmith or Mr.
Wurlitzer is in Italy, they have some money at their disposal without having to go through all the red tape of

currency regulations. Sometimes I bring paintings back to London. This means that Dad's nephew has sterling available to him. It's all perfectly foolproof, and this way neither party loses on the exchange. Both currencies stay in their own countries."

"Humph. We'll have to think about that one," murmured the super. "So what happened next, Miss Harwick?"

"Gee left for the gallery and I popped into Selfridge's to go to the ladies. I tried to be sick, stuck my fingers down my throat, but no luck. Everything seemed so stuffy. It was unbearable. I knew I ought to have gone right home. I live with my father and stepmother, but you probably know that. I took a taxi, but on the way I changed my mind and asked to be driven to the Princess Gallery instead. I knew my father and Maria would be there. And Gee. Besides, this was a special afternoon for both of us and I didn't want to let him down. But the taxi finished me. The smell of petrol fumes in Oxford Street. I kept the window shut, which only made me feel worse. So I just ran into the gallery and downstairs to the little lavatory opposite the office. My father and Maria were talking to a fat lady. I don't think either of them noticed my arrival. I know Gee didn't. He told me so. Which was just as well because I only just made it in time. I was horribly sick. I felt I wanted to die! I didn't lose consciousness, but very nearly. I just collapsed onto the toilet seat. I was shaking all over."

"And you saw nobody downstairs?" Superintendent Graham watched her closely. She seemed to be telling the truth.

"I washed my face and then was sick again. Didn't see or hear anyone. I was violently sick till I could only retch. Worse than the first time. My eyes were burning and I was shivering one minute and sweating the next."

"How long were you downstairs?" asked Purvis.

"How would I know? Fifteen minutes? Half an hour? All I know was that I'd made a mistake in going to the gallery. I

134

was in no condition to meet the private viewing guests. Certainly to be there and announce our engagement in my present state would have been ludicrous. I decided to go upstairs, ask Gee to meet me at his car, which I knew he would have parked in the mews behind the gallery, and take me home. But when I opened the door I saw Charles."

"How did you know it was him?" asked the super.

"He'd been round to our house very early that morning. Before breakfast. I'd opened the door and told him to wait while I fetched my father. He and my father had been squabbling. Charles wasn't invited into the house. He was asking for money. Something to do with paying for photographs. When father didn't pay, Charles refused to hand them over." Trudi stopped for a moment and then continued her story.

"He didn't see me when he came out of the gallery office. Had his back to me. He was looking at an old painting on an easel. Then he heard my father coming downstairs and hurried back into the office. He was trying to hide, I think."

"What did Doctor Edinburgh do?"

"He stuck a red seal on two of the watercolors. Then he too looked at the painting on the easel. Only for a second. Because he could see through the glass brick wall that there was someone in the office. You must remember, I couldn't see too much because I'd almost closed the door. Just left it open a crack. My father reacted in a funny sort of way. He seemed to look at the person on the other side of the glass blocks, then tiptoed toward the office door and opened it. Charles must have seen him coming and he just stood there. Father shut the door, and I couldn't hear what was being said but I could tell from their movements that they were arguing. The glass blocks play peculiar optical tricks. Father seemed enormous."

"Did they come to blows?" the super questioned Trudi.

"No. Father was only in the office a minute or so, then he

came out, followed by Charles. Charles was saying something like 'I'm not bloody well coming upstairs to go through that sham. You'd better have the money tonight when I come round.' He said something like that. I was a bit shocked at a young boy using the word 'bloody,' though I don't know why I should have been. More likely to have used a four-letter word, like the rest of the kids. Funny how one reacts in such a silly way. If I'd gone out and let them know that I was there, then nothing would have happened, probably. At least Charles wouldn't be dead! I seemed to be paralyzed. Couldn't move. It was like watching a play rehearsal. Then it was all over. Charles turned to go back into the office and my father half sprang at him, like a leopard. He had his left arm pulling Charles's neck, while his right hand pressed the head forward and down. I heard the neck snap.'

For the first time, Trudi seemed to lose control. Her eyes filled with tears. She leaned toward Gee and nestled against his shoulder.

"Are you able to tell us what happened next, Miss Harwick?" The super nodded at Policewoman Maitland. "Perhaps Miss Harwick would like a cup of tea. Better still, see if there's something stronger will you, constable, brandy, or whisky?"

"I have some Strega in the kitchen cupboard," said Gee. "It's very similar to chartreuse and as you'll learn, a favorite with my countrymen. Or I can offer you Greek brandy? What about the rest of you?"

"I don't want anything," said Trudi. "I'm feeling sick again. Just get me a glass of water, please."

Until Maitland returned with the water, Trudi sat dabbing her eyes with Gee's handkerchief.

"My father carefully lowered Charles to the floor. Then he pulled him into the office," she continued. "When he came out again he closed the door, didn't lock it, and went

136

back upstairs. He was so calm. So casual. As though he was used to killing people! He walked up the stairs, just as if nothing had happened. It was horrid! It was then that I knew how much I hated him. He wasn't my father. He was a monster!"

"His commando training had come in handy," observed Purvis to no one in particular. "Well, he's got his comeuppance now."

"Mind what you're saying, sergeant," the super admonished. 'Watch your language. You are probably correct, all the same. When Mr. Finnegan told us that Doctor Edinburgh had been medical officer to a commando unit during the war, there was no mention of Edinburgh's being anything more than a doctor." The super was about to add that the only operations Edinburgh had probably assisted with were medical rather than military. He checked himself. This was no time for puns. He had to watch his language also. This was a serious moment. No time for quips.

"He saw action, all right," Cyrus said. "I know, because we compared notes about our war experiences. He received the Distinguished Service Order."

"I waited," Trudi interrupted them, anxious to complete her statement. "Then I ran to the office. I had some crazy idea that Charles wasn't dead. That I could get help. I took him by the heels and dragged him toward the bottom of the stairs. Quite mad, of course! I shouldn't have touched him. It never occurred to me to run and get help. But I couldn't do that. I could see there was no point in it. Charles was dead. I felt absolutely paralyzed. But I couldn't stay downstairs either. I'll never understand why nobody, not one of the visitors, had come down into the lower gallery. Then I remembered Maria's telling everybody that they'd be invited downstairs later, for champagne cocktails. I suppose nobody would have thought it very polite to go downstairs before that."

137

"So you screamed," Superintendent Graham reminded her.

"Did I? I guess so. I have no recollection. All I knew was that I just had to get a million miles away from the body. But I do remember my father's expression. He knew that I must have seen everything. At that second his eyes looked like two pits, brimming with evil. I knew that I would be his next victim unless I could get right away from London. Someplace where he wouldn't find me. I also knew that I would have to tell the police what I'd seen. But doing that would be almost the same as killing one's own father with one's own hands. I was utterly confused and petrified!"

"Patricide," Cyrus Finnegan said grimly. "Not nearly as uncommon a crime as one would wish."

It was with considerable annoyance that they heard the telephone. Its ring was not only jarring, it could not have sounded at a worse time. It broke across all their thoughts, interrupting each reaction to what they had just been told.

"Answer the damned thing, will you, Purvis."

"Sir!"

Detective Sergeant Purvis listened.

"Sorry, ma'am. I can't help you. He's not here." He replaced the receiver.

"That was Mrs. Edinburgh. She was trying to find her husband. Something about Mrs. Winterhalter going there for supper. And I wasn't lying when I told her he isn't here. He'll be in the morgue by now. Our next unpleasant duty will be to tell your stepmother, Miss Harwick, that her husband is dead."

An hour later, when it was nearly nine o'clock, Superintendent Graham, Purvis, and Finnegan sealed the flat and made their way to the nearest pub. Two constables had been posted outside the building. It was the establishment, a pub serving Watney's beer, where Mr. Gordon, the caretaker, usually spent his evenings when there was nothing to watch on the telly and the dogs weren't running. This evening, although the saloon was packed with its Saturday crowd, Finnegan found them an almost empty private bar. He felt that it was his turn to offer some liquid consolation to her majesty's police, so he bought three double scotches and three bottles of Watney's best India Pale Ale as chasers.

Policewoman Helen Maitland went along in the police car to the Edinburgh flat in Haverstock Hill. She sat in front with the driver. Gee and Trudi were in the back. Helen knew that she would see no more of her fiancé that night. It was her duty to tell Mrs. Edinburgh that the doctor was dead. Superintendent Graham had suggested that she should stay all night if either Maria Edinburgh or Trudi looked as if they would need her presence. Gee, of course, would be staying there also. He had no intention of returning to the flat ever again, except to pack his things and take Trudi back to Italy with him. He would switch to the university at Turin. He had decided this as soon as he had heard the grisly details of Trudi's ghastly experience. Well, it was a comfort to have the policewoman there. An attractive girl, with that special attraction that English girls have. And while he had sat comforting Trudi, he had not failed to notice that Policewoman Maitland had a most inviting figure. He wondered what she would look like out of uniform, thoughts that caused him guiltily to reconcentrate his attentions on Trudi.

In the pub, Superintendent Graham, finally acknowledging that his back was miserable, his shoulder aching like a thousand abscesses, and his mind blank with fatigue, downed his whisky and asked Cyrus to be a good chap and get him another double.

"I thought you had men watching the block? Clowns!" He controlled his temper with difficulty, trying not to sound too reproachful. He would discipline the constables later. "Sounds like the old shell game to me! Now you see the pea, now you don't. How in God's name did you let the three of them get into the flat without being seen?"

"Beat's me, Sir. Had men back and front. The flat's curtains were drawn all day. I was still trying to get hold of a search warrant when Mr. Dagerra telephoned. You know how difficult it is to have a search warrant signed on a week-end. Doesn't take much to distract one's attention."

"Apparently," Graham snapped bitterly. "No use crying over uncrossed bridges." He liked to reshuffle cliché metaphors. "You saw Mrs. Edinburgh earlier, Constable Maitland told me. By the way, tell Maitland I appreciate her rallying round like this, giving up her weekend off duty, just as I am."

"Yes, sir. Thank you, sir." Purvis would be only too happy to convey the super's appreciation. A good word from high places is never out of order. "I saw Mrs. Edinburgh at her house. Still in bed. Had a neighbor looking after her because Doctor Edinburgh had been lunching with Mrs. Winterhalter and then had a couple of patients to see. She wasn't expecting him home till this evening."

"Mrs. Winterhalter told me on our way back from High Wycombe that Doctor Edinburgh had delivered the picture to her but had declined her invitation to lunch," said Cyrus.

"Well, Mrs. Winterhalter will be with Maria Edinburgh this evening," the super reminded them. "Probably will be there still when Policewoman Maitland arrives with Miss Harwick and Mr. Dagerra."

"It'll be a damned short visit," Cyrus Finnegan said. "She really has a ticket for tonight's show at the National Theatre; that's where she'll be."

The three men drank in silence.

"So? What did Maria Edinburgh have to say for herself?" The super recalled that Purvis had told him that he had

140

gone to Haverstock Hill. The super seemed to be more relaxed.

"She was pretty doped up," Purvis answered. "Difficult to hear, the words sort of slurred. A few minutes after I arrived there, Doctor Edinburgh telephoned and asked how she was feeling. Fine, she said. Told him to pick up some pork sausages from Walls in Jermyn Street, then remembered it would be closed on Saturday afternoons. Thought Mrs. Winterhalter would like English toad-in-the-hole for super! Blimey. Imagine giving a Yankee a sausage in dough!" Sergeant Purvis was even more relaxed than the super. He chuckled, then became serious. "Which means that Maria must have been the last person to speak to him. Aside from the patients he was seeing, though probably not on a Saturday afternoon."

"Let's forget the patients," Cyrus said. "Forgive me for butting in like this on police talk, but frankly I agree with you. I don't think he had any patients to see. He'd gone to the flat for some other purpose. He was up to something, but what? And what did he go home for? Why didn't he go straight to his flat, after delivering Mrs. Winterhalter's picture to the Savoy?"

"Perhaps he was still worried about her. You said she was heavily sedated?" said the super.

"Very much so." Purvis looked reflectively at his empty beer glass and then at his watch. "I think Maria suspected he had a lady friend. Got quite steamed up at one point, despite the drugs. Jealous Italian spitfire, I imagine, when she gets going. Of course, it could have been something far more serious. Doing abortions on the side? Something the British Medical Association is pretty touchy about."

"You're tired, Purvis," Superintendent Graham said, looking at his watch. "We're all tired and none of us is thinking straight. Almost closing time anyway. Let's all go home and get a bit of shuteye."

"Answer me this one, sir, if you please," Purvis said to Cyrus Finnegan. He was being most formal. Probably to impress the super. "Those photo transparencies. What would a medical doctor, a psychiatrist no less, be doing with a set of meaningless pictures like those? Porno. Now that's different. I'd understand that!"

"I'll come round to your office and look at them again, tomorrow morning, Mr. Purvis. I've a hunch this is the first proper lead we've had so far. It would be nice if all of us could stop thinking in riddles!"

"If you want my opinion," said the super, starting to feel the full effects of mixing hops and barley, "they looked like intestines. Pink, blue, purple, red! Guts."

"Red herrings, more likely," said Purvis. "And not for the first time, believe me, what with the lies people tell."

"There probably is a very simple explanation," Superintendent Graham answered. "Mind you, I'm not totally convinced that Trudi Harwick didn't kill Charles and is now blaming her father. Knowing he can't contradict her."

"For that matter," Purvis said sourly, "why not tell us that it was she who killed Charles and in that way she'd be protecting her late father. Say it had been self-defense. Charles had attacked her."

"Both of you are talking rubbish," said Cyrus. "You're twisting yourselves into knots, like a couple of addlepated boa constrictors. As the super's just said, let's get some sleep. We'll think more logically in daylight. I've no doubt whatever that Trudi told us the truth. She merely confirms what I've felt from the beginning, that Doctor Edinburgh did exactly what she said he did. What we have to do now is learn why. Even ex-commandos don't just go around killing people, especially budding young painters."

142

9

"Helga," Cyrus asked his housekeeper later that evening, "just why do young women wear wigs?"

He was sprawled in the deepest and most comfortable of his armchairs. He'd taken off shoes, jacket, and tie. Sometimes beer made him sweat in hot weather.

"To make themselves prettier, I suppose."

"Oh Helga, that's a damned silly answer!"

"Ach! Not so, not so. We women must always consider such points, which is why I am not a women's libber. Going dirty and unwashed and wearing those dreadful clothes and no make-up. It's not decent. No wonder men prefer men! Who can blame them! Look at me, almost fifty-six and I still take trouble, even though you don't seem to notice. It's my pride. Maybe I'm not quite as blonde as I used to be when I was younger. So, maybe I ought to wear a wig, eh? You prefer your housekeeper to be black hair, auburn, carrot?"

"I like you as you are, Helga. And this is what I'm getting

143

at. When we saw Trudi Harwick earlier this evening, she was no longer a blonde. Her real hair is rich, warm, brown, full of natural waves, must be a delight for her hairdresser. She looks quite aristocratic. The blonde wig makes her rather artificial, stagy in a vulgar sort of way."

"But she's in the chorus, ja?"

"Yes, indeed. And that probably accounts for why she was wearing her wig yesterday at the Princess Gallery. Had put it on in the morning for a rehearsal she didn't go to. Anyway, any chorus girl I've met has been a smasher, and for my money, if Trudi has any sense she'll throw her wig away."

"And her young man prefers her as a brunette?"

"Obviously. So, let me tell you about my day."

Helga was a good listener. She could listen while cooking. She could listen while pasting things in her scrapbook. She could listen now when it was late evening and she would rather be in bed.

"I think the superintendent was just leading you on. Joking, eh? If that young lady had been as ill as you say she was, she would not have had the strength to kill. Certainly she screamed, and she may have moved the body. Naturally she was shocked and hysterical, but she would not kill. And something else . . ."

"What?"

"That poisoning. Probably it had nothing to do with the dish she'd eaten earlier."

"So back to the wig, Helga. My guess is that it is her stage look. Don't ask me why. Perhaps she's heard some cock and bull tale about producers' preferring blondes. Certainly in the short time she's been in England, she's made quite an inroad on the London stage. At least, that's what Edinburgh told Purvis."

"Vanity!" Helga exclaimed disgustedly. "I'm not contradicting myself. Looking one's best is one thing. Wearing

144

blonde wigs is just female folly. But there. You are right. She wears it for the stage."

"Which implies something else," Cyrus pointed out. "When she left home yesterday morning, she'd had every intention of going to the theater. A rehearsal. The stage manager wasn't being fair to her, was he?"

"But she didn't go. And she missed performances in the past. I'd say he was being fair. How was he to know she'd been taken ill with fish-casserole poisoning? Silly dish to order in a restaurant, anyway."

"Just because you make the best cod soufflé and halibut crêpes, don't be so uppity."

"And about what the super was saying," said Helga, ignoring his remark. "I think that young lady was telling the truth. She would have been too hysterical to make up such a story to save her father."

"Even supposing she loved her father?"

"But she doesn't. She said that. What that Trudi has been through in her short life! How must it feel, when you are grown up, to be reunited with your father and realize you don't like him? That perhaps you don't even trust him?"

"I'll concede your point, Helga. Look at her tale from another angle. Suppose it was she who killed Charles. That, for the reasons you've just stated, she decided to blame Doctor Edinburgh."

"Why would she kill that nice young man?"

"But we don't know if he was nice, do we?"

"So young to be murdered. On the first step of his career! Cynthia Tomkins in her 'Tomkins Table Talk' says that Charles was a genius."

"And Cynthia bloody Tomkins said that I was in Dublin hunting I.R.A. thugs planning to steal the Lane Collection from the National Gallery of Ireland. Did you give her that rubbish?"

145

"Superintendent Graham told me to say that you were out of town for the weekend. You know he did."

"Oh, Helga, what would I do without you! Now I'll have the I.R.A. gunning for me."

"Well! Anyway! Trudi didn't kill Charles! Of that I'm sure! That poisoning, what do you call it?"

"Ptomaine. She could have got it from something she'd eaten earlier. For breakfast, or last night's supper. Despite your Norwegian snobbishness, fish casseroles are perfectly safe in good restaurants."

There was a pause, neither Cyrus nor Helga feeling that this conversation was constructive. As both of them were tired, one of them might say something which would lead to a quarrel. It had happened before.

"If you want to know who I think is behind all this," said Helga, picking up her scrapbook and heading toward the corridor and bed, "my instinct is working for me. You wait!"

But at that moment the doorbell rang.

"God almighty, who's calling at this hour! Find out who it is, Helga. Tell whoever it is I've gone to Dublin."

As she so often did when she knew that she was winning an argument, Helga chose to ignore his instructions. She returned with Mr. Grossmith and Mr. Wurlitzer. By previous arrangement, apparently, it was Grossmith who spoke first.

"Our regrets at calling to see you so late, and on a Saturday night. We're worried. We think you should know why."

"Then take a pew," Cyrus pointed at two empty chairs. "How about a drop of brandy? Or scotch?"

"Brandy would do nicely," said Wurlitzer, "but not too big."

Cyrus heard Helga's door being shut like a pistol shot. As he'd told the super, he quite liked Grossmith and Wurlitzer. They were both so openly and proudly Jewish. And in the world of art, without Jewish foresight, intellectual leadership, and generous patronage, many people would be in a pretty sorry mess. Jews were not cautious gamblers, but imaginative and daring. They took risks. If some of them liked to show off and others were greedy, they were no different from the rest of humanity. At least they were direct, and free of hocus-pocus and pretense.

This didn't blind Cyrus to the reality that, like Englishmen, some Jews are out-and-out bastards. While he didn't like rumors he'd heard of the unethical activities of Grossmith and Wurlitzer, as he'd also told Superintendent Graham, these two had never tried to pull a fast one on him. He knew there was faint proof that they had raised their first capital by selling Tanagra figurines, faked in Paris; and that, when Peter Knowles was employed by them, there had been rumors of a fake Gainsborough's being sold to an Australian with no questions asked. The story went that Knowles disappeared a couple of days later, taking with him a liberal pile of banknotes. Like so much of the Bond Street gossip—tales of mock bids at auction, faked provenances for stolen works, fabulous manipulations in currency, and dealers who flitted from one bankruptcy to another, choosing a different country each time—it was all part of the art scene, and one learned to live with what one heard and do nothing about it.

When Cyrus had poured their brandy and a double scotch for himself, it was midnight. There was only a little beer left in his tankard.

"We won't stay long, Mr. Finnegan," Grossmith said, downing his drink with one swift movement. "There are a couple of points we feel will have to be cleared up."

"Sooner or later, with the police," Wurlitzer interposed. He usually let Grossmith do the talking. "It's about some photographs we took for Doctor Edinburgh."

Cyrus didn't say anything. Doubt if they've heard of

Edinburgh's death, he was thinking. Damned suspicious if they have, though.

"Color film. Developed in our own lab."

"And what was the subject?"

"Subjects. Subjects in the plural. Five paintings in all, by that unfortunate young man, Charles. Not what we like, naturally. But photography is our new sideline. More profitable than framing. These days everybody is into framing. Cheap do-it-yourself rubbish. Mass-produced. Not the high-quality framing we do for our special clients. We still do a bit, but now the photography is really catching on. Only for the trade."

"Very lucrative," observed Grossmith. "Very interesting too. Now when Tony Kershaw brought those paintings round—"

"I thought you said Edinburgh asked you to take the photographs?"

"It was for Doctor Edinburgh, yes. But it was Kershaw who told us the pictures were for the doctor and that he'd been asked by Charles to bring them to our gallery."

"Did something go wrong?"

"That's it. You see, we don't understand what has happened. The photographs were taken last Monday, and we personally delivered the five canvases to the Princess Gallery on the Tuesday. Which gave the Edinburghs three days before the private viewing." Grossmith, feeling the effect of the brandy and the warm room, mopped his brow. Wurlitzer, sipping slowly, had by now finished his drink also.

"I don't follow," Cyrus remarked. "What's gone wrong?"

"The photographs are missing. All original transparencies. Can't take them again, unless we get the paintings back." Wurlitzer looked anxiously at his fingernails, while Grossmith continued.

148

"Edinburgh telephoned us this afternoon. At our house. Our gallery is closed on Saturdays. In a real panic. Wanted to know where the slides were. I told him that we'd given them to Charles yesterday morning. The day of the private viewing. The day it happened. Edinburgh said yes, he knew we'd given them to Charles, but they'd disappeared. Could we do him another set today! As we're bachelors and have no family responsibilities the doctor seemed to think we'd hop to it. Not mind doing a Saturday afternoon rush job. Breaking the Sabbath, I ask you! So we told him it couldn't be done. We'd have to have the paintings back." Grossmith licked his lips and mopped his brow again. "I'm afraid Doctor Edinburgh thought we were lying. He swore and shouted, as though the world was coming to an end. So that's what we wanted to tell you, Mr. Finnegan."

"What do you expect me to do?" Cyrus was puzzled. "They're your photographs. You've told Edinburgh you can't make duplicates without the originals. Maybe they'll turn up."

"And will you report this to Superintendent Graham or to Sergeant Purvis?" asked Wurlitzer. "Not that we've anything to hide. Our lab is perfectly legit, understand."

"No dirty photos?" Cyrus grinned at their shocked expressions.

"Certainly not, Mr. Finnegan."

"Then I'll decide whether to tell the police later," said Cyrus reassuringly. "Doesn't sound as if you've committed any crime. If you'd been up to monkey business, photographing stolen works, that sort of shenanigan, it would be a very different matter. In that case, the police would undoubtedly be most anxious to have a few words with you."

Grossmith and Wurlitzer both stood up.

"Well, at least it's off our conscience," Wurlitzer remarked. "Having you in on the picture makes us feel better. Thank you for being so understanding, Mr. Finnegan."

"Being understanding is part of my job," said Cyrus.

Later, as he slid thankfully into his bed, he said to himself that perhaps he was beginning to get the picture after all.

"I think it's bloody shameful the way people think we're crooks." Larry Grossmith pressed his foot on the accelerator and beat the caution light. "Even Finnegan doesn't trust us."

"Balls!" Morris countered. "Finnegan has his brains in his head, not between his legs."

"Then why didn't he ask us more about Charles?"

"Because he's shrewd. He knows we're in the clear."

"Clear soup, you mean. No, I'm kidding. Finnegan's been around, and what he's learned on his rounds is to hold back. When he gives, he's sure of his facts."

"Then perhaps we should have told him about Edinburgh's offer?"

"Let's sleep on that one, shall we?"

It was after one A.M. Larry carefully drove north toward Finchley, where he and Morris Wurlitzer shared a luxuriously appointed flat in a posh, eight-story condominium. Their late-night meeting with Cyrus Finnegan had left both of them depressed. It would have been prudent to wait until morning. Finnegan had been tired. Too tired, perhaps, to fully understand the significance of what they were telling him.

The car passed alongside Lords Cricket Ground in the direction of Swiss Cottage. Although it was late, there was a steady flow of traffic.

"It's that damned idiot Kershaw," said Morris, while they waited at the next set of lights. "Can't keep his hands off Maria. And the doctor knows it. He's not missed what's been going on these years."

"Two or three at least. Just after Kershaw got back from that tour he conducted in Holland—Rotterdam, Amsterdam, Everdingen, Nijmegen, The Hague. Got tired of hearing about it."

"That's about the time Maria got her first fix." Grossmith eased out into the center lane. "Do you think Kershaw got her onto the stuff? Could have been the doctor himself. He's a drug merchant. But no, no man would do that to his own wife."

"Want to bet? And how about Trudi? She arrived on the scene just about then. Perhaps she's the supplier. She's pretty high-strung and edgy, that one. Bundle of nerves."

"My money's on Tony Kershaw. He was all right when he worked for us. We shouldn't have given him time off to conduct those tours. But we must still remember how useful he was to us, visiting those foreign dealers. Put some good deals our way. I'm grateful to him for that. If he's working a drug racket on the side, then I suppose it's none of our business. We haven't proof."

"We haven't proof, yet we know." Wurlitzer glanced sideways at his friend. "Which doesn't help Maria Edinburgh."

Grossmith countered, "If she keeps on doping at this rate, she's not long for this world. I'd like to pin it on Kershaw and turn him in to the drug squad. Really, we would be doing the human race a favor. We'll just have to wait."

It was an unpleasant subject for both of them.

"When Kershaw passed along Edinburgh's offer to sell us the Princess Gallery, didn't you smell something fishy?" Grossmith guided the car down the ramp into the basement garage.

"You know we did. Both of us were surprised as hell. Getting a business off to a good start, then suddenly quitting. Doesn't make for commercial goodwill. The pur-

151

chaser is buying nothing, just vacant premises. And as for those photographs. Suppose we've not heard the end of that. All seemed aboveboard."

"Otherwise we wouldn't have touched the job, would we?"

"No sir. Keeping our noses clean. That's our trademark!"

"With a couple of legit exceptions?"

"Of course."

Mrs. Winterhalter was a light sleeper. Heartburn and indigestion responded to a tumbler full of soda bicarbonate before retiring. Geting rid of wind at either end was a self-imposed treatment for flatulence that sometimes worked and sometimes didn't. Tonight, wind still bounced about inside her. She rolled restlessly, disturbing the sheets, going over in her mind the many surprises and spontaneous actions that had enveloped her since her arrival in London.

It had been a good touch, ordering a nurse. The young doctor and the hotel staff apparently had fallen for the bait. Clever. Very clever. But she knew that! Peter would be proud.

It had been extravagant, buying that luxury hamper at Fortnum's to take as a gift to the Edinburghs. They had both been so very kind to her. A twinge of conscience tickled lightly at her drowsy mind, like a wink. Well, Maria would get over it. Widows, if they thought positively, could be remarkably resilient through not brooding. Time was indeed a fast healer. And people thought that she herself was a widow! As a renowned Mexican plaintiff, she had successfully disposed of three husbands in divorce proceedings with substantial settlements, and two separate awards of magnificent alimony. Well, in a way people were half right when they ascribed to her a widow's role. Divorces could be deadly! And now Peter had changed all that, once again. Pity about killing Peter's wife, though!

But poor Maria! Mrs. Winterhalter had personally unpacked the food hamper in the Edinburghs' quaint old-world kitchen. A pressed pheasant in aspic, with foie gras and truffles. Delicious! And Maria refusing even a spoonful. Bursting into tears at the sight of food. Not even a nibble of Russian eggs and cold asparagus vinaigrette. She had written the name in her notebook. *Buisson d'asperges en croustade à la Carème.* Gorgeous! Nor would Maria touch the fruit or the Stilton, though she had accepted a glass of chilled wine—*Gewürztraminer.*

At least Trudi had managed to peck at her food, while that pretty young Italian boy fairly wolfed down everything. Thank goodness that young policewoman was on a diet! Maria, however, continued to be inconsolable. So much so that Mrs. Winterhalter suspected that she was putting on an act. The whole scene seemed too melodramatic. No woman in her right mind should allow herself to grieve quite so loudly. To Mrs. Winterhalter, who had a heart of lead, such emotional carryings-on were ridiculous. Of course, Maria was Italian, and they were a race of wailers, like the Spaniards.

Maria had taken to her bed, which was the best place to be in her state. And Trudi had telephoned that strange Mr. Kershaw and asked him to come up to London as her stepmother wished to see him. Trudi said that Mr. Kershaw had sounded quite unnerved when she told him Edinburgh had been murdered. Mrs. Winterhalter wondered whether Kershaw was dependable. At least she knew he had a rotten streak. Peter had told her that Kershaw was an addict and that his wife, Peter's sister, had made up her mind to leave him because their marriage was at rock bottom. "Good for her," Mrs. Winterhalter had remarked gleefully.

It was a pity she had to waste the theater ticket. She had been looking forward to seeing the National Theatre and the huge Olivier Auditorium. She'd heard that the pre-theater snacks and wine bar were exceptionally good. Perhaps on her next visit? Now, of course, there would have to be a change in plans. She'd sent the cable, as a night letter, from the all-night post office near Charing Cross. That would make two inquests. Fortunately she wouldn't have to stay for the Edinburgh one.

She thought for a few minutes about how she would handle Mr. Cyrus Finnegan's visit. A very nice person. He'd been quite witty on their drive from High Wycombe. Most amusing. Well, having a nurse present would convince even the most skeptical. Nurses could be hired so cheaply. They qualified as a kind of servant. They could be bossed around and they distracted people—even Cyrus. Not that she considered Mr. Finnegan a skeptic, but she had noted that he was certainly observant. Who else could have so quickly identified the flowers in all the other paintings?

Suddenly the bicarbonate of soda took effect. Mrs. Winterhalter belched, then contentedly settled herself for sleep. She looked forward to her breakfast of *oeufs à la bénédictine*.

10

On Sundays when Cyrus knew he would be too busy to attend matins in a small church near Gloucester Road he made a point of going to the early communion service at eight A.M. This morning, walking back to the flat, where Helga would have breakfast waiting for him, he reviewed Grossmith and Wurltzer's visit. They had given the photographs to Charles. So how did the transparencies turn up in Edinburgh's flat off Harley Street? There were two possibilities. Charles had taken them to Edinburgh at the Belsize Park address. When Edinburgh refused to pay, he'd then turned them over to Kershaw. In which case, had Kershaw given them to Edinburgh at the private viewing? Or had Doctor Edinburgh taken them from one of Charles's pockets after killing him? Trudi had said she hadn't been able to see what her father was doing while bending over the artist's body. She had been too scared to move closer.

Blackmail? Had Charles been putting pressure on the doctor? If so, for what reason?

An hour later, when Cyrus arrived at the Princess Gallery, a young constable was waiting with the key to let him in. He told the constable not to wait, he would drop the key off at Savile Row on his way to the Savoy for lunch with Mrs. Winterhalter.

"Excuse me, sir," said the constable. "You're wearing your necktie inside out. I can read the label." Cyrus looked surprised, then chuckled.

It was good having the gallery to himself. Switching on the overhead track brought the paintings to glowing life with rich, voluptuous colors. The ingenious lighting, the artificially elegant proportions of the room, where only the mantelpiece and molded ceiling were original, were the hallmark of one of London's most brilliant interior decorators. Even the most jaded gallery-goer would surely react favorably to such elegance. The only touch of sadness in the midst of such lush color was the small wreath on the mantelpiece beneath the empty space last occupied by Mrs. Winterhalter's picture.

There was no disputing, on this evidence alone, that Charles had been good painter. That is, if it was indeed he who had created these vividly impressionistic abstractions. Naturally the super had been taken in, thinking they were nonobjective. The super, like Sergeant Purvis, would obviously prefer realism. Cyrus remembered what Raymond Chandler, the mystery writer, had written: "Of all forms of art, realism is the easiest to practice, because of all forms of mind the dull mind is commonest." He must remember to pass that onto the super the next time he accused Cyrus of being highbrow.

Other styles? What did it matter, whether one did action painting or nonobjective art? Spilling your paint pots at random did not necessarily mean that you couldn't have quality. Quality in art came with better control, with discipline. And quality was what Cyrus looked for, with the results that he discounted much that he saw on his rounds of the galleries. One year alone he had totaled the score and found that he had seen eighteen thousand canvases, in group exhibitions and commercial galleries, excluding those masterpieces in the National and Tate and other art museums. Of those eighteen thousand, there were far too few worth the wall space given to them.

Even if there had been no murder, would he still have accepted this present exhibition for inclusion in his column? Yes, he thought he would, for there was an abundance of quality. That he always looked for first, the controlled ebb and flow of colors, the interplay of form, the painterly use of blurred lines blended, diffusing planes of light into light. These were not works by some immature splasher of paint.

Cyrus walked slowly from picture to picture, once in a while writing in his notebook, assessing each optical contrivance where skillful illusion had been used to disguise the flowers or plants depicted. Once the flower's identity had been established, the image stayed in focus and filled one with pleasure.

Downstairs in the lower gallery, the message, if there was one, was less obscure: good, technically efficient watercolor drawings, each one a Thames Valley landscape. Cyrus recognized scenes familiar to him. The lawn at Marlow mentioned in The Compleat Angler, the church at Ipsden, a high-walled topiary garden near Nettlebed, bridges at Reading and Henley. These clean, uncluttered pictures, totally conventional, were worthy successors to the earlier schools of British watercolor painters. They would be suitable in sedate drawing rooms, would look impressive in offices and modest flats. Only their titles were whimsical and Whistlerian. The lock at Bourne End was called *Study in Blue and Gold*. A view of Cookham bore the ridiculous title, *Nectarine Space consummated*.

Cyrus lifted one of the pictures off its hook and examined the back. There was no label to identify the framer. Only the title, the name "Charles," a price in code, and the date were given.

What was unusual was that not one of the watercolors had been signed. This applied also to the canvases upstairs. Many modern artists eschewed signing their canvases, though they would sign watercolors and given edition numbers for prints. To a layman, it might have seemed strange that these works in the upper and lower galleries should be so different yet still by the same artist. Cyrus had noticed this oddity often enough. Some artists seemed to change their personalities when using different techniques, and so their watercolors and oils might seem to have been painted by two individuals instead of one. But if you studied the pictures carefully, you quickly recognized a common denominator. In the case of Charles Knowles, it was the predominance of certain colors. Ultramarine, pink, red, bluish-white, apple green, yellow ochre recurred time and time again. It would be difficult explaining this to Superintendent Graham; like telling a color-blind person that one could usually identify Murillo by his blues. How many people knew the Spaniard Murillo had invented his own blue?

There was a further and more obvious disparity in style. Little evidence of good drawing was apparent in the upstairs oils; in the lower gallery the drawing was controlled and first-class.

Cyrus was about to go upstairs when he decided to recheck the storage area. The Dutch seascape was still on its easel. Grossmith and Wurlitzer had been a bit fretful last night, wondering how soon they could get it back. Cyrus was sure the super would let them remove it on Monday morning. Meanwhile he had another look, this time using his pocket magnifying glass. He was pretty well satisfied that the painting was authentic.

He bent and turned over one of the watercolors that was on the floor facing the wall. There it was! The school! He recognized it, a sprawling red-brick Victorian building with numerous gables and at least thirty chimneys. At the back of what was formerly a stable yard were three greenhouses. St. Justin's. This must be the school where Mary Kershaw's husband taught, although she pretended not to know its name. This in itself was either a deliberate lie or total indifference on her part. How could a wife not know where her husband worked? Sheer nonsense. She was bluffing because she had guessed that this was the school where Kershaw had taken Charles whom she was too priggish to have anything to do with. Yet she felt she ought to protect her husband. Why?

Cyrus knew the school by sight. It was situated between Twyford and Reading near Twyford Junction. He had heard that the school had fallen on bad times. It was now little better than an expensive storage place for upper-class delinquents, a place where the wealthy could hide criminally inclined progeny with the hope that if they were made to work hard, some learning might rub off on them. For an extra fee, the boys could be kept at the school during holidays, even Christmas. Cyrus had forgotten all about the place until now.

He replaced the watercolor against the wall and turned his attention to the rest of the converted coal cellar. The small pile of coal was still in the middle of the linoleum-covered floor. Looking up, he saw that the retaining bar which prevented the manhole from being opened from outside was back in position. It could have been Edinburgh who had replaced it after he had killed Charles. It wouldn't have taken him more than a few seconds. The police would have checked this and probably taken fingerprints.

It was all so obvious! Cyrus and the super had entered Newton Street and both noticed that all the manholes were open. The horse with its coal cart and sacks was at the far end of the street near Mrs. Winterhalter's Rolls. Cyrus made a note to find out the name of the coal company and have a word with the delivery man. Nothing could have been easier for Charles than to wait until the street was clear of pedestrians and then lower himself in the cellar.

It was too late to alter his program now. In fifteen minutes he was due at the Savoy, and he must also drop off the gallery key at the Savile Row police station. This afternoon he planned to take advantage of the Sunday emptiness of the Adelphi Club's writing room and prepare his first report for Detective Sergeant Purvis. That would take two or three hours at least, as there were many facets and angles for conjecture.

He was only certain about one point. He remembered Mary Kershaw's comment that her husband was a frustrated painter, a *peintre manqué*. It seemed to Cyrus Finnegan that Kershaw had worked out his frustrations very nicely indeed. Why on earth the mysterious anonymity?

Tomorrow morning, Cyrus decided, he would take an early train to Twyford Junction and visit the school. After all, as he kept telling his art students, Superintendent Graham, Sergeant Purvis, and anybody else who bothered to listen, the closer one looked, the greater one's insight.

He hoped Mrs. Winterhalter would serve champagne. He felt like celebrating. Although he was only halfway in his foraging for clues, he was confident that by the end of the day the picture would be different. Meanwhile a spot of champagne would do very nicely, thank you.

A nurse opened the door of Mrs. Winterhalter's suite. A middle-aged "special," she looked powerfully athletic, like a discus thrower, with close-cropped black hair, a delicate moustache, and a complexion the color of port wine.

Cyrus followed her into a large sitting room, beautifully

furnished in Regency style, and with an extensive view of the Thames. Mrs. Winterhalter was lying on a sofa, her shoulders propped up by four pillows, her knees covered by a Shetland rug. She was very pale, with darkish-blue circles accentuating the bags under her eyes.

"So kind of you to come, Mr. Finnegan. Take a chair. Make yourself comfortable. Nurse, do you know how to mix martinis?"

"You shouldn't have anything alcoholic, ma'am." The nurse tried to be firm but obviously had decided earlier that this particular patient would take orders from no one. "Orange juice is more suited for your condition."

"But we haven't any vodka! Don't be so ridiculous! Who ever heard of drinking orange juice without vodka! Cyrus Finnegan, you look intelligent enough to make a very dry martini. Or shall I send for some champagne, which I usually drink for my heart. But before lunch martinis are just what the doctor ordered."

"Not any doctor I know of," the nurse spoke sharply. "When he asked me to report this morning, I was to see that you rested and not get overstimulated. This gentleman can mix all the martinis he wishes. But for you it's orange juice."

"In that case, Cyrus, mix me a strong screwdriver, O.K.?"

"One screwdriver with gin and one very double dry martini on their way," said Cyrus heading towards the well-stocked bar, temporarily placed on an elegant tripod table, with bird-cage boxing round its edge.

"Let any fatal results be on you, sir!" snapped the nurse.

"Fatal, my aunt's tit!" Mrs. Winterhalter was delighted to spot the nurse pale. "Now run along, and leave Mr. Finnegan and me alone. Go and sit in my bedroom. Say! Why don't you let him fix you a martini?"

"For two reasons, dammit, ma'am. I'm on duty and I'm an abstainer. Carry on being rude to me, and you can get

161

yourself another bloody nurse!" She managed her exit with dignity.

"If I'd known you were ill, I'd have suggested postponing our meeting," Cyrus apologized.

"No way, Cyrus. This is one of my usual attacks. I came on all faint last night in the elevator and flipped over. Gave the hotel staff a god-awful fright, I bet. But they were ever so kind. Called the house doctor. He wanted to pack me off to the London Clinic, but no way! I just get breathless, as I did in the car yesterday, remember? Just too much excitement. Two killings in twenty-four hours. And an inquest on Tuesday. And of course I'm real sorry, and all that, about Charles and Hans—I like to call him Hansy, somehow suited him! Well, at least I have my fine painting, and that's the reason for your visit, correct?"

The painting, which Cyrus had noticed immediately when entering the room, was hung on the wall facing him. The hotel's picture had been removed.

"It's for my article. I need to see it in leisure and in daylight."

"Yes, you explained all that. Lunch will be served when I phone for it, so take your time. Have a good look. Meanwhile, as that bitch is out of the room, pour this damned drink into that vase over there and mix me a martini. Make it a triple."

"Then as nurse said, let the fatal consequences be on your head."

"That's my boy! and don't hold back on the ice." Mrs. Winterhalter was already a better color. "The doctor, such a nice man, is just being cautious. Nurse wouldn't even let me look at the Sunday newspapers. Fancy that! And I'd planned to take in one of your English churches this morning. St. Paul's or Westminster Cathedral or Abbey, I forget which has all those famous people under the floor. This

162

afternoon the Rolls was booked to take me to have a gander at Stratford-upon-Avon where your Bard lived with Ann what's-her-name."

"Hathaway. You've been trying to do too much. Save it till your next visit and take at least a couple of weeks. These twenty-one-day holiday flights would suit you admirably."

"But I told you. I detest flying. That's why I'm booked to go back on the *Queen E.* on Wednesday. The inquest couldn't have been timed better."

"I compliment you on your planning. When did you learn Doctor Edinburgh had been murdered?"

"Yesterday evening. I went to visit them in that dumpy old place near Hampstead; do you know it? Fortunately the driver knew the dead-end street." Mrs. Winterhalter had a large sip of her martini and continued. "Meant to be a surprise visit. I'd arranged a real dandy of a fancy supper hamper from Fortnum's. So you can just guess my disappointment. I arrived just as a young policewoman was making tea. She'd brought Trudi and the young Italian home. Had told Maria about her husband being dead. Maria had gone all to pieces, believe me. What with one thing and another, I didn't get to the theater after all. You'll remember my intention to see a play at the National? Then having this crazy attack as soon as I got back to the Savoy sure put the lid on things."

"You have my sympathy." Cyrus didn't know what else to say so he crossed over to look closely at Charles's painting. It looked better in daylight. The gallery lighting, while good, somehow had exaggerated certain tonal balances. In daylight the colors seemed softer. Paint applied by palette knife, unless the impasto was of a certain thickness, tended to look shiny and flat. But here the artist had worked swiftly and with knowledge and self-assurance. Even so, there was something off about the treatment of the surface. The appli-

163

cation of paint was thinner close to the frame. The center of the canvas was a wild swirl of heavy strokes, the paint as thick as icing.

"Have you a photograph of this? I'd like one in color for my own records. For the newspaper, black and white would do nicely, unless the editor decided to work it into our magazine supplement."

"Now that's something else again," Mrs. Winterhalter complained. "Hansy Edinburgh said he would get a photographer to come here tomorrow, Monday, and take a few shots, black and white and in color. So now I've no way of knowing whether he arranged for a photographer or not."

"Then I'll arrange it for you. Grossmith and Wurlitzer are the best. I'll get them."

"Will you really? That's swell. I've been buying simply dozens of those little souvenir slides while here, Tower of London, Windsor Castle, Kew Gardens. Even though I haven't had time to visit these places, slides are always handy when you want to show people what an interesting holiday you've had. I've even got one of those little viewers over there by the mirror. See? Make sure they take slides I can use in my viewer."

"I'll have the photographer come round here, but I'll have him telephone first, make sure you're well enough. He'll manage it before you sail on Wednesday."

Mrs. Winterhalter used the house phone and told room service to send up lunch, reminding them to be sure the wine was chilled. A brave woman to say that in the Savoy.

"We're having Lobster Newburg. I hope that's all right Cyrus."

"Perfect!"

His eyes kept straying back to the painting. Gloxinia. And on top of what he recognized as a Regency adaptation of a Carlton House writing table was the gloxinia plant itself.

"To think that it is the very last painting Charles fin-

164

ished." Mrs. Winterhalter slightly slurred her words, betraying the effect of her triple martini. "That was what Doctor Edinburgh told me when he explained why there just hadn't been time to have it photographed. The paint's still wet, too. I can smell it from here! And of course it was that nice Mr. Kershaw who found the plant to match it. Hansy Edinburgh brought it with him and insisted I enjoy looking at it while I'm still in London."

Cyrus wondered whether she thought that every male was a nice man. It was not an adjective he would associate with Tony Kershaw.

"A good subject for a still life. That's one good thing about having a greenhouse, you can grow your favorite plants whatever the season."

"I guess so. The poor thing's not doing so well here close to the window. I remember our gardener in our Long Island home, that's when I was married to my second husband, telling me gloxinias bloom best in artificial light. That's why it looked so healthy in the Princess Gallery. Now, fancy me remembering that!"

"Funny how some facts seem to stick in one's mind forever." Cyrus tried to guide the conversation elsewhere. "If you're feeling ill, you probably don't want company, but it's not much fun being ill when you're alone in a hotel room. I don't mean to be nosy, but has anybody else been to visit you?"

"Well, now, I have that bossy nurse. While she doesn't seem to have much sympathy for a person who might be dying, she's at least here when I want her. But to answer your question. Yes, that nice young police sergeant left here about ten minutes before you arrived. Called soon after I'd moved in here from my bedroom. Seeing how ill I was, he only stayed for a few minutes. He said that I was probably the last person to see Hansy. Which sounded real queer, because Doctor Edinburgh—it's so hard to think of

165

him now as one of the dear departed, isn't it—well, I told Sergeant Purvis that Hansy had refused my invitation to lunch. Said he had too much to attend to. Had to get home to look after Maria, and I suppose it would have been he who had to arrange for Charles's funeral. Now somebody will be having to arrange for his! Just fancy!"

"Was that all Purvis wanted to know?"

"Nope. He asked me if Doctor Edinburgh had given me any photographs, and I told him that Hansy was arranging to have one taken before I left for home, just as I've been saying to you. Told him how the American Express had confirmed my sailing next Wednesday. Boy, is this drink everstrong! They'd better hurry with that lunch! Purvis took a good look at the painting, asked where I'd been yesterday afternoon, so I told him I'd been with you in High Wycombe. And then I remembered Hansy saying he and Maria would be selling the gallery, now that this terrible thing had happened. If they stayed, it would always remind them of that horrid murder, not that murders aren't always horrid."

"I'm surprised the Edinburghs would make such a drastic decision so soon." Cyrus wondered whether it was just a spur of the moment reaction. "Did Purvis seem surprised?"

"Hell, no. Have you ever seen one of your nice young policemen looking surprised? He just asked me a couple of questions and left. Sort of checking up on my movements, I guess. At least that's how it appeared to me. Though I've got nothing to hide."

I wonder, Cyrus Finnegan was thinking, when a discreet knock on the door and the sound of trolley wheels squeaking to a halt indicated that lunch had arrived.

"Nurse!" Mrs. Winterhalter shouted her command in the direction of the bedroom. "Let the man in! Mr. Finnegan and I are famished. You can go downstairs and grab a sandwich!"

"I'll wait till your visitor has left," the nurse snapped back. When the waiter had served and wheeled away the trolley, the nurse tooked disapprovingly at the dishes. "As for you, ma'am, you should be having only a cup of broth, if that. Not this rich spicy rubbish."

The lunch was in every way delicious, though neither Cyrus nor his hostess could finish the wine. The meal was leisurely and caused him to stay longer than he had intended.

"Now back to your bed, ma'am," the nurse said firmly when they'd finished coffee. "I'll see the gentleman to the door, then I'll give you a little something to make you relax and sleep. Though if you ask me, what you ought to have is an extra-strong enema."

Mrs. Winterhalter scowled disapprovingly at the nurse, then took Cyrus Finnegan's hand between both of hers.

"I do hope we meet again before I leave."

"I'll see you at the inquest on Tuesday," answered Cyrus. "I've so enjoyed our chat. And thank you so much for lunch. Well up to Savoy standards."

"Life is so short, one should always travel first class. That's what my last husband, Mr. Winterhalter, believed. Do things on the cheap and you'll feel cheap."

"All right for those who can afford such extravagances, which must be tough if one's in a swank hotel like this," the nurse cut in. She waited while Cyrus said farewell, then accompanied him into the corridor. Her eyes were aflame with indignation.

"Revolting creature! I know I shouldn't discuss my patients. Most unprofessional of me, but I can hardly wait till I'm off duty."

"It's a pity she's ill."

"Ill! My Aunt Fanny! She's strong as a Hereford bull!"

"Then what about her breathlessness? She had quite a bad attack yesterday afternoon, when she gave me a lift back

167

from the country. Told me then that her heart's a bit dicey."

"Dicey? Did you say dicey? That lady, if one can refer to her as such, is one fat, overstuffed sham. And that's the opinion I'll be telling doctor when I check out. She's a bully. Goes right to the jugular. She's got enough spare breath for that! Spiteful bitch!"

Cyrus saw tears in her eyes. Her lips trembled.

"I'm sorry for you," he said. "Must be hard sometimes, not knowing how patients are going to react. But I've noticed a good side in her after only knowing her a couple of days. She's generous. Likes to give people gifts, even when they're strangers."

"She can bloody well afford to," the nurse snapped at him.

"Even so, please take good care of her," Cyrus said placatingly. "We don't want to lose her."

Before leaving the hotel Cyrus had a word with the head porter.

"The name of the company, sir, that rents Mrs. Winterhalter her Rolls?" The porter thought. "Do you know the number of her suite?"

Cyrus told him, and the head porter checked his guest list.

"No trouble at all, sir. That's the largish lady from New York. She hires from Peerless Aristocratic Car Hire and Continental Tours Limited. You'll find them in Mayfair, sir. I can telephone them now, if you'd like me to."

"Don't they sound grand!" Cyrus chuckled. "That's all right, thank you very much. I won't be needing a car till tomorrow."

"They've only got Rolls-Royces, sir. I can give you the name of a company that's cheaper."

"They'll do nicely for my purposes," said Cyrus. A name guaranteed to tickle the fancy of any rubberneck tourist with money to burn, he was thinking. It was a play on words to delight the super, pompous pretentiousness. "Peerless" could mean getting rid of the House of Lords!

As he turned left along the Strand a surprise awaited him. He came face to face with Grossmith and Wurlitzer.

"How fortunate!" Grossmith exclaimed. "We telephoned your housekeeper and she said you were lunching at the Savoy. Didn't say who with, but we took a chance. Afraid we'd timed it wrong."

"You've timed it perfectly."

"I guessed you must be visiting that Yank who bought Charles's painting," added Wurlitzer. "We've got something important to show you."

"Urgent!" Grossmith handed Cyrus a telegram. "We got this yesterday afternoon, about tea time."

The message read: ARRANGEMENTS SATISFAC- TORILY CONCLUDED NO FURTHER NEED OF YOUR SERVICES STOP OFFER CANCELED STOP EDINBURGH.

"What does that mean?" asked Cyrus. "Explain."

"We ought to have mentioned it when we visited last night," said Wurlitzer. "Edinburgh wanted to sell us his gallery. Not asking much, either. Driving back home after we'd left you, it struck us as a strange coincidence, our getting that message just about the time he was murdered."

"So you've heard?"

"Naturally. It was on the news, and in the Sunday papers. We thought you should hear about the offer first. That's why we telephoned your flat. We didn't want to disturb you on a Sunday, but felt it was too important to wait."

"Thanks for the thought, anyway. Mind if I keep this to show the police?"

"Go ahead. No use to us anymore, now that Edinburgh's dead. Maria will want to sell, though possibly not to us.

169

Best thing for her would be to turn it over to Gee and Trudi as a wedding gift."

The two dealers waited for Finnegan's comments.

"What's the telegram getting at; that bit about no further need for your services?"

"It puzzled us," Grossmith replied. "Guess it means he wouldn't use us for photography again. As we told you, he was hopping mad because we didn't have his transparencies. Guess he was feeling hotheaded when he wrote that. No doubt he would have changed his mind later and come back. We're the best there is."

"How many prints were on the roll?" asked Cyrus.

"Twenty. We find twenty is the most practical."

"I'm glad you contacted me," said Cyrus. "You've gone to a lot of trouble. Anything else to add?"

"Don't think so," Wurlitzer answered, after a sideways glance at his partner. "Except there is one other thing. Don't know how to put it."

"We're worried about Maria Edinburgh, that's what Morris wants to convey."

"Now Laurie, you know that you feel just as badly as I do about her. You see, Mr. Finnegan, she's an addict."

"How long have you known this?"

"A year, possibly longer. She's changed very little in her appearance, though. Still quite plump and jolly. Not thin and scrawny like so many dopers. But some days she's real down and edgy."

"Do you see a lot of her?" Cyrus was curious.

"We're often in and out of the Princess Gallery," Grossmith replied drily. "But that's stating the obvious. We're in trade. No idea where she gets the stuff from. Can't be hard to find, London's plugged to the guts with dope. We don't think she gets it from the doctor. Unless he's a fiend, like that Scotland Yard pathologist who did away with himself rather than go to prison over that girl he'd got hooked."

"Has she many friends, over and above the acquaintances she'd know through the gallery?"

"I reckon Tony Kershaw is closest to both of them," said Wurlitzer. "But one wouldn't make accusations about him. Not to the police, for example. Letting oneself in for slander or whatever, saying things like that."

"You've given me plenty to think about. Thanks again. I'll be in touch, and while I've got you here, will one of you pop up to Mrs. Winterhalter's suite tomorrow and photograph her painting? Glossy eight-by-ten's for me, also color transparencies. She'll say what she wants. But phone first."

After they had separated, Cyrus Finnegan continued his walk towards the Adelphi. He liked clubs and belonged to three. They were good places to entertain and to meet an interesting cross section of society, from bishop to tea planter, from author to film star. But best of all, clubs provided an instant oasis; they were places where one could think without interruption, unlike the crowded streets, where people could stop and give you unpleasant information, uninvited, as Grossmith and Wurlitzer had just done. In a club one had basic protection from intruders, however well intentioned. In a club you were acknowledged with civility, so long as you behaved yourself and recognized the rules. You could doze or sleep or talk, play cards or billiards, swim or read. Or you could use the club's stationery and make notes.

At about the time that Cyrus Finnegan was settled at a table in the club writing room with a supply of lined paper before him, Mr. Peter Knowles, in New York, was handed a night-letter cable by a diminutive bellhop, to whom he gave a dollar. The message was clear and, unlike the cable he had received the previous day, contained no hidden code.

He made his way to the bar and ordered a bourbon

manhattan. He was thinking that he wouldn't have to stay in Manhattan much longer. Perhaps he would try Toronto. He'd been told that Canadians were beginning to take an interest in art and that there were one or two good paintings in different parts of the country. He remembered the Rembrandts in Montreal and Toronto. Might even be one in Ottawa at the National Gallery.

By the time this caper was completed, in about three months, it would be winter. Mr. Peter Knowles remembered visiting Montreal during winter, an enforced visit to try and get information to an inmate in St. Vincent de Paul Penitentiary. He'd been stranded for three days because of a strike by snow shovelers at the airports. No, he'd give the art lovers of Canada a miss. He ordered another manhattan. This time he would try Sydney. Better give Melbourne a wide berth, after the Gainsborough letdown. Too bad it had to go to a private collector rather than to the Melbourne Art Gallery. Trouble was, curators sometimes knew too bloody much.

But what to do about Melita? Bit awkward having to trot her along, but something would work out, it always did. Too bad about the boy, though. He'd have to leave him in England. One of these days he'd send for him. Tony would take care of the kid for as long as he was told to do so. Nothing like a bit of know-how to put the squeeze on one's brother-in-law. Brother-in-lawlessness was more like it.

Well, once he got down under he would forget the lot of them. He paused momentarily in his thoughts, then ordered his third manhattan. He wondered how Tony Kershaw would fit in in Australia or the U.S.A.? Not very well, he decided. Yet he was coming after all. A brief visit. Peter Knowles hoped it would turn out profitably. For even at the last minute, and with perfect logistics, plans could go awry. Of mice and men? Peter knew which side he was on. To hell with the mice.

172

11

Tony Darling,

I am going home to Mummy and Daddy. Now! Forever!
I am leaving this letter which you will probably think is a
suicide note. It isn't. I hope it scared you when you found it
on the kitchen table.

Not true! Because I love you even though you've been a
bastard. Not at first you weren't. Why do I use that word,
which means one thing about Peter's son (he's well out of it,
God rest his soul) while with you it means being a louse.
You're off your rocker! Do you know that I realize you've
never loved me from the start? When Peter took me to that
supper at the Edinburghs, how long ago it seems, five years
since we married, and for what? Why did you pick on me or
was it me who picked? Still, why? But this past six months
topped everything, with your secret comings and goings
and self-pity for what you might have been, if only people
believed in you, meaning little me! No time for painting,
yet you come here late at night reeking of turps. Better

than scent and lipstick, not that I'd care, I'm beyond caring for anything except to get away from your lies. This weekend is it! What was that patronizing Yank visiting us for? What reason? To bring me a box of chocolates or to see our cottage garden? And Finnegan? Drops in like we'd seen each other only yesterday, all very familiar. Thinks no end of himself and asking funny sort of questions. I pretended I didn't know your school's St. Justin's. Wonder why I did that?

So now you've taken your suitcase. Just shirts and underthings and a spare suit and socks. And your toilet things and Philoshave, so I estimate you've gone for a short time only. Not worth telling your wife where you're off to and when she can expect you back, so that she can have supper ready, and her pill swallowed. Sorry I won't be here. Like hell! But you'd better hurry! I am writing to our landlord giving a month's notice that we won't be renewing the lease, which is in Daddy's name anyway. How does that hit you? What will you do with your silly books and silly pictures and all the other silly junk if you've nowhere to lay your fuzzy little head? And don't come running to me for help. Daddy will turn you over to the knackers. If he doesn't I will, even though I do still love you, though less than at first.

Well, Mr. Smarty, what do you think I've been doing while you've been acting ever so mysterious and brooding? Gardening? No Tony, my pet, I've been checking up on you. How d'you like that? Little old me following you up to London twice in one week. Your headmaster told me what train you and Charles took from Twyford Junction, so I was there at Paddington ahead of you. Saw you going into that block of flats. If I didn't know you were only interested in women, I'd have been worried! But I am worried because I know you're up to no good. Another thing Headmaster Robertson told me surprised me very much. He says you've been teaching chemistry and math. And I've been thinking all along you teach art, and that's why you feel too sapped to do any painting of your own.

174

Now for one last shock, my darling, so hold on. Kept this till the end. When I saw you with your suitcase driving off in the taxi this afternoon, I knew you realized that the law had rumbled you. Painter or pusher? Didn't think I knew that one, did you? It was Peter who tipped me off about eighteen months ago in one of his rare letters to me. Marked "private," so I burned it, even though I didn't understand what he was hinting at. Said Edinburgh had a hold over you, about something you were doing for him.

Peter said you had a racket of your own, that's the word he used, which you thought nobody knew about, something about your trips abroad on art tours, and that you'd let something slip when you and he were in Holland a couple of years ago. So talk about funny coincidences! While you and Mrs. Winterhalter were jawing away in the garden yesterday and Mr. la-di-dah Finnegan was asking me those questions, her chauffeur got out of the Rolls and strolled across to watch the cricket match.

Seems he was recognized by Mr. Watts who owns our pub. I go there quite a bit when I'm on my own, and last night when I popped over to get us a bottle of Gordon's gin I heard him telling old Yarrow, the hedge trimmer, that milady's chauffeur was a policeman like Mr. Watts had been himself. They'd had quite a little chat, seeing as how they had worked together. He'd told Mr. Watts he still was given the odd assignment, undercover works, mostly with the drug squad. Works for the car rental firm as a regular. Not very discreet, I thought, but then old Yarrow is deaf as a doorknob, so it didn't matter. Then I remembered hearing a couple of weeks ago, while in the butcher's, that the drug squad had been carrying out some raids hereabouts, and the High Wycombe police had been "making inquiries" in the village, though they hadn't called at the cottage. Strange!

Am I just guessing this terrible thing? I hope I'm wrong! I can see you as a thief, even a killer, which shows how low an opinion I have of you, even though I love you. Anyway, as soon as I've finished with this letter I'm going to get in

175

touch with Mr. Finnegan, as he asked me to phone if I am worried, which I am. I'm frightened, and want to get as far away from you as I can. Somehow I can't bring myself to believe you are a pusher.

Don't worry looking for anything valuable. I'm taking everything that's worth more than a few pence. These days, money just vanishes, doesn't it? And thank you for leaving me the two hundred quid. Do you realize you've given me a thousand since January?

One final word! I think you are mad. Rotten demented. You should get yourself committed before it's too late!

Your not so affectionate wife,
Mary

P.S. Don't feel sorry for me. I'm not the type of person
people feel sorry for. I'm the type who makes her
bed and lies in it. Oh boy!

Cyrus Finnegan had the writing room entirely to himself. He stared at the paintings on the dark mahogany paneling: two portraits by Sir Peter Lely; a view of Bombay Harbor, associated with the East India Company, artist unknown; a decorative Far Eastern scene by George Chinnery, probably Canton or Macao; and a group of eight *fin de siécle* caricatures of club members by Beerbohm.

A steward had served him a pot of Earl Grey tea and a plate of digestive biscuits and slices of Dundee fruitcake. Cyrus drank the tea, nibbled the biscuits and fruitcake, and reviewed the events of the past few days. The eighteenth-century regulator next to the bust of Mr. Gladstone showed that he had been at the writing table for an hour and fifteen minutes.

Cyrus focused his eye on the Lely. Sir Peter Lely. Peter Knowles. He began to write.

After Cyrus reread his notes, he sat for several minutes recalling all he knew about Tony Kershaw. He had never

176

really cared for the man, nor had he actively disliked him. He regarded him as a moderately good art critic, sincerely enthusiastic and occasionally pretty astute in his judgments, even if he arrived at them accidentally. Cyrus was too broadminded to accuse Kershaw of favoring any group of painters over another. That did happen, but for the justifiable reason that one group was indeed better than another. Cyrus, on the other hand, preferred to deal with individual artists, to disassociate each one from any group or school. To him the artist's survival depended on the personal development of a strong individual style, superior and enduring.

But now Cyrus was faced with a personality who was not only sensitive to art, fine art if you wanted to elevate it, but who was accused of pushing hard drugs. Cyrus found this impossible to accept, at least for the time being. Kershaw seemed far too nondescript a person to take such risks. Let Sergeant Purvis get an inkling of this and Kershaw would be behind bars with his shoe laces and belt removed.

Grossmith and Wurlitzer had left the next move up to him. He knew now what he would have to do. It would be risky, certainly unlawful, and the super would swallow his umbrella when he was told. On the other hand, he might not.

Detective Sergeant Purvis and Policewoman Helen Maitland were lying side by side on the sergeant's divan bed. He had removed his jacket and tie and taken off his slippers. Helen had allowed him to unbutton her blouse. They had completed twenty minutes of intense necking and had arrived at a point of further exploration and development when his landlady knocked on the door. Had she known the extent of his angry frustration when she handed him the envelope, she would have fled in terror.

"Message for you, Mr. Purvis. Cabby brought it with

177

instructions to give it to you personally. He'd been to the police station first."

The envelope bore the crest of a famous club and was addressed in the barely legible scrawl that passed as Finnegan's handwriting. While Purvis tore open the envelope and began to read, his fiancée put on the kettle for tea and returned to the divan to repair the wreckage to her make-up. In about twenty-four hours, with any luck, she might once again feel calm and normal.

"Listen to this, sweetheart," Sergeant Purvis sounded bewildered. "Tell me what it means."

> *Upon further examination I find the paintings are divided into two groups stylistically which, for expediency and to make my point clear, I shall designate group (a) sincere, group (b) contrived. Sincerity, a regrettably lost term, is recognized in both amateur and professional work and has no association with techniques employed. It is a quality achieved from the combined mental and emotional personality of the artist. Thus a person who is mature, in the worldly sense, through his greater technical skill might appear to the uninformed as immature when he or she deliberately tries to be so.*

"Do you understand what the hell Finnegan's getting at? I used to think I was the only one who's barmy. Now I've got company."

"I'll have to think about that!" Helen, whose thoughts had been elsewhere, had him reread the passage.

"And what about this next bit? Listen to this!

> A naturally talented artist who has advanced through proper instruction, and in many cases with a follow-up in graduate studies and higher academic qualifications

178

is no longer capable of going back to his beginnings. Through intense formal schooling and discipline, he loses all trace of earlier freshness of vision and emotion. He reaches a point of stabilization, his work is intellectual and boring because it has been gutted of those qualities of emotional spirit and drive, passion if you wish, that are the very foundation of the greatest art throughout the ages of Western civilization.

"There's quite a bit more. Shall I go on?"

"Please do. I'm beginning to get the gist, at least I think so."

"Then you're even smarter than I thought. Kettle's boiling. You make the tea, and listen to the next steamy passage.

There are those who regard all formal training in art as retrogressive. The boredom of so much "international" art is through sameness. The better artists everywhere are free spirits. There is failure and confusion, sickness of mind. The only escape is a form of anarchy. You reject what you have learned about theory and only retain those foundation facts to facilitate your thrust as an individual. Henry Moore, I suppose, is a good example, though even he had a period of intense emotional crisis, a nervous breakdown before he found himself. That the world is now filled with his imitators, increasing our boredom with contemporary internationalism, is our tough luck. There are those who invent and those who imitate.

"Moore's the fellow who discovered the human orifices, isn't he? A real ripoff, if you ask me." Purvis gulped his tea gratefully. "Is this getting us anywhere, sweetheart, or shall we go to bed?"

"Later! Mr. Finnegan's not the man to go to all this trouble for nothing."

"I hope you're right. I asked for a report, some facts the super and I can use as grapples. What we get is a lot of high-falutin' highbrow balderdash, if you ask me. I guess these critics have to have pretty wonky brains to begin with to be able to write the arse off a turkey. It takes a lot of knock-brained experts like themselves to understand such jargon."

"Let's hear the conclusions, shall we? And don't be so scornful."

"He really is long-winded. Writes quite a bit about maturity and the fact that some of the world's masterpieces were created by men who in any other profession would have been put out to grass. Calls the use of the word "genius" by dealers and media the world's greatest misnomer cliché. Quite a bit about his opinions of Kershaw both as man and critic. 'Journalists write at you, with facts. Critics write round you, with cant.' I like that. Bit of sense there. Finnegan can't understand why Kershaw went overboard in his enthusiasm for the paintings by Charles. Suggests ulterior motive. Something at back of Finnegan's mind troubling him. Something he spotted in Mrs. Winterhalter's picture when he looked at it again this morning. Peculiarly odd that it is the only work by Charles done with palette knife. Ah! Here we are. Findings!

I find it impossible to accept that Charles Knowles painted either the watercolors or the oils and acrylics. Mary Kershaw informed me that her husband is self-taught. His formal education was in chemistry but he dropped it in favor of a career as schoolmaster and art critic. He sketches, or used to do so, on weekends. He hasn't touched painting for well over a year. So if

180

Charles was not the artist the Edinburghs and Kershaw claimed, what was he being used for? To bolster Kershaw's ego by having a disciple? Unlikely.

The exhibition, in both the lower and upper galleries, was arranged as a front, but for what? Dr. Hans Edinburgh and his wife were the most unlikely people to become art dealers. I informed Superintendent Graham of my high regard for dealers as shrewd representatives of intellectualism and salesmanship. The Edinburghs struck me, on my several visits to their gallery, as playing parts, though not very convincingly. Edinburgh, with his extensive practice as a psychiatrist specializing in artists, undoubtedly would have learned quite a bit about art in general. Kershaw is the person to watch.

In conclusion. The Princess Gallery was opened expressly for the purpose of eventually holding this exhibition, over which a great deal of time, labor, and promotion has been involved. This would indicate that a substantial financial gain was anticipated. Not through the sale of contemporary paintings by unknowns such as Charles. Side dealings, making deals on canvases such as the van de Velde with Grossmith and Wurlitzer, are not involved. If they are, then it is without their knowledge. I have reservations about Mrs. Winterhalter. I would suggest you contact the New York police and find out what they know, if anything. Ask New York to check again Mary Kershaw's brother, Peter Knowles, the boy's father. Edinburgh seemed to think he was still in Australia or South Africa.

I think that nobody expected there would be murder. The survivors are caught off guard.

"That's all." Purvis stuffed the report back into its envelope. "I'll have to take this and show it to the super right away. Sorry, pet. Love loses out to work every time."

"It would be a better society if it was the other way round," pouted Helen. "You'd better find out why Kershaw pretended he hadn't painted those pictures when obviously, from Finnegan's report, he wants the world to know how brilliant an artist he is."

"It's a mystery. Seems to be covering up something. But what?"

Cyrus Finnegan let himself into his flat shortly after six o'clock and found that Helga had retired to her bedroom.

"I think I'm coming down with flu," she called through her closed door.

"You'd better not! I've a job for you first thing tomorrow."

"Then mix me a hot whisky toddy. My tummy's upset and I've aches and pains all over. Back feels hot as an ironing board."

"Toddy and aspirins. Three aspirins." Cyrus went in search of the ingredients. In a few minutes he returned with a full tumbler. "Made it extra-strength. And put these two thick blankets on your bed. They'll help you sweat the bugs out of your system. You can be as sick as you want later, but tomorrow I can't be in two places at once. I'll need your help, old girl, so bottoms up. Drink up while it's piping hot."

"You'd have done well in the Gestapo. Ugh! This tastes horrid."

"*Skol*, Helga! Sleep well. Early breakfast for both of us. No later than seven."

"I'll be dead long before then. Just let an old woman die in peace."

Cyrus closed her door. She had a fever, no doubt about that. Running a high temperature. He himself had unshakable faith in the curative powers of a whisky toddy. They were best made with pure malt whisky rather than a blend. A hundred-proof black Jamaica rum was the only alternative.

As he cut himself a sandwich and poured a glass of cold beer in the kitchen, he let the telephone extension ring several times before answering.

"Mr. Finnegan. This is Mary Kershaw. I'm calling you from the station. I'm on my way to Nottingham. I've written you a letter, but after posting it I thought I'd better correct a couple of things I wrote. First, about the drugs. I don't think Tony would ever go for that. I can't see him destroying lives like that. He's too fond of people, well, most of them. He's a pacifist, did you know that?"

"Doesn't surprise me."

"I also said in my letter that he wasn't teaching art. Tony was teaching applied science, chemistry and math."

"Thank you, Mrs. Kershaw. Why are you on your way to Nottingham?"

"Because I've had it with Tony. Some couples just never ought to get married, and we're one of them. It's bad enough having a crook for a brother, but to have a crook for a husband, well, that's something else."

"What makes you think Tony is a crook?"

"Because he hasn't got the guts nor the stamina to be straight. He ought to consult a shrink again. Edinburgh had him as a patient before we married. Wish I'd known."

"Is he still at the cottage?"

"He's hopped it, suitcase and all. Just as well, otherwise I'd have had trouble getting away. Gone to London, most likely."

"What did you mean, when you said you have a crook for a brother?"

"Exactly what I said."

She hung up.

Cyrus finished making his sandwich, poured another glass of beer and went into the living room. He ate slowly, trying to order his jumbled thoughts. He remembered Peter Knowles clearly enough. He thought of Charles and the view of the lad's school from the train window. Somehow all three memories merged into what he had seen in Mrs. Winterhalter's painting. He saw himself standing on the rostrum, working the carousel projector by its remote-control cord while he lectured to the group of students at summer school. He enjoyed using one of those clever German flashlights that threw an illuminated arrow onto the screen's surface, enabling one to point exactly at the section of the object under discussion. A very clever invention!

Was it that summer or the next that Tony Kershaw had asked to sit in on a couple of classes as an auditor? Cyrus finished his sandwich and carried the empty plate and glass back to the kitchen. He had one more call to make before telephoning Trudi. He must get word to the super.

It was Stella who answered.

"How's your dad?"

"He's fine, Mr. Finnegan. Taken it easy all day. He's in the sitting room watching telly. Mum's not back from evensong. She usually drops in at the rectory afterwards. Do you want to talk to him?"

"Just give him a message, please, Stella. No need to disturb him. I want to meet with him and Sergeant Purvis later tonight. Probably round about eleven. If I'm not at your house by eleven-fifteen, then I want the super and Purvis to go immediately to Doctor Edinburgh's house in Hampstead. Clear?"

"Sounds terribly exciting. Just like those gangster movies."

"Not at all," Cyrus reassured her. Funny what imagination kids have. What he was doing wasn't illegal, not the first part of it anyway. It was the second part that would raise official eyebrows. This way, he was covering the odds. He hoped he could get away with it. Stella was saying something.

"Sergeant Purvis and that nice policewoman girlfriend of his are coming round here for supper. He telephoned Dad and said he wanted him to read a report you'd written." Stella sounded amused. "Told Dad you were too smart for your britches, and asked if Dad could read Zulu!"

"Guess I didn't make myself clear."

"Guess not! Anything else?"

"Yes, please. Will you ask your dad to have the police get in touch with Peerless Aristocratic Tours Limited, tonight. They'll probably have to go right to the man at the top. I want it arranged so that the same Rolls-Royce and driver engaged by Mrs. Winterhalter are outside my flat tomorrow morning at eight-thirty. If that driver isn't available, no matter. They can send somebody else, but I would prefer him. It's both urgent and important."

"Roger! Message received loud and clear. I'll wait up till you get here, as I don't have early school tomorrow. I'll tell Dad that if he won't let me stay up and listen to what you've been up to, I won't cook supper for Sergeant Purvis and his girl."

"Better not, Stella. I'd hate to have the super charge his only daughter with blackmail. Don't put him on the spot. When it's all over, I'll take you to tea at Rumplemeyer's cafe and tell you all about it. But on one condition."

"What?"

"That you've reached the age of twenty-one!"

He didn't have time to wait for her answer.

12

Sure enough, the weather forecast had been right. It was a miserable night. Bt the time Cyrus had walked the quarter mile from the Chalk Farm underground station to the cul-de-sac where the Edinburghs lived, he was wet. It was a good night for staying indoors. Apparently everybody else agreed, for Cyrus Finnegan was the only pedestrian in sight.

He was not particularly surprised when the door was opened by Tony Kershaw. He'd half expected it. He had not, however, expected Grossmith and Wurlitzer to be visiting with Maria, Gee, and Trudi in the small sitting room. The surprise was mutual. There was a seat for everyone except himself.

"Let me fetch you a chair from the dining room." It was Trudi who went to get it, and as she passed him Cyrus thought she was trying to signal to him with her eyes. A warning? He'd liked Trudi from their first meeting in Gee's flat, under circumstances that were hardly sociable. When she returned with the chair, Cyrus had no doubt that she, by frowning and slowly lowering her eyelids, was hinting that he had barged in where he was least welcome.

"We are having coffee. Would you care for some?" Kershaw made the invitation, pointing at the low table on which were six half-filled demitasse cups, plus a bottle of schnapps and four liqueur glasses for the men.

"Something stronger, if you wish? Whisky?"

"No thanks." Cyrus found himself staring at Maria and checked himself. He shook hands with her and Gee, who was at her side on a rather uncomfortable loveseat, and sat down. She was dressed entirely in black, as she had been at the private viewing. This time, her white face was blotched with puffiness, the result of crying, no doubt. The pupils of her eyes were enormously dilated, and Cyrus wondered whether she realized that he was in the room and that they had just shaken hands.

"You seem to be addicted to surprise visits," Kershaw said curtly. "But I must warn you that Maria has been told to have complete rest and no visitors till after the funeral. As you can see, she's heavily sedated. Gee and Trudi were just preparing to escort her up to her room when you arrived."

"Then I apologize for the intrusion."

"That's what we've been doing also," said Grossmith, leaning across to tap his partner on the shoulder. "We've been here less than five minutes. Wouldn't have come if we'd known that Mrs. Edinburgh was so poorly. Just dropped by to convey condolences." He and Wurlitzer stood and solemnly shook hands with Maria, Gee, and then Trudi.

"We'll be back in a few days, Trudi dear, when your stepmother will feel more capable of talking business. We had no intention of raising anything tonight."

"Do you refer to the telegram Hans sent you?" Although

her words were slightly slurred, Maria's voice was sharp. "He meant it, you know. Deal's off." The effort required to talk was too much for her. She toppled sideways against Gee's shoulder.

"Come on, Mums. Up to bed with you. I'll bring you some hot Ovaltine for your pill."

By the time Grossmith was sufficiently recovered to answer Maria, it was too late.

Maria allowed herself to be led from the room, Gee and Trudi supporting her on either side. Kershaw, whom Cyrus thought had grown thinner, stood still, sharp-eyed and stiff as an ice pick, watching every movement, his clenched lips cold with disdain or hatred. The fellow looked crazy! It was Cyrus who caught him off guard.

"Didn't expect to find you here, Kershaw. Assumed you'd be home at your cottage with Mary. She must find it lonely."

"Well I'm here. You can see that for yourself. I'm staying the night, as Maria needs someone of her own age to turn to, not a pair of children."

"They seem to be coping very nicely. What say you, fellows?"

"Exactly. Perfectly. Very understanding for their age, both of them." Grossmith and Wurlitzer stood near the open door. They looked trapped, like two trout in a net. Grossmith turned and faced Kershaw.

"It was you who put Hans up to sending the message that our services are no longer required."

"Of course not! Don't talk rubbish."

"Like hell. You're lying through your teeth."

"Now look here, Grossmith!"

"I'm looking. So's my partner, and we don't like what we see, do we Morrie? And don't worry about Mr. Finnegan here. He knows what the message said. He's given it to the sergeant, haven't you Mr. Finnegan?"

"It's on its way." Cyrus could see that Kershaw was certainly frightened of the two art dealers. If only he knew why. They'd seemed chummy enough at the private viewing, bobbing and smiling at each other like ducks on a pond.

"Well, leave the coppers to find out, boy-o." Morrie Wurlitzer couldn't resist thrusting his own barb. "See you at Charles's inquest!"

"Bugger off!" Kershaw's face was ashen. "You sound like a ghoul. As though the inquest was a bloody dance."

"We'll get even with you. Sooner than later, you'll see."

With this parting shot, Grossmith turned toward the doorway and almost collided with Trudi and Gee.

"Maria would like to have a word with you, Mr. Finnegan. You'd better hurry, before she drops off. Her room's at the front, upstairs. I'll fix a night-light for her when I take up her Ovaltine. Don't stay too long."

"I'd leave her be if I were you. Doesn't know what she's saying." Kershaw tried to stop him.

"I'll be right back." Cyrus was happy to see the beginning of a smile on Trudi's mouth.

The first thing he noticed was the clear, soft smoothness of Maria's arms and shoulders. There were no telltale scars or scabs, no signs of rubber tube and hypodermic. Her head was propped up by three pillows; while her eyes seemed to have difficulty in focusing and her appearance was languid, Cyrus sensed that her general condition was improving.

"I sent for you because I wanted you to know that I sent Larry and Morrie the telegram saying we wouldn't want their services. I sent it without Hans knowing. I was going to telephone them, but thought that a telegram would be proof in writing. I was about to tell them when you arrived."

"What exactly were the services you refer to?"

"Lending us money. Hans and I are flat broke."

189

"What about the Princess Gallery? Everybody thinks you're rolling."

"Rolling!" Maria snorted with disgust. "Hans should have filed bankruptcy papers six months ago! He kept saying that I must be patient, that one day soon our luck would turn and everything would be better." Tears suddenly trickled slowly down her cheeks. She made no attempt to brush them away.

"How do Grossmith and Wurlitzer come into the picture?"

"As soon as Hans got this wild scheme of opening the Princess Gallery, building up a good business, goodwill he called it, then selling out as soon as possible to the highest bidder. I couldn't make him see sense. No way. Trudi was so cross with him she moved away. Only came back between shows, to save money on rent."

"So Grossmith and Wurlitzer were prepared to back Doctor Edinburgh's crazy idea. Is that what you're implying?"

"They didn't back it in the recognized way. They lent and charged an outrageous rate of interest. Real loan sharks! In less than three months they owned the gallery. Hans and I were merely employees. So I took the only step I could think of. It meant swallowing my pride. It was a bitter moment to ask my ex-husband, Signor Dagerra, to give, not lend, two hundred thousand pounds."

"Why such a large sum?" Cyrus was flabbergasted.

"Because Larry and Morrie wanted half of that to cancel our arrangement. Our mortgages at the bank are another sixty thousand."

"And your ex-husband was willing to give you this?"

"He's always been a kind, generous person. He still loves me and I still love him. But as I once told you, Mr. Finnegan, we'd already separated long ago. I was light-headed and infatuated. For a time I was the same about Tony

190

Kershaw. But that's over too, now. I've always been flighty when it comes to sex. My son, Gee, wants us to go back to Milan, so I suppose that's what I'll do."

Trudi came into the room with the Ovaltine. She handed a small yellow capsule to her stepmother and watched while she swallowed it.

"I've just one more thing to say to Mr. Finnegan, Trudi. Wait outside and he'll join you."

"I didn't tell you about the flat," Maria kept her voice low. She knew that Trudi was possibly eavesdropping. "Another crazy scheme. He and Kershaw were up to something, but I couldn't get a word from either of them. Whatever it was, I'm sure it was Kershaw's mad brainwave and that he'd roped Hans into it. Another madman's scheme for making a fortune. Something bad."

"Could it in any way be connected with the Princess Gallery?"

"I've no idea." Maria paused, as though uncertain whether she had said too much already. She continued. "This will shock you, Mr. Finnegan! I wasn't really surprised when Hans was murdered. Some of the crazy artists and actors who've been coming to this house for years are really maniacs. They should be under lock and key. I've warned Hans a thousand times. One of these days, one of your crazies will stick a knife in you!"

With that, Maria suddenly closed her eyes and fell asleep.

Trudi was waiting for Cyrus on the landing. He was glad of this because it gave him the opportunity of carrying out his plan to gain access to Doctor Edinburgh's consulting room and files. When he arrived at the house, he had seen that the consulting room had a separate entrance. In former years, it had probably been the waiting room and surgery.

"I want you to do something for me, Trudi. I'm just going

191

downstairs to say good-bye to Mr. Kershaw and Gee. One must be able to enter your father's consulting room from the house?"

"Of course. There's a door leading to it from the sitting room. I'll show you."

"I'm not allowed to do this, Trudi. I should leave it to the police. They'd have to have a warrant, but something tells me that time is closing in on us. I want to look at the files."

"But they're locked. There isn't a spare key that I know of."

"Then I'll have to have a go at them anyway." Cyrus hoped that his early training in picking locks was not entirely forgotten. He hadn't made use of this skill since Berlin. "I'll have to explain to you later, Trudi. Things seem to be gaining momentum. I only hope to hell I find what I'm looking for. When I go into the sitting room, will you set the dining room door slightly ajar. I don't want anyone to see or hear me enter, especially Kershaw. You'll accompany me to the front door when I'm ready. If either Kershaw or Gee insist on seeing me off the premises, then I'll have to find another way in. But if you are the one, then leave the front door ajar. Then go back into the room and try and prevent them from coming to into the hallway."

"What if either of them wants to pee?"

"Let's not anticipate. Just keep them in the sitting room. Once I get into the consulting room, which shouldn't take more than a couple of minutes, I'll lock the door from the inside and let myself out through the patients' entrance."

"I've a suggestion. Instead of coming back via the front door, come in via the kitchen. I'll unlock it now. As for keeping Gee and Mr. Kershaw out of the way, I'll ask them to hear me recite something I'm learning for my next audition. Gosh! This is exciting! With me letting you into the house, it wouldn't be breaking and entering would it?"

"My guess is that forced entry into confidential medical

192

files should earn me ten years in the clink, at the very least."

"Then take care!" Trudi half opened the dining room door, then went toward the kitchen.

It was Kershaw who helped Cyrus Finnegan with his raincoat, obviously anxious to see him leave.

"I had lunch with Mrs. Winterhalter. Too bad she's so ill." Cyrus dropped the information casually. "Be in her bed for a few days more, I'd imagine."

"Good God!" Kershaw's mouth opened with a gasp. "But she was fit as they come when we saw her yesterday, wasn't she?"

"Seemed that Way. Had a bit of an attack on the way back to London, though. She has a nurse looking after her."

"Oh God! I'll call and see her first thing tomorrow morning."

"Do that. I'm sure she'd appreciate it." Something told him that Kershaw knew all about Mrs. Winterhalter's illness and that it was a put-up job. Maybe the nurse was right after all. Cyrus had still to be convinced that her illness wasn't genuine, though he would have been unable to say why. Just instinct. Just as he sensed that Kershaw and Mrs. Winterhalter had been in touch since their meeting at High Wycombe.

The room was much as he had expected. An extra-long couch against one wall, a desk and chair placed so that Doctor Edinburgh could see the face of the person lying there. There were lamps at either end of the couch and an adjustable-angle light on the desk itself. Cyrus switched this on and angled it in the direction of the three filing cabinets. As Trudi had said, they were locked.

He looked carefully at the rest of the room. There were the usual framed diplomas, photographs of Trudi and Maria and two watercolors, very stiff and amateurish, signed A. Kershaw. They were dated 1950. Kershaw had progressed a thousand-fold since then. The furnishings generally were quiet and restful, chosen to put patients at their ease. The locks were what his sergeant instructor had called "jerk virgins." A tickle, a shove and a push and any jerk could open them. It took Cyrus four minutes to open the middle cabinet, the one whose top drawer, according to the outside card, filed names beginning with the letter K.

"Kershaw, Anthony Ethelred." The profession "chemist" had been crossed out and the words "artist/writer" substituted. This was interesting. It meant that Edinburgh had first known his patient as a chemist and not as an artist. In a way, the record was almost like a curriculum vitae, a series of signposts presenting a toneless, unreal abstraction of a person's life, the emotional guts of human existence deleted. Kershaw's signposts indicated a variety of side-roads. Schoolmaster; national service was two years Air Force, including a stint in West Germany; good at languages; correspondence school, biochemistry and fine arts. A real humdinger, that one. Tour guide during long vacations from Manchester University. Developing interests in art history and restoration. Dissertation for masters of science on "Adverse Pigmentation Response in Macrophotographic Analysis." Six months' hospitalization during which art therapy classes proved effective in overcoming sense of inadequacy. Primary signs of dementia praecox. Employed for six months by a firm of manufacturing chemists in the Midlands. Second breakdown. Referral to Dr. Edinburgh, who diagnosed positive manic depression and schizophrenia. Weekly sessions of ninety minutes on a regular basis during next three years. Marked improvement. Patient employed as chemistry teacher in Leeds grammar school. Quits after one term. Employed as analyst with manufacturers of oil paints, expanding production in acrylics. Consultations cease abruptly at request of patient. Resumed shortly after patient employed as picture restorer employed by Messrs. Grossmith and Wurlitzer, dealers in fine art, specializing in sixteenth-, seventeenth-, and eighteenth-century Dutch and Flemish paintings. Marriage to Mary Knowles of Shepton-cum-Nass, Nottinghamshire, sister of Peter Knowles, company director.

Only one tour abroad as tour guide during past three years. Some notes about sexual difficulties with marriage. (Cyrus skipped these, feeling that such intimate comments should remain where they belonged, in the confidential files in a psychiatrist's office.) Developing aggressiveness. Edinburgh had made a marginal notation in red ink. "Patient under stress. Evasive in answers. Lies! Lies! Now I've got him. I'll get my share. I'll see to that."

If Kershaw had been pushing drugs, then there was no doubt Edinburgh would have noted the fact. His notes, several pages going back over a twelve-year period, were detailed, and as far as Cyrus could judge, comprehensive and objective. There was at no time any suggestion of friendship outside the consulting room. A strictly professional, doctor-patient relationship.

The second file was further back in the drawer. Knowles, Peter. It was empty. That there was a folder bearing that name was proof that at one time there were notes here also.

Surely Knowles would never have consulted a psychiatrist. Cyrus remembered him as an extrovert, self-confident and cocksure, well camouflaged behind his polished behavior as an English gentleman. Company director, my foot! Small timer and swindler was more like it! So why the missing file? Cyrus glanced at his watch. Almost ten-thirty. Trudi would be at the end of her recitation by now. He must hurry. Gently he slid the file drawer back into position. Pity the lock could no longer be pushed more than halfway back. In the old days the sergeant instructor would have given him hell if the lock didn't work after being tampered with. Switching off the lights, Cyrus found his way through the waiting room to the outside door. He let himself into the garden.

He felt rather silly at having left that message with Stella. All so melodramatic. The super and Purvis would be watching the clock, ready to pile into the sergeant's car as soon as time was up. He'd behaved like an idiot. Everything had gone smoothly, without a hitch. What he had learned from the file, and what Maria Edinburgh had told him, went a long way to proving that his own theories were probably not so far from the truth. It will be interesting to compare notes with the super and Sergeant Purvis. He'd taken a chance. He'd undoubtedly broken a law. But what the heck! He'd gotten away with it!

As he turned to close the front gate, Cyrus Finnegan glanced towards the house, then jerked his head back in shock. Tony Kershaw had opened the sitting room curtains and was watching him through the gentle summer rain. Cyrus waved, then set off to find the nearest taxi stand. With luck he'd be in St. John's Wood within fifteen minutes.

"Come on in, Cyrus. Pour yourself a scotch." Superintendent Graham indicated decanter and glasses on a Queen Anne crescent table. It was the one good piece of furniture that Mrs. Graham had inherited from her grandmother. "Mum's gone to bed. I'm letting Stella stay up so that she could see for herself you hadn't come to any harm."

Cyrus poured himself a double with a splash of soda. He knew better than to ask for ice in the Graham household.

"Another five minutes and we'd have been on our way." As she spoke, Policewoman Maitland looked at him anxiously.

"You looked whacked. But, before you begin: all's clear

with the car-hire firm. I contacted the manager. Your Rolls will be waiting promptly at eight-thirty."

"Interpol have quite a story on Knowles. Last heard of in Texas six months ago." Sergeant Purvis read from his notebook. He never trusted his own memory. "F.B.I. are checking. While they're at it, I've asked for anything they've got on Mrs. Winterhalter." Purvis snapped shut his notebook. "The super's read your report."

"Report, nonsense." Superintendent Graham chuckled. "Lot of bunkum. Ask Purvis and Maitland what they think! You agree it's a lot of tosh, sergeant?" Purvis and Helen sat side by side on two uncomfortable chairs. They wished they could hold hands. It was reassuring at times like this, when one was feeling shy.

"That bit about old age and art was a bit hard to follow, Mr. Finnegan." Purvis ran his finger inside his shirt collar. "But I must say, I was interested when you made the point that Charles wouldn't have, couldn't have, painted these works because he was too young."

"That's right." Cyrus noticed that they were all staring at him. This must be a diversionary tactic. They didn't wish to appear too eager to hear about the evening. Not yet. They were maneuvering.

"Constructionist bunkum," growled the Super. "Paint a length of rusty railing and call it sculpture. Maybe our victim Charles had better taste and judgment than we reckoned he had."

"Well, I like funky art! So there!" Stella rallied to the defense. "I like funk art, junk art, found art. Rusty railings and all. It reflects the uncertainty of the age we live in. The nuclear age. Not knowing what's waiting round the corner. I think Charles Knowles was for the birds."

The super grinned at his daughter, then laughed.

"Don't let your mum know we've got a cuckoo in our nest! Life's neither better nor worse than it ever was. Just

197

the same as when I was a lad, and my dad a lad before that!
Here, give me a kiss and up you go to bed. And another
thing, young lady. Blame Cyrus. And blame yourself, for
asking him to give your poor old dad a gander at art appreciation. I should have stuck to cricket. And now, Cyrus, let's
hear it. What have you been up to?"

13

"Good morning, Mr. Smith."

"Brown, sir. Good morning."

"Sorry about that." Cyrus climbed into the back of the Rolls. Ordinarily he would have chosen to sit beside the chauffeur. "Glad you could take me, Mr. Brown. We should be back here by lunch."

"Yes, sir. Where to, sir?"

"St. Justin's Academy. It's between Twyford and Reading. Stick to the motorway the first part. I'll tell you when to turn off."

"Very good, sir." They moved off in the direction of Cromwell Road, heading west. "That was a nasty spell the American lady had on Saturday." Mr. Brown kept his eyes on the traffic. The morning was warm, the windows closed and the air conditioning turned on. Brown spoke with a soft, west country accent—Cornwall or Devon, Cyrus supposed.

"Still ill, I'm afraid," Cyrus informed the driver.

"I'm sorry. Very sorry indeed, sir. I enjoyed driving her. I'm booked to drive her to Southampton next Wednesday. Hope she'll make it." His brown-silver hair was tidily cut in a straight line above his coat collar. He wore a dark-blue uniform, a peaked cap, and white gloves. His neck, like his face, was sunburned and not what one would have expected in a chauffeur who hung around London. His next remark caught Cyrus off guard.

"That gentleman she visited in High Wycombe on Saturday, sir. Mr. Kershaw. Isn't he one of the masters at St. Justin's Academy?"

"Yes."

"A funny bloke, that one. Pretended he'd never seen me before, on Saturday, he did. I've even dropped him back at St. Justin's a couple of times in the minibus."

"Mini?"

"Peerless Aristocratic Culture Tours, sir. That's one of the firm's lines. I've driven him to the Continent twice. Very restricted group of 'connoisseurs,' I think they call themselves. Never more than six, plus guide. Cost a pretty packet, a real whopper. But I can't understand Mr. Kershaw cutting me like that. Not like him at all. Used to be real matey and good to chum along with."

"When was the last trip you made together?"

"Getting on for three years. All of that. Two weeks in the Low Countries. Now come to think of it, sir, there were two short trips since then, but I wasn't driving. One more to Holland and one to Denmark. My last trip was to Spain and North Africa. Museum directors from the U.S. studying Moorish architecture. Away a month. Just back."

They were approaching the Henley turnoff. There was little traffic going in their direction, and what little there was was no match for the elegant Rolls-Royce hogging the passing lane. Cyrus let Brown concentrate on the driving.

200

My God, he'd been lucky. The super had chewed his nuts off, a real dressing-down for tampering with the files. Well, he'd expected as much. Having accepted offence, neither the super nor Purvis referred to it again, and for the next hour they'd reviewed every detail of the day's activities. Sergeant Purvis had investigated Mrs. Winterhalter's fainting spell with the hotel staff. He'd had a word with the house doctor and nurse, the latter saying that her patient was indeed seriously ill. Cyrus wondered why she had so freely expressed her view to him. Poor Purvis. He'd made all the routine checks and double checks. Everything tallied, including the time Mrs. Winterhalter had paid off her driver and the number of the taxi she'd taken from the Savoy to the Edinburghs'. But why hadn't she kept the Rolls engaged for the evening?

"On Saturday afternoon, after you let me out at Marble Arch," Cyrus addressed Brown, "where did you take Mrs. Winterhalter after that? Back to the Savoy?"

"No, sir. She had me drop her at Portman Square. Said the weather was so nice, she'd like to go for a walk. Do some window-shopping." Brown moved back into the center lane. Their exit was coming up.

"Did you try and stop her? I mean, after that coughing spell, did you think she should be wandering about London on her own?"

"Seemed fine to me, sir. Dear me! Never known anybody so crazy about shops. Seemed to spend my time passing to and from Fortnum's, Harrods, Peter Jackson's, and Selfridges. Always the food counters. Parcel after parcel back to the States. What it must be to have plenty of lolly!"

They had left the motorway and now entered a series of short, twisting roads, little better than lanes, almost too narrow for such a large vehicle. Cyrus decided to risk the next questions.

201

"Were you in the services, Brown?"

"Yes, sir. Field Security and Port Control. Pretty dull stuff mostly."

"When you were demobbed, what then?"

"Into the police. Devon Constabulary. River police and coastal patrols. Lot of smuggling just after VE Day, sir. And drugs. I was awarded two good conduct medals and mentioned a couple of times in the *Police Gazette*. I enjoyed police work. Still help out once in a while."

"I suppose these art and culture tours abroad provide plenty of opportunity for all types of illegal trafficking. I was told once that all you chaps are bonded. Correct?"

"We have to be. Insurance insists on it. And people do talk carelessly. Especially these culture vultures, jet set. After they've had a few glasses of vino, down comes the old hair and they puff grass and sniff coke like merry England's off her perishing rocker. Anything goes when you're abroad. Americans, Irish, Canadians, Frogs, Blacks. All the same, sir.

"One thing I do insist, though. When we're approaching customs, it's down with the windows to let in fresh air. I've no pity for those who push hard stuff. I've tipped off the lads once in a while. Capital punishment is too gentle for that lot. A good lashing and fifty years solitary, even that's too soft for them."

"How did Mr. Kershaw react on these occasions?"

"Paid no attention. Bit of a dreamer and a bit of a money snob, he is. Mixing with this bunch of high timers, he wouldn't want to be prudish."

Classes were in progress. Cyrus was shown into the headmaster's study and informed that Mr. Robertson would be free in about fifteen minutes. Even with the windows open, the room was stuffy, impregnated with stale tobacco smoke and the acids of inks and chalk.

Mr. Robertson kept him waiting only five minutes. A plump, jolly-faced, bespectacled little man, trim and neat as a candlewick, his complexion the color of McIntosh apples, he seemed to bounce into the room. Cyrus had expected a giant. There was only one thing out of character. He wasn't smiling.

"You've come about young Knowles. I was expecting you." Mr. Robertson seated himself on the swivel chair behind his desk. "Our mutual friend Johnny Graham telephoned at breakfast time and said you were on your way. Coffee? Only instant, I'm afraid. All I can offer parents and guests. Matron keeps everything under lock."

"No thanks. I'd like to inspect his room, if I may, sir."

"By all means. However, you won't find anything there. Matron had it cleaned and scrubbed on Saturday. After we'd heard about the tragedy in the newspapers."

"How did you know it was him? Stories only gave his Christian name."

"It was through Mrs. Kershaw, she's the wife of one of my staff. She telephoned. They are related to the boy in some way. Acting guardians. We send all bills to them. It was Kershaw who had the boy admitted as a special pupil. A slow learner. Very slow in class, believe me. Though Mr. Spokes, our head gardener, thought the boy was bright. Very good in the potting shed, and gardening generally. Green thumb with vegetables!"

"Do all boys garden?"

"At present, only a dozen of the lads are allowed anywhere near the garden. The rest have extra study and parades. Our training corps is famous for its smart turnout on parade. Square-bashing whips even the most unruly into shape. That, plus study. This is one of the few schools where we insist on a good grounding in Latin, Greek, and scripture. Classics plus math, chemistry, and grammar. All a boy needs."

"No arts or crafts? I thought that was pretty standard these days?"

"Standard for other schools, perhaps. No such fripperies for us. Now, let me have matron show you Knowles's room. She has his personal property under lock."

Mr. Robertson stood and led Cyrus along a corridor painted in institutional green and brown.

"I must explain something," said Mr. Robertson after he had introduced Cyrus to matron, who could have been the twin sister of Mrs. Winterhalter's nurse. "Our Mr. Kershaw, although he taught chemistry and mathematics, was allowed to give art lessons to one or two boys for whom everything else was hopeless."

"Then how do you account for Charles Knowles's being an artist, having a one-man show in a West End art gallery?"

"But I don't, Mr. Finnegan. Not for one second would I believe that! Would you, matron?"

"No, head. Though Mr. Kershaw was giving him art lessons and I did find a grip full of paint tubes and brushes and bits of scrap canvas in his cell. I mean room!"

"Unfortunately, Charles had been misbehaving himself and neither matron nor I thought he should be allowed to sleep in the dormitories with the other boys until his psychiatrist thought it would be safe. The boys call our individual rooms cells. We don't lock them in. Mr. Kershaw took Knowles to London three evenings a week for treatment by a well-known specialist in nervous disorders. Spokes thought the best treatment would be to leave the lad to help with the garden and greenhouses. But Kershaw insisted. Very expensive treatments, thrice weekly. And now I must leave you and get back to my duties."

Mr. Robertson did not shake hands. Nor had he smiled once. Later, as matron showed Cyrus a shortcut through the stable yard to where the Rolls was parked, she handed him the small airline travel bag in which young Charles had kept his paints.

"The head's taking this badly," Matron said grimly. "So far we've managed to keep the school out of the newspapers. I think he's counting on Superintendent Graham of New Scotland Yard to see there are no leaks about Knowles's having been one of our boys." She cleared her throat. "I never did like that boy. He was cunning. And a thief. Stole one of Mr. Spokes's prize-winning gloxinias the morning he ran off to London. No, you couldn't trust him. I feel the same about Mr. Kershaw. I just hope we've seen the last of him, too. What's more, I've had the strangest feeling about those two. You'd expect Kershaw, being a master, would have the upper hand with the lad, wouldn't you? Well, I think it was the other way round. Knowles had a hold on Kershaw; the man was scared of the nipper!"

God bless the Rolls-Royce, where nothing disturbs those who wish to contemplate once they have closed the dividing glass partition and transmogrified the chauffeur into a creature in outer space. What was even more conducive to Cyrus's analysis of the events and circumstances was the bottle of sherry and two glasses that he found in the concealed bar. This was peerless service indeed, fit for aristocrats who have problems to solve and must solve them fast. Very fast.

The fact that his theory was developing into something totally preposterous did not make it nevertheless impossible. There was a logical pattern involving several suppositions, not one of which would be acceptable to either the super or Sergeant Purvis.

The previous night had been a long one, not ending until two A.M., when Cyrus had gotten Purvis, reluctantly, to agree to bring Kershaw to Savile Row for questioning first thing in the morning. Not so much for questioning, Cyrus had insisted, but to haul him in for his own good. Protective custody was a grand coverall. Of course, you had to play it carefully. Get him to the station, then hang onto him as long as the laws of habeas corpus permitted. *Habendum et tenendum*, to have and to hold. If Mr. Robertson had but known it, Cyrus was still pretty handy with Latin phrases.

It would be necessary to obtain proof. The immediate question was how to set about obtaining it without flushing out the enemy. For there was an enemy, an enemy of society who plotted and made others precipitate the action.

He reopened the glass partition and saw Brown watching him in the rearview mirror.

"Has this battleship got a telephone, Brown? Ship to shore?"

"In the left armrest, sir. You can dial direct."

"Long distance? Overseas?"

"If you have a credit card, sir."

"Where are we now?"

"About twelve miles from Chiswick Broadway."

"Then step on it, please. Home by noon, if possible."

Cyrus closed the partition, got his telephone service credit card from his wallet, then checked the telephone numbers at the end of his pocket diary.

The first call, to The Hague, was placed without delay. His second call, to Hampstead, took longer. He was about to replace the receiver when he heard Trudi's voice. She sounded a hundred miles away.

"Oh, I'm so glad it's you, Mr. Finnegan. I've tried your flat but there's no answer. Superintendent Graham and Sergeant Purvis left here fifteen minutes ago. It's Maria. Overdose. Fortunately I took her up a cup of tea at eight. Another half hour and I might have been too late."

"Where is she?"

"Hampstead General. Intensive care. Gee is with her.

206

He telephoned to say she's showing signs of coming out of her coma."

"Christ, I'm sorry. Can I have a word with Kershaw?"

"He left long ago. Before any of us were up."

"No indication where he might have gone? Back to the cottage?"

"Could be. He's taken his suitcase. Can't understand how Maria has put up with him all these years."

The third call was to Savile Row. Sergeant Purvis and Policewoman Maitland, who was now transferred to the case officially, were at New Scotland Yard with Superintendent Graham.

Cyrus thanked the constable on duty at the switchboard.

"If any of them check in," he instructed her, "please ask them to come to my flat at two o'clock. Tell whoever calls that it's urgent. Extremely urgent. My name is Finnegan."

"Very good, sir." There was a pause. "Are you the Mr. Finnegan who is giving Superintendent Graham art lessons?"

"You could say that. How did you hear?"

"It's all over the service, sir. We all think you're terribly brave. If you ever need a model, my name's Phyllis."

Cyrus replaced the telephone in its hiding place, then poured himself another sherry, once again opening the glass partition. So simple, these electronic buttons. Every house should have windows operated by remote control!

"Brown—I've changed my mind. Instead of taking me to my flat, head for the Savoy. Strand entrance. When I go inside, I want you to park in the courtyard. Tell the doorman it's official police business. And should you spot Mrs. Winterhalter, detain her till I come out. Understood?"

"Detain her, sir?"

"I don't mean chop her to bits. Just ask her to step into this cavernous vehicle of yours and make sure that she bloody well doesn't escape."

207

14

What had begun pleasantly enough, with several people gathered together to admire paintings by a previously unknown painter, had emerged unequivocally as a nightmare. For the protagonists on the other side, they were running scared.

Not Mary Kershaw. Back home with her parents, she fed the hens their mixture of bran and corn. She went into the village to shop for groceries, for kidneys and stewing beef from the butcher, and to post two letters, one to her lawyer and the second to their landlord. From the public telephone box outside the post office and confectionary shop, she placed a toll call to their cottage. She was not surprised when there was no answer. She hadn't really expected Tony to be there.

Not Trudi Harwick. She sat in the kitchen because Superintendent Graham had asked her not to leave the house. She was fully dressed and wore her blonde wig. She would

208

take it off when Gee returned from the hospital. As regular as a bouncing ball, one image kept coming back to her—her father, the handle of the paper knife sunk up to its hilt—and she would begin to shake.

Not Gee Dagerra. His mother was out of the emergency intensive care unit and had a room to herself, from which she could have seen Hampstead Heath, had she wanted to. She didn't. It seemed that all she wanted to do was hold his hand. Sometimes squeezing so hard he could feel his knuckles crack. He had telephoned Milan as soon as the nurses had wheeled her away. His father was flying to Croydon in his Lear Executive and would be landing at midday. Gee had ordered a limousine to bring Mr. Dagerra to the hospital. After that, he would have to see what he could do for Trudi. He didn't look forward to spending another night in Edinburgh's house. The doctor's flat had been sealed by the police. Gee didn't want to see that place again either.

Gee realized he had been played for a sucker, but couldn't see how or why. He felt very young and unprotected. His racing schedule would have to be scrapped for this season at any rate. He wasn't too worried about missing classes. He knew people who took a whole year off from university and their marks improved as a result. He hoped his father would approve of Trudi. No reason why he shouldn't once he heard she was a converted Catholic. This time it was he who pressed his mother's hand. She was looking at him. She was trying to smile, but somehow her smile lacked warmth. He leaned across and kissed her on the cheek nearest to him. He kissed her again. For the first time he sensed what it must be like to be vulnerable, to fight one's own battles alone, in a foreign city when neither husband nor lover were to be trusted. He had never realized that his mother had courage and fight. She would recover.

Sergeant Purvis methodically rearranged his notes and read them with satisfaction. Times tallied. Events followed in sequence. Both postmortem reports were filed as Appendix A. There was one note that the constable clerk should have deleted. It was his note that Policewoman Maitland's birthday was only a week away. He thought he would buy her one of Charles's water colors, the View of Kingston Bridge. She'd liked that, and it wasn't expensive. Then he remembered that the Princess Gallery was closed. If this case moved in the direction, he guessed, it would never reopen.

During his tea break at eleven o'clock, Superintendent John Graham flipped through the pages of *Art and Society* by Herbert Read. Stella was always handing him books from the school library. He particularly liked the pictures, especially that one of Calais Gate by Hogarth. The super wondered whether he would ever understand art as Stella wanted him to. Art and society? They were best kept apart. No good for one another, not one bit.

On Monday morning, Peter Knowles stayed in bed until ten o'clock. Then he packed. He was slightly hung over—not too badly, but enough to make him take a double dose of bromos. If only he had stopped after three manhattans. And the girl. He shouldn't have touched that one. Picked her up while he was trying to negotiate the ramp in the Guggenheim. Picked? It was she who had come to his rescue before he fell face-down under the largest bloody Kandinsky he'd ever seen.

It was supper next at a Japanese restaurant on East Fifty-fourth. A good-looking brunette went well with the warm Saki. How many flasks between them? Four at least, and he drank two of them. Then another bar and a cab downtown to Chelsea, where she lived in surroundings rather too elegant for a twenty-seven-year-old sculptor.

That was the age she'd told him. Not much sculpture on display either. All he could see was her king-size water bed and black satin sheets. For two hundred bucks it hadn't been too bad a shakedown. He didn't believe she was self-supporting as an artist. For that matter, she probably didn't believe that he was in advertising. Manhattan was full of surprises on Sunday afternoons. It was best to accept and not question good luck if the chemistry was right.

Peter Knowles checked out of his hotel at one o'clock. His Exxon credit card was in the name of Mr. John Brown and it was genuine. He had two others in his name and made sure the payments didn't lapse. Only a fool played around with credit companies.

According to the cable he had four hours to wait, which would make the rendezvous at five o'clock New York time. No more manhattans this time. No more found companions. It was back to business.

Although Cyrus had eaten a breakfast of grilled kidneys, bacon, scrambled eggs, and toast plastered with chunky Oxford marmalade and had drunk three cups of tea, Helga found that she could only bring herself to swallow half a mug of black coffee and two aspirin. She'd nibbled at unbuttered toast but had managed only half a slice before giving up. On other mornings she would have enjoyed cooking Cyrus Finnegan's breakfast. This morning, her stomach weaving like a weathervane in a gale, she cursed the world of male chauvinists who kept women in thralldom. She hoped she would be dead by lunchtime.

"You look rough, Helga."

"Headache, backache, upset tummy and the sweats; otherwise I'm feeling fine."

"That's the girl! Glad you're feeling better. This is what I want you to do."

At ten o'clock, Helga found herself outside the Haymarket offices of American Express. She'd already been to Cook's and Lunn's and three lesser agencies. Everywhere she'd drawn a blank. So now she stood on the pavement and decided that perhaps Cyrus had been mistaken. Thank goodness the aspirin had taken effect. They always did.

There was no sign of Mrs. Winterhalter. Helga had seen several expensively dressed and overweight ladies going in and out of travel agents, but not one of them really fitting Cyrus's description.

Fifteen minutes later Helga spotted her. Unmistakable. There she was, squeezing her bulk from a taxicab right into Helga's lap, as it were, in front of the office of Pan Am. Helga had been up and down, back and forth along a dozen streets or more, with increasing desperation, ready to give up. Victory! She followed Mrs. Winterhalter inside and saw her take a numbered card off a hook. Number eighteen. Helga took number nineteen and sat down near enough to the counter so that she could overhear the booking agents and their customers. A young man pocketed his tickets and moved away, and a moment later a voice said "Number twelve, please," and a middle-aged couple took their turn. Five numbers to go before Mrs. Winterhalter would be called. A busy place. Agents tapping away at their computers, a steady flow of customers, telephones ringing constantly, and Mrs. Winterhalter sitting there, fat and complacent, not a trace of anxiety or worry, as though she was quite prepared to wait all day if necessary, filled with love for all mankind.

But why come here in person. That puzzled Helga. Surely it would have been more convenient to telephone from the hotel and have a manager pick up the tickets. Yes, Cyrus had mentioned that as a possibility, but somehow he felt that Mrs. Winterhalter would enjoy the diversion of attending to the tickets personally. It would give her something to do. Ten minutes. Helga was filled with admiration for the calm efficiency with which the different clerks consulted thick books and price schedules. She heard English, French, German, Spanish being spoken. She felt she'd go crazy having to work at such a clip. It made cooking big breakfasts an act of joy. Helga clutched her handbag. Bringing her Colt .22 was against all rules. Hadn't Cyrus told her often enough that it was illegal to carry weapons, particularly an unlicensed handgun that was formerly the property of the Norwegian armed forces, had its number filed off, and featured special barreling in the chamber? Helga looked at Mrs. Winterhalter and inwardly smirked with satisfaction. "Number eighteen." Good clear tone. Nothing cheap about this sound system. Mrs. Winterhalter wobbled her way towards the counter and Helga switched on her hearing aid. That was another piece of special equipment she should have handed in. Its inventor boasted one could hear a thimble drop in the middle of an air raid.

"The name is Winterhalter. Mr. and Mrs. Winterhalter. I telephoned earlier."

"Certainly, madam. You're confirmed on flight sixty-three at eighteen hundred hours. Be at Heathrow at least one hour before flight time and check in with our agent for seat allocations. You're a U.S. citizen, so you'll go right through. May I see your passport?"

Helga saw Mrs. Winterhalter hand the clerk two passports.

"Thank you, madam. I hope you've enjoyed your visit to England."

"I've had a lovely time. Everybody's been so kind and hospitable. Still, my husband and I will be glad to get home. He misses those Kansas strip steaks. The restaurants here just don't seem to know of them."

Helga heard her own number being called. Mrs. Winterhalter was leaving, and walking fairly rapidly for a woman of her size. "Number nineteen, please."

As Helga passed the young lady at the reception desk, she placed her card number on the desk.

"I'll come back later, thank you." Through the window she saw Mrs. Winterhalter turn left. For a moment Helga thought she'd lost her, the pavement was so crowded with people. A moment later she saw that Mrs. Winterhalter had reached the island in the middle of the pedestrian crossing. She held up her arm to stop the traffic and trotted with remarkable speed to the opposite pavement. To her amazement, Helga saw her enter the offices of British Airways.

This time Helga did not take a number. Mrs. Winterhalter was over on the far side, once again seated, waiting her turn in the line. Here the busy scene repeated itself, following the same pattern of airline offices all over the world. Standardization. Without it, the system would collapse.

Helga, who was leafing idly through some travel brochures on a stand near the door, turned up the volume of her receiver when Mrs. Winterhalter went up to the counter.

"The name is Winterhalter. Mr. and Mrs. Winterhalter. I telephoned earlier."

"Certainly, madam. You're confirmed on flight number four. Departure time eighteen hundred hours. Try and be at the air terminal at least one hour before scheduled departure time. And, can I see your passport?"

"If I am forced to change my plans, the tickets are refundable?"

"Of course, madam. Less a deduction for last-minute cancellation. We have to protect ourselves. But in your case, as you're flying first class, this will not apply."

Helga was almost prepared when a few minutes later she followed Mrs. Winterhalter into Trans World Airways. TWA was just as busily efficient as the other two. Helga

214

kept her distance. She felt it unnecessary to switch on her receiver but did it anyway.

Although Mrs. Winterhalter was overweight, she was not unobservant, especially when she spotted the woman who looked well built and athletic. The Scandinavian lady whom Mrs. Winterhalter had observed in three different airline offices had been either following her around or had been, like herself, purchasing tickets on three separate flights, with expected times of arrival at John F. Kennedy within half an hour of each other. This she considered as being most improbable. If she was indeed being followed, then she wondered why? Why, when her movements in England had been beyond suspicion. She had shopped, paid visits, entertained and been entertained by others. She had taken one trip into the country.

Certainly it was a fact that she had been present at the scene of a most unpleasant murder, not that murders were ever pleasant. She had been subjected to routine questioning by a charming superintendent and a very nice young police sergeant and had agreed, as a matter of courtesy, to remain in England till after the inquest. As she was an American citizen, they were not in a position to hold her against her will. Mrs. Winterhalter was indeed puzzled. For the first time since Saturday afternoon, when the caretaker let her inside Doctor Edinburgh's flat, she felt a moment of panic. Just a fluttering flick of guilt that passed as quickly as it had come. Mrs. Winterhalter had never been troubled by conscience.

Mrs. Winterhalter wobbled her way along Lower Regent Street, passed within screaming distance of Savile Row police station, turned right at Vigo Street and then left down to Piccadilly, and Jermyn Street, and entered the store so favored by her patronage, Fortnum and Mason.

Mrs. Winterhalter took the lift to the restaurant and would have been only too happy to order one of their delicious watercress salads and a slice of their exquisite veal and ham pie, but there was no time. The lift had made another descent and was now on its return journey. It would be bringing the Scandinavian up with it. She had been just too late to board it the first time. Mrs. Winterhalter opened the door to the fire exit and bounded down the stairs as fast as her weight allowed her. A minute later, she left by the side entrance, stopped a passing taxi and drove off in the direction of Leicester Square underground station, where she purchased a ticket to Epping. She doubted very much that the Scandinavian lady or anybody else would expect to find her walking in Epping Forest. It would be a good place to pass the intervening hours till her rendezvous with Tony Kershaw at the West London Air Terminal. She would have a pub lunch, which she had been told about but had never tried.

As for Kershaw, it was irritating that she must take him with her. When Peter learned how much Kershaw knew, undoubtedly he would deal with the matter expeditiously. Meanwhile, Kershaw had better look after what she had given him in exchange for his passport. It was as much as his life was worth.

15

Kershaw was seated on a bench in Hyde Park facing that very delightful lake, the Serpentine. He had been there since nine A.M. and was shivering. Not because it was cold. The day was warming into a scorcher, and London in summertime was only bearable because of its parks. Green Park, Regents Park, St. James's Park and Kensington Gardens. In Central London these were a paradise for loafing amidst the trees and flowers and shrubs. Kershaw planned that his day should be spent taking a bus from one park to another. He was shivering now because he had been awake all night and was exhausted. He was also scared.

As a precaution, just in case he fell asleep, he had slipped Mrs. Winterhalter's package under his cardigan and buttoned all three buttons of his jacket so no one could filch the package. His raincoat and suitcase were on the seat. A knitted cardigan was not exactly made for summer wear, but it had been chilly when he had left Edinburgh's house before dawn. It had taken him almost an hour to walk to The Victoria Embankment gardens below the Savoy, and there had been another hour spent on a bench near Cleopatra's Needle, where Mrs. Winterhalter had arranged to meet him. He had drunk two cups of tea and eaten half a raisin bun at the all-night coffee stall beneath Charing Cross Bridge, but that had taken less than fifteen minutes. The remainder of the time he had spent thinking.

What thoughts they were! If it weren't for just that one careless mistake on his part, Edinburgh would never have been involved. On the other hand, Edinburgh had certainly provided the flat where he could work, with Charles keeping a lookout. Edinburgh had stored the canvases and had been extremely useful; his murder had been completely unexpected, and Kershaw wondered for the millionth time who had killed him. Naturally, when the police learned that he had been having an affair with Maria they would be inclined to suspect him, when, of course, logically it ought to have been the other way round, with himself the victim and Edinburgh the murderer. But Kershaw knew that Hans Edinburgh's affection for his wife was mostly on the surface. After the tumult of their early passion for one another—the opposition of Signor Dagerra, a devout Roman Catholic, to divorce and the complications of obtaining an annulment—Edinburgh had become pretty well indifferent to his wife. She was an attractive person to have around the house. She made an affectionate stepmother for his daughter. She was a good cook and useful in the Princess Gallery and, before they opened the gallery, as a receptionist in his office. Kershaw knew all this from Maria.

Kershaw dozed in the heat haze of midmorning. Mary and Maria. Two women as different as tweed and velvet. Mary, country woman, daughter of a Baptist minister. Or was it Methodist? He couldn't remember because he'd never had any use for the man. But she was a good girl, could turn her hand to anything. And patient. Only in recent months had he begun to feel her pent-up resentment, suspicion. She had been unsophisticated when he married her. And uncomplaining. He'd at one time deluded himself into believing that everything he did, however underhanded it might appear to others, was for her sake. That it was she who was behind everything, his eagerness to become rich and be able to buy her anything she desired. What rubbish! All his motivations were his own passionate wish fulfillments. He enjoyed her flattery. The way she encouraged him to take up painting again. If she only knew what he'd been up to. Silly bitch! Silly bitch! Silly bitch! Inwardly Tony Kershaw exploded with hatred for her and the whole world. The way she kept watching him. Asking those questions! Why didn't she trust him? And it had all been so jolly at first. Cozy pretense. The way she joined him on weekend sketching expeditions, packing a picnic basket with tasty sandwiches and bottles of beer.

While he sketched she would read, or gather wild flowers, berries, branches of autumn leaves or spring blossoms, never interrupting him. They were quite devoted one to the other. It was in the middle of one of his breakdowns, what Edinburgh, his psychiatrist, referred to as a "temporary disassociation," that he began to think of her as nosy. Next, he thought of her as being selfishly possessive. That she wanted to take over his life and run it. What was worse, she would not acknowledge that he was a genius, that he was superior to and better than any of their clever friends. She only pretended to enjoy reading the articles he wrote as an art critic. He'd never once seen her open his book about Victorian bric-a-brac, which no publisher would touch. It was later that he realized that his dear wife Mary had sided with the publisher all along.

Little by little, Tony Kershaw retraced the up-and-down graph of their marriage and why he stopped confiding in her. Sending him to that hospital must have been Mary's idea. Edinburgh and Mary connived together to keep him out of the way. It must have been difficult for them to know how to deal with a genius like himself. At least Hans Edinburgh's wife, Maria, had understood, had been wonderful in fact, at any rate at the beginning. In the end, all three were plotting against him. They refused to accept that being a painter was his true vocation, that art was his métier. Couldn't they see that art was his life! The only books he bought were about art. He had taught himself Italian and German so that he could study the history of art in depth.

Here he was, trying to discover a way to earn more money to buy her gifts, while Mary was scheming and plotting behind his back. His articles were almost given away, newspapers and magazines paid such low rates. Where he made his money was through those summer jobs. Peerless Aristocratic Tours was not exactly generous. But the perks! His own idea entirely. Where he made his mistake was letting it slip out during one of his consultations with Edinburgh. He was lying there completely relaxed, talking his brain out, with an occasional probe from the doctor, and he'd let it slip.

First, Peter had got to him through his sister. Then Edinburgh. Closing his eyes to his relationship with Maria gave Edinburgh a further hold on him. It was another form of blackmail. Maria had been so loving and sweet to him to begin with. He couldn't exactly pinpoint the moment when he had realized she had also turned against him. Must have been something she had said, and which made him aware that Edinburgh must have told Maria what he himself had learned during that fateful session. Kershaw wondered how many psychiatrists breached the professional trust of confidentiality between doctor and patient. The majority of them, he'd bet!

It was a godsend, that teaching post at St. Justin's. It provided him with a retreat, a room where he could keep his art books. And he liked young Charles! It would have been much better, of course, if Mary had accepted her brother's bastard child and the lad could have lived with them at the cottage. He was a slow learner, progressed with the speed of a tortoise, but once he had learned, he didn't forget. That was something else again. When Charles learned what his guardian-teacher did during their thrice-weekly visits to London, he had tried some tricks on his own. Grossmith and Wurlitzer should never have given the lad those photographs. There were many blanks in his mind nowadays.

But those tour trips abroad, he could remember every detail. The galleries and art museums visited. The churches and cathedrals so richly endowed with altar pieces and other furnishings. The Hague, Rotterdam, Everdingen, Utrecht, Ghent, Bruges, Antwerp, and Amsterdam.

Edinburgh had suggested that they spread a rumor that he used these trips for smuggling drugs. Kershaw had been horrified at the suggestion. Then Peter got into the act. When they met in Amsterdam and Kershaw told him what Edinburgh had suggested, he had agreed it would provide wonderful cover. Tony the drug pusher. What better cover for Tony the thief!

It was now eleven-thirty. Tony Kershaw picked up his raincoat and suitcase and made his way toward Green Park. All around him he could hear the pulsating throb of passing traffic. It matched the throbbing within his head. The horses with their elegantly attired riders, two of them even riding sidesaddle, made him think of Stubbs, Herring, Munnings and that interesting lecture Cyrus Finnegan had delivered at the Reading University summer school, "The

Horse in British Art." How surprised Cyrus would have been had he known that one of his listeners had been enthralled by the torch with its indicator arrow.

As Kershaw entered the pedestrian subway at Hyde Park Corner, he recalled how offhand Cyrus had been with him on Friday at the private viewing. Looked right through him, as if he wasn't there. One by one, people were turning against him—his enemies were everywhere. Heaven forbid that Mrs. Winterhalter should turn against him also!

"Yes, sir, Mrs. Winterhalter checked out shortly after breakfast." The young lady cashier at the Savoy Hotel had personally receipted Mrs. Winterhalter's bill, for which she had used her Bank of America card. Her forwarding address was care of a postal box in New Britain, Connecticut. Her baggage, according to the hall porter, had been forwarded to the West London Air Terminal. Mrs. Winterhalter only had her handbag with her when she left. She had not taken a taxi. She had walked.

The assistant manager, who had just come on duty, checked with the housekeeper. The painters were at work redecorating Mrs. Winterhalter's suite. All the others on that floor had been done. They had been waiting for Mrs. Winterhalter's departure and had therefore scheduled the redecoration for after Wednesday. Her departure at an earlier date was most welcome. Mr. Finnegan could certainly take a look at the suite if he wished.

The furniture had been moved to the center of the room. Pictures and mirrors had been taken off the walls and, like the furniture, covered with dust sheets. It was the same in the bedroom. The bed hadn't been moved, but it had been stripped down to the mattress. The shelves and bathroom cupboard were empty. Even the tumblers had been taken away. The painters could swing their brushes and tilt their ladders; there was nothing for them to break.

Further along the corridor, a service cart was standing outside a door. A maid came out of one of the rooms and tipped the contents of a wastepaper basket into a plastic bag hanging from the side of her cart. She stared at Cyrus for a second, then picked up a bottle of Windex and a polishing cloth. She went back into the room and Cyrus followed her.

"I'm afraid you'll have to ask the housekeeper about that, sir." She was a pretty young creature. She spoke with an accent that might have been Swiss or Austrian. "All the trash is taken away by one of the men. They come every fifteen minutes or so to empty the garbage bags on our trolleys."

"Did you do that suite the men are painting?"

"Yes, sir."

"Did you notice anything unusual among the stuff the last occupant threw out?"

"Not that I can think of, sir. You'd better ask the housekeeper about that. We're not permitted to engage in conversation with strangers."

"But would the housekeeper have a record of what the guests leave for you to clean up?"

"I wouldn't know about that, sir. You'd better ask the housekeeper. Her office is on the sixth floor."

The housekeeper's office turned out to be a combination linen cupboard and sewing room. She herself was checking a pillowcase that had been torn across its middle.

"Beats me how some people manage to wreck everything. What sort of homes do they come from? Bet they don't treat their own pillows like this. Whole bottom's missing. Lower half, see?"

"Was that from the suite the men are redecorating?"

"It was. An American lady. She was sick over the weekend. Had to have her own nurse. But well enough to rip this thing apart."

"It would take some doing!" Cyrus examined the torn material. "I've never tried, but somehow I don't think I could manage it."

"A pigsty is a polite way of describing the mess some of our guests make of their rooms. Real horror stories, any hotel housekeeper could tell you of things we've seen that are beyond imagination." Suddenly, having given vent to her bitterness, the housekeeper became curious. "Did you know that lady, sir?"

"Yes."

"She was a good tipper, I'll say that for her. Me and the girls did very well out of her. But she was messy in her habits. Excuse me, sir, for commenting about one of your friends. I've no business to do so. It's just that I'm angry about the pillowcase."

"She was an acquaintance rather than a friend," Cyrus informed her. "We are involved in the same business, as it were. I am making some inquiries on behalf of the police. For the time being, they prefer to keep out of the way."

"What is it exactly you want, sir?"

"To rummage through that lady's trash."

"Rather you than me, sir." The housekeeper put her forefinger against her temple. "Nutty. That's what you must be, sir. But you realize you're too late. We can't have rubbish left lying around in the corridors. It would stink the place out. All downstairs in the subbasement. Probably outside in the containers by now."

"I'd still like to look."

"Then take the service lift to the subbasement and ask the back-door janitor. You'd better hurry. It might still be in one of the bags taken from this floor. Once it gets mixed up in the city's collector, you'd never sort it out."

Cyrus was in luck. There were thirty bags still inside the building. The janitor told him to help himself.

"Just put everything back inside each bag when you've found what you are looking for. Valuable ring, is it, sir? Found a Cartier necklace myself once. Worth seventy thousand I learned later. Owner gave me a five-shilling reward. I should have hung on to it and given it to my old lady to wear on Bingo nights."

It was in bag number seven. Dropped between the empty gin, brandy, and vermouth bottles were four sections of wooden stretchers, four two-by-two-inch color transparencies, and what remained of the canvas the stretcher had once supported. Cyrus unrolled the canvas and turned it face upwards. It was badly creased where it had been carelessly folded before being rolled, but the colors were unmistakable. They were the same colors as the paints in Charles's airline bag. A small section in the center of the canvas had been neatly removed. The edges of the hole were straight, as if meticulously cut along a ruler with a razor blade.

Cyrus pressed the surrounding impasto. It was still soft. Taking out his pocket magnifier, he peered intently at the surrounding areas at each corner of the hole.

"The clever bastard!" Painted into the impasto in such a way that they blended perfectly were four arrows. One dark pink, one green like a leaf, the third the color of a gloxinia stamen, the fourth arrow clay-red like a plant pot.

"Be a chum and put this trash back for me, will you." Before the janitor could answer, Cyrus handed him a fiver and ran upstairs, canvas and stretchers in his hand. He wondered what had become of the frame. Probably the janitor had it stashed away somewhere.

Mr. Brown was leaning against the Rolls, talking to another chauffeur wearing the same uniform.

"No sign of her, sir."

"Can't be helped." Cyrus climbed inside the car. "Back

225

to my flat, Mr. Brown. Sorry to have kept you waiting so long, but I got rather caught up. I've enjoyed driving with you very much."

"It's been a pleasure, sir."

Cyrus poured himself another glass of sherry. As the Rolls swung through Trafalgar Square, he raised his glass and toasted Admiral Nelson on his column.

"Here's the fuzz back again, your honor. This time you can bloody well cope. It's your job."

Mr. Gordon answered his wife's summons in his undershirt. His hair was tousled, his jaw covered with graying stubble, and his breath sour with the fumes of stale beer. On Monday morning, because he was on duty, he didn't go to the boozer till noon. The coppers were lucky to find him in. And a nice bit of whistlestop that one, he thought, eyeing Policewoman Helen Maitland. Uniform showed off her boobs nicely. But the specimen with her looked like a real meany. Could be a boxer or a wrestler. Probably a judo expert. They all were, these days. Even a high-tit dolly like this one. Karate, black belt, certainly. Better be civil. Don't want them trying their chop-chop round here.

"Yes. What d'you want? Are you the same fuzz that was bothering my missus about that artist bloke who got done in?" Mr. Gordon spat contemptuously on the steps that his wife had just finished scrubbing. She took pride in the entrance to the block of flats.

"You were here on Saturday afternoon, Mr. Gordon, or did you go to watch the soccer match?" Detective Sergeant Purvis was polite, yet firm. He would not tolerate rudeness with Helen present.

"Here. Upstairs. When I've had one over the eight, I usually nip into one of the empty flats and nip off. That way the missus doesn't see me. What she don't know about me don't hurt me, get it."

226

"We checked with the pubs you usually go to. Nobody remembers seeing you."

"Is that so?" Gordon was about to turn cocky, but thought better of it.

"Where were you?"

"Out shopping. Tomorrow's our anniversary. That old fart I'm married to thinks I wouldn't remember, but this year I did. I bought her a pair of glass cats at Woolworths. I've hidden them in the furnace room."

Policewoman Maitland smiled. "That was very thoughtful of you. And you weren't drinking?"

"Sure I was drinking. But not in my usual. Was in Kensington High Street. Got back here about four and lay down, after I'd hidden the cats in the furnace room."

"When did you come downstairs?" Funny how the policewoman was asking the questions.

"About five."

"Notice anything unusual?"

"Jesus! Why don't you coppers stop asking questions? My missus and I have had a bellyful of questions since Saturday night. Coppers here, questions at the boozer. Jesus!"

"We feel that in the excitement following the discovery of Doctor Edinburgh's murder, you may have forgotten something. Something out of the ordinary, which at the time you didn't pay much attention to."

"Like the doctor himself being here, do you mean? Never see him around. Usually only that young wop who lives in the flat, he's all I see, and his girl. Spends the night there sometimes, she does."

"Please think."

Blimey! The police skirt was appealing to him. Even so, he did his best to think back. He knew what they were after.

On the Saturday when the police first questioned him,

227

he had been too frightened to tell them about letting that fat American lady into the Doctor's flat. If he'd been sober, he would never have been so foolish. Once the management heard what he'd done, he'd be out on his arse as fast as a flying saucer. A master key was his most important badge of office, as valuable as the Lord Mayor's chain. It was only given to people who could be trusted not to abuse it. That's what he'd done. Abused his responsibility as a caretaker. Letting himself be hoodwinked, pretending it was a prank. Going along with her story that she wished to sneak in and surprise her dear old pal, the doctor. Known each other for years. Been one of his patients. Crap!

Well, better not hold out any longer. These coppers could smell a hole in a lump of cheese. No putting them off the scent, once they'd begun sniffing. Using his master pass key, for the sake of a few lousy quid. Mr. Smart. Right smart he'd been.

Well, he'd better tell what happened. He felt himself begin to sweat. From the armpits, across his belly, between his legs, across his cheeks perspiration oozed, as from a sponge. They'd book him! A bloody accomplice, that's the sort of goat he was! Book the wife too, probably.

While Mr. Gordon revealed what he had kept secret all weekend, Detective Sergeant Purvis wrote in his notebook. He was not surprised at what he heard. His only surprise was finding how long it took to obtain evidence that wasn't circumstantial, and how guilty some people looked when the moment of truth hit them between the eyeballs.

Gordon didn't particularly enjoy spilling the beans about one copper to another, but he had his own hide to save. That business with the master key would finish him. But all's fair in crime and law.

"That copper posted out back, an old timer he was, nipped into the pub for a half-pint while I was there. Didn't

228

spot me. Or, if he did, guess he wasn't thinking right. But it takes all sorts. Not that I'm saying he was 'bent' as the saying goes; just thirsty." Gordon chuckled. Not so hard after all to betray and turn a man in.

"You realize what you've just told me?" Purvis was shocked, knowing that if this were true, and Gordon wasn't bluffing, then his fellow officer would be kicked off the Force. Dismissed without pension, probably. He'd get the works, poor bugger.

"This is a serious accusation. God help you if you are just inventing this. I'll personally see you're chopped to bits."

"It's true, Gov. I ought to have spoke up sooner. Anyone familiar with the building could 'ave nipped in an' out smartly as Bob's me uncle!"

"I'll have to ask you to come with us. I'll want you to sign your statement, once it has been typed."

"Will I be charged?"

"That will be up to the inspector on duty. Put on your shirt and jacket. We'll wait. And don't try any tricks. Just tell your wife, and come quietly."

16

At two o'clock that Monday afternoon Superintendent Graham and Detective Sergeant Purvis arrived at Cyrus Finnegan's flat. He was on the phone.

"Thanks, Charlie. What did you say is the name of the curator? Joos van der Graaf. Yes, I know how to spell it. If KLM can't get you here, you'd better charter a plane. Tell your chief what's up, that it's an exclusive. We'll be at Heathrow when you get here. Ask for us at Security."

Cyrus Finnegan put down the receiver and lit a cigarette. His expression was grim.

"It's what I suspected. That was Charlie Averkamp. Dutch press bureau. Used to be subeditor with a paper over there. He's confirmed what I asked him on the telephone this morning. But we'll have to wait till the expert he's bringing with him gives his opinion. Meanwhile, I've something I want to show you. Any news of Kershaw?"

"Not a sign. General alert issued an hour ago." The super

nodded towards Helga. "She did a good job, Finnegan. Telephoned me as soon as Mrs. Winterhalter gave her the slip. She's undoubtedly told you about the air tickets. All three lines have her listed. She must be pretty damned confident to expect to get away with it. Playing us for suckers! Doesn't she realize that all we have to do is hold the plane she boards? And whom do you suppose she's taking with her? Helga said there were two passports. Kershaw. We'll grab both of them."

"I hope you're right, that there's no slipup." Cyrus watched Helga set up the projector and screen. She still looked a bit green and washed out. Stomach flu was the very devil. You were meant to rest, not exert yourself, and here she'd been following that Winterhalter creature. Probably taken that Colt .22 with her. He wouldn't try to find out. What was the point? He'd fixed it so that it wouldn't fire. "This could be a put-on, you realize that?"

"How?" It was the first time Purvis had spoken.

"Buying air tickets like that. Wouldn't cost her a penny, as long as she cancels them. She could be on her way to France by hydroplane. A bluff."

"And take Kershaw with her? She has his passport."

"We'll have to wait and see. I just don't like the way things are working out. Switch on the projector, Helga. Let's have a look at those transparencies."

Cyrus took his German flashlight from a drawer and pointed an arrow. "Spot anything, either of you?"

"Just blobs of color, like the other slides we found on the doctor's desk."

"Not quite. The others were also of different sections of the same painting. The still life of the gloxinia that Mrs. Winterhalter purchased. O.K.?"

"Shoot." Purvis and the super strained their eyes. They could see nothing except patterns of different colors. Blobs, as the super called them.

"Explain, damn it, man. What the hell are you trying to tell me and Purvis? More of your highbrow claptrap?"

"Look at the tip of the arrow. It's pointing at another arrow; only this is in color, not flashlight. Next three slides, Helga. Quickly. Four separate arrows, each different. Now switch off, and we'll look at what remains of Mrs. Winterhalter's picture."

Cyrus spread the canvas on the table. "Look carefully while I touch each arrow with the tip of my pencil. They were signals. They indicated where to cut."

"But why on earth cut the middle out of a picture?" The super was trying to calm down and make sense of what he was hearing.

"The section that has been removed was thickly painted impasto. You remember I showed it to you. You can see the rest of it on the remains of the canvas. It's my guess that the impasto was covering another painting. Something quite small. It could have been lightly glued to the other canvas, which would then be painted over. The trick would be to partly hold the hidden picture with impasto. Not long enough for the paint to harden. Just long enough to get it to its final destination. And now we come to the million-dollar question. What painting is so valuable that it is worth going to all this trouble and expense for? Flights across the Atlantic. First-class hotels."

"How did you guess about the arrows?"

"A hunch, Purvis. Simple as that. First clue, I suppose, was the fact that when we found Edinburgh, there were only sixteen photographs. I learned later that the film roll was for twenty; therefore, there must have been four other photographs that were missing. You were good enough to let me borrow the sixteen, after they had been dusted for fingerprints. I projected them, blew them up as far as I could without losing focus. They told me nothing. They were just different sections of Mrs. Winterhalter's picture.

I tried fitting them together from memory, after my visit to her hotel, and after I had looked at the painting again. It didn't work. But I did notice a couple of strokes which made me think of arrows. Very subtle painting. Looked accidental. A phone call to Wurlitzer at their house gave me the information I wanted. Kershaw had told them to photograph the canvas all over with overlapping shots, except for the very center. For this he wanted four separate shots. He watched over them while the photographs were being taken."

"Why didn't they just take one or two full views?"

"For a very obvious reason. In a single photograph, the arrows wouldn't have been visible, for quick identification."

"So when Mrs. Winterhalter visited Doctor Edinburgh's flat, she knew what to look for?"

"Possibly." Cyrus placed the canvas in the carrier bag and dropped in the four transparencies and pieces of stretcher as well. "My guess is that Edinburgh also knew what to look for. By the time Mrs. Winterhalter sneaked in on him, he had already separated the four arrow photographs and put them to one side. He was merely checking the others to see if there were any duplicates when she stabbed him."

"Callous! A monster." Purvis was flushed with anger. "And we let her slip out from under."

"But we don't know that, do we?" Cyrus tried to sound confident. "She's a monster, no doubt about that. So is her accomplice, whoever he is."

"Or accomplices," mumbled the super. "What are your views about Kershaw, Cyrus? Batty as a clapperboard?"

"According to Edinburgh's diagnosis, yes. But also quite brilliant. I think he's been doing this sort of thing for years and getting away with it. On his own. I think that once we catch up with him he'll start bragging. Same as Van Meergeren, who forged those Vermeers. He was extremely pleased and proud at being clever enough to fool so many experts. He'll talk. I think our present concern is that Mrs. Winterhalter doesn't get hold of him first! She'll either kill him or make use of him. Fifty-fifty which route she takes."

"Incredible." Superintendent John Graham was finally getting the picture in perspective. "How did you guess about the arrows, Cyrus?"

"I've already told you part of it. The second part happened this morning on my drive back to London from Twyford. I was letting my mind idle along in rhythm with the motor. Suddenly I was thinking about my lectures at summer school and how Kershaw, after one of them, I forget which, asked me about my torch. I told him they were in common use and gave him the name of the maker. Then flash! I thought of the faint arrows I'd seen in Mrs. Winterhalter's picture. Of course, it was a legitimate purchase. She had paid for it and had a receipt for cash payment, to show the customs. If she planned to take it back to the States with her, then she would have asked Edinburgh to have it crated and shipped to her later."

"Instead," Purvis cut in, "she decided to make a bolt for it today. No time to have it crated and too bulky to put inside her baggage. If she was only interested in the small section. You've suggested what probably happened next."

"Then what the devil is under that impasto, as you call it."

"For that, we must wait for Mr. Joos van der Graaf. He's curator at the Everdingen Museum."

"Isn't that the place where the Rembrandt was stolen? The one they got back."

"That's the place."

Helga, who had left the room after putting away the projector and portable screen, returned with three cups of steaming coffee. To each she had added a tablespoon of Tia Maria. The three men looked badly in need of a pick-me-up.

234

It was Superintendent Graham who produced a genuine nugget of information. He had visited the Peerless Aristocratic Car Hire and Continental Tours head office in Jermyn Street. He had inquired about one of the tour guides, Mr. Anthony Kershaw. Worked for their company off and on during the summer for seven years. Mostly in Holland, Belgium, and Italy. He had come to their notice through Mr. Peter Knowles, a director of the company and their overseas representative. In addition to his salary, Knowles was paid a commission on American clients who booked their vehicles with the company during their visits to Europe. Mr. Knowles hadn't visited England for a considerable time, though he had been in Holland two years ago and last year attended the Strasbourg Festival with his friends, Dr. and Mrs. Hans Edinburgh.

"Thought you'd like to know that," said the super, delighted at the surprised look on both their faces. "Any news of Maria?"

"Yes, sir. Policewoman Maitland visited her in hospital this morning, acting on my instructions." Sometimes Purvis couldn't help sounding pompous. "Made a quick recovery. She's taking Gee and Trudi back to Italy with her after Edinburgh's funeral."

"Did she deliberately swallow an overdose?" Cyrus recounted how he had seen Trudi give her stepmother the yellow pill, along with a cup of Ovaltine.

"Helen said that Maria was quite vague about what had happened. Seemed part dream, part reality. She thinks she may have dreamed that Kershaw came into her room either very late at night or early in the morning. He shook her shoulders and asked her what she had done with the photographs Edinburgh had taken from Charles's pocket. She didn't know anything about photographs. Kershaw slapped her quite hard. There was a bruise on her left cheek, which meant that she wasn't dreaming. Then he kissed her rather

235

roughly and suddenly knelt beside her bed. He was sobbing. Asking God to forgive him for betraying Mary. He blamed himself for everything having gone wrong. That he was responsible for Charles and Hans Edinburgh being killed. Maria thinks she fell asleep. Next thing she knew, Kershaw was leaning over her, stroking her hair. He had some pills in his hand. He also had a glass of milk. He was praying again, asking forgiveness and explaining to God that what he was doing was best for both of them. They both would be better off in the next world."

"Did she swallow the pills?" asked Cyrus.

"She remembers swallowing two of them." Purvis replied. "They made her feel sick. Her mind's a blank about from then on, till she awakened in hospital. Doesn't remember going there or how long Kershaw was in her bedroom."

"Then if he asked for the photographs, obviously he didn't know that Mrs. Winterhalter had taken them!" exclaimed the super. "When he puts two and two together he will know that Mrs. Winterhalter knows which section of the canvas to cut out. That she will not need him anymore. That she can cut the picture out herself and sell it. He won't get a penny for his efforts. The only thing he can do now is stick close and steal it back."

"I sincerely hope he doesn't try anything so foolish," said Cyrus. "It would be fatal."

Anthony Kershaw sat on a bench in Kensington Gardens. He was gazing at the statue of Peter Pan. Peter, the boy who didn't want to grow up. Kershaw had often felt like that. His thoughts turned to the other Peter, his brother-in-law.

Sixteen paintings had passed through their hands. He stole and Peter sold. It had been so easy. One always took the smallest. Security in many art museums was astonishingly lax—during the day, that is. At night it was different. Thieves were expected to strike at night, so one switched on the fancy electronic systems, the infrared and television scanners, and went to sleep. It took a genius like himself to rumble that one. Mix in with crowds. Be a tour guide and bring your own crowd with you. Give them a free period to roam about on their own and get mixed in with the other visitors. That was the time he liked best. It was a challenge. It was a thrill. He made friends with the customs at the different borders by giving an occasional tipoff. Had to be very discreet, but favors granted usually meant favors received. He could count on the fingers of one hand the times his minibus had been inspected. Nowadays, with terrorists on the loose, the inspections and searches were pretty thorough. There were metal detectors, baggage searches, body frisking. The once friendly customs officers were not quite so friendly, the less so when there was a security agent close by. These security people were quite unlike the rest of the human race. They were hawks. They could do as they bloody well liked, and often did. Probably they could shoot you if they didn't like the color of your hair and get away with it after an official hushed-up inquiry.

Kershaw was quite content to leave the selling to Peter. Not this time, however. This was different. This was big. It called for teamwork, a scheme of total deception. It required capital, and this the Edinburghs had provided. Or so it had seemed at first, until Maria told him about Grossmith and Wurlitzer. Well, that was their worry, not his.

This last theft was the most dangerous of all and gave him the opportunity of trying his hand at something he had studied but never actually done. It had taken him two years. If the picture had been bigger, he'd have given up. Charles had made the stretchers for all the canvases in the school workshop. He had a green thumb and a steady hand and eye for carpentry. Charles fetched and carried. Charles ordered the paints and went to the post office to pick up the parcels when they arrived. It was Charles who kept him company during those boring journeys by train and who was posted guard at the flat.

Kershaw also bought a very old painting at a country auction because the canvas was more or less what he needed. He ought not to have let Charles see what he was doing with that old piece of canvas and the hand-ground pigments. No harm in the lad watching him paint those abstractions. He allowed him to try painting one of his own, but the lad was hopeless. Still, it had given him an idea about the exhibition. Hans Edinburgh was enthusiastic, and between them they wrote press releases and spread the word in the proper circles, that there was a new painter who would soon be holding his first one-man exhibition.

Then Charles outsmarted himself and just about ruined everything for everyone. He'd been present when Grossmith and Wurlitzer were photographing the pictures; all of them, including the gloxinia. Charles hadn't actually seen him applying the heavy impasto and carefully placing the arrows. He must have guessed that there was something special about the painting of the gloxinia. It was the only picture he hadn't been allowed to handle. Kershaw had done the framing, had supervised the photography and delivered it personally to the Princess Gallery. So Charles stole the photographs. He tried to sell them to Edinburgh, who had shouted at him and slammed the door in his face. When Charles had brought the gloxinia plant round to the gallery on Friday morning, he had tried to sell the photographs to him as well. The lad had been thoroughly unpleasant to deal with. Spiteful, foulmouthed, threatening, refusing to hand over the photographs. When the Edinburghs arrived to take them both out to lunch, Charles had turned his back and walked out of the room.

At least he had brought the gloxinia. Only a genius would

have thought of that one, Tony congratulated himself. When Tony and Peter had last spoken on the transatlantic phone, he'd told Peter about his plan. Peter had refused to tell him whom he was sending over to buy the painting. He might come himself. This person had been told to buy a painting of a plant. The plant displayed in the gallery would indicate which one. Brilliant, said Peter, and Kershaw had agreed with him.

Tony Kershaw looked at his watch. It was time to make his way to the West London Air Terminal for the bus to Heathrow. He touched the painting under his cardigan. It was still there. He wouldn't give it back to her. After all, she was only an intermediary between himself and Peter. The final settlement would have to be made in New York. Peter had always been understanding and cooperative in the past. He'd dealt with him fairly. He just hoped that Peter hadn't turned against him, like everyone else.

Mrs. Winterhalter's feet hurt. Her Madison Avenue shoes were fine on the sidewalks of New York. They were a disaster in Epping Forest. Epping Woods was more like it. It had hardly any trees, compared with forest back home in New England. She'd expected to see Robin Hood and his merry men, then remembered that they haunted Sherwood Forest. The town of Epping itself she quite enjoyed.

Her pub lunch was everything she could have wished her last meal in England to be. Mulligatawny soup, potted shrimp, smoked salmon, pork-pie-with-mayonnaise salad, rice pudding, Stilton and water biscuits, washed down with three tankards of Guinness. Some of the other customers had stared at her. She didn't mind. She was accustomed to it.

She was feeling slightly lightheaded as she made her way to the ladies room. Outside in Epping High Street she continued to be cautious. If she saw a policeman, or one of their cars, those funny little minis, she would dodge into a doorway. She even entered one or two shops to get out of their way. The underground seemed the fastest way back to the West End. Or perhaps she should take a taxi all the way to the West London Air Terminal? It would be safer. Less chance of her being spotted. It was already past two o'clock. She was limping now, quite painfully. By the time she found a taxi she was almost back where she had started, at the underground. Two policemen and a policewoman stood near a newsstand. As she boarded her taxi, she saw that the police were looking at her. As she drove away, they resumed their conversation.

It was two ten already. She had wasted a full ten minutes. It had been at ten minutes past two during the night when Kershaw had telephoned. Stupid ass. Asking her if she knew where he could find the photographs. They were his own photographs. He'd paid for them. Not only that, he was asking her to return the picture. Wanted to buy it back. Said that there's been a mistake. That the signal plant should have been an azalea. That she'd bought the wrong painting.

"Then why the hell do you want to buy it back?"

That had stopped him. Almost. He was still in Hampstead and was expected to sleep on the settee in Edinburgh's sitting room. On and on he went; the man was raving. A lunatic! Mrs. Winterhalter found herself very wide awake indeed. This man was dangerous. Unless she could calm him down, get through to him somehow, he might give the whole show away.

"You can't possibly come here now," she heard herself saying. "You'd better keep away from the hotel. Not safe."

"Why not?" he was asking. "You haven't done anything wrong, have you? I'm the one who is evil."

"How come? You been a bad boy?" She must try and jolly him along. He talked for half an hour about all the people who were plotting against him. He even feared for his life. Everywhere he went, he could feel eyes watching him. Then she hit on the solution.

"Let's meet in the morning, early? Alongside Cleopatra's Needle. It's that kooky obelisk on the Embankment. Say, eight o'clock sharp."

"Why should I meet you? Are you trying to trick me?"

"For Pete's sake! Get a hold of yourself." She could hear him breathing.

"You want to kill me, too?" he said.

For a second her heart fluttered. Surely he couldn't have guessed. Who would ever suspect her?

"I don't get it. Why do you think I've killed somebody?"

"I didn't mean that. Sorry. I'm a little confused."

"I'll say." He sounded normal again. "Eight o'clock. I've got something to give you, then I'll explain what you and I are going to do. And bring your passport. Or haven't you..."

"I always carry it with me. Never know when I'm off on another tour."

So she had given him the cut-out section of the painting and told him they would fly to New York that evening. Peter Knowles would meet both of them at J.F.K. She hadn't intended to tell him that Peter was her fourth husband. It would be worth it, however, just to see the shocked expression on his idiot face.

He'd better be there at the terminal. He'd better have the picture with him, otherwise she'd track him to the ends of the earth.

241

17

Since the terrorists, all the fun has gone out of airports. Most observation decks are closed. Windows are bricked in. One has no idea how many planes are on the tarmac. How many are landing and taking off. How many stacked. There are lineups everywhere. The air is charged with frustration and rage. Names are told to report here and yonder, under the green light, at the information desk. It is all one huge jamboree of let's get the hell out of here. What's the holdup, buster? Another flight canceled. Why put up with all the inconvenience. Better if the whole world were grounded.

Mrs. Winterhalter and her companion stood in line. They had introduced themselves at the bus terminal. Kershaw. Winterhalter. Flying to New York, are you? Mrs. Winterhalter needed a double seat to herself. She sat next to the window. Tony Kershaw squeezed in beside her. Just.

From her seat at the rear of the bus, Helga had watched

the scene with satisfaction. That was the woman all right. She remembered Kershaw coming to the flat once to ask Cyrus for advice about an art criticism he was writing for *The Observer*. In the lineup at Pan Am, Helga stood a few paces behind them. Very slightly, she inclined her head. A plainclothesman took note of her signal and took the escalator up to the departure lounge.

Mrs. Winterhalter was not going to argue. Kershaw could hang onto his picturn for all she cared. It would be quite handy having him carry it through customs when they got to the other side. This was a direct flight. All the same, she felt uncomfortable. The man's nerves were in a shocking state. His hands trembled so much that she was afraid he'd give the whole show away when he handed his ticket to the girl who allocated seats and issued a boarding pass. Mrs. Winterhalter had had to give him back his passport. She'd get it back from him later, once they'd cleared immigration. It was her insurance against one small painting valued in six figures.

There was another wait. They passed the second barrier, where they were asked their nationality, their destination, how much English currency they had on them. Simple straightforward questions asked so nonchalantly that one wondered whether anybody listened to the answers.

"Where were you born, madam?"

"Nebraska. U.S.A."

"Where do you normally reside?"

"New Britain, Connecticut."

"Thank you, madam. Enjoy your flight."

Kershaw had no difficulty either. They walked toward the duty-free shop. Kershaw bought cigarettes and a bottle of Dimple Haig for himself. She bought a couple of neckties, a Dunhill lighter, and a bottle of Rémy-Martin for Peter. They paid at the checkout, then sat in two uncomfortable plastic chairs to await the calling of their flight.

Only little children seemed happy in airports. They could run and shriek, watched glumly by their parents. So simple. So easy. In a few more minutes they would board the airport bus that would take them to their plane. Mrs. Winterhalter looked forward to her glass of champagne.

"Mrs. Winterhalter?"

"That's right." She looked up to see who was addressing her and got the shock of her life. She was staring into the unblinking eyes of Detective Sergeant Purvis. The young policewoman at his side looked as though she meant business also.

"And Mr. Kershaw? What are you doing here, sir? Are you also flying to America." Purvis didn't expect a reply, and didn't get one. Kershaw clutched his cardigan and stood up. "Will you both follow me, please. There's some query about your luggage."

"But it's been cleared downstairs. I don't have to open it till I get to the States. You just don't search baggage belonging to U.S. citizens when they leave England. You've got a nerve. Our flight is due out any minute."

"Don't worry, madam. They'll hold the plane if we ask them to. That is, if everything is aboveboard."

"For Christ's sake!"

It was all pretense, she realized that. Play-acting, so as not to attract the attention of the other travelers. Well, she'd go along with it, act out her part. They could search her baggage, tear out the linings, rip everything apart. They would find nothing on her.

They seemed to be walking forever. Her feet ached. They were leaden. With total naturalness, the policewoman had fallen into step at her side. Purvis had done the same with Kershaw.

Her baggage was certainly there. It had been placed unopened on a low counter. Kershaw's suitcase was there

244

also. There were people everywhere, and none of them were smiling.

She saw Superintendent Graham and that nice Mr. Finnegan. There were a policeman in uniform and two inspectors from Her Majesty's customs. The other men, whom Mrs. Winterhalter thought were either Dutch or German, were standing next to Mr. Finnegan. Beyond them was the Scandinavian woman who had followed her that morning. With the young policeman on her left and Sergeant Purvis standing alongside Kershaw on her right, Mrs. Winterhalter realized that she had been trapped. All she could do now was to bluff her way out. She felt it would be pretty useless, but worth trying.

"What the hell's happening?" She fired her question at Superintendent Graham.

"You are being held for questioning, madam, in connection with our inquiries into the circumstances of the late Doctor Edinburgh's death. I warn you that anything you say may be recorded and possibly used in evidence at a later date. You are at liberty to remain silent. You have permission to telephone your embassy and obtain the services of a lawyer. Meanwhile, I have a warrant for your arrest."

"You can't get away with this. I'll sue. I'll throw the book at you. I'm an American citizen and I demand my rights."

"I've already explained those rights to you, Mrs. Winterhalter. Do you wish to telephone your embassy?"

"I sure do. Get me the ambassador."

Tony Kershaw had been listening to Superintendent Graham. He knew his nerves would not hold out much longer. He must get out of here. Just long enough to get rid of the painting. Silently he counted to three, then dashed towards the door. To reach it, he had to pass between the counter and Finnegan's housekeeper. Helga made a slight movement with her hand, at the same time lifting her knee.

245

Kershaw toppled forward, his shoulder feeling the full impact of her hand. Her knee gouged him in the groin. Kershaw fainted.

"I'd almost forgotten how to do that," Helga said to no one in particular.

The policewoman was attending to Kershaw. She unbuttoned his collar and undid the buttons of his cardigan. Gingerly, she removed the package he was carrying. She untied the length of ribbon Mrs. Winterhalter had used to prevent the picture from slipping out of the pillowcase.

"Is this what we've been looking for?" Helen Maitland gave the painting to Cyrus Finnegan.

"I don't know. Let's find out. Let's give it to Mr. Joos van der Graaf. He's the expert. Got your camera with you, Charlie? We'd better keep a record of this, step by step."

Charlie Averkamp didn't have one camera, he had two of them and an electric flash.

Joos worked slowly. From his briefcase he took a pack of orange sticks, cotton, and several squat bottles filled with solvents and turpentine.

Kershaw was barely conscious. A St. John's Ambulance Service first-aid man had been sent for and had covered the shivering figure with a blanket. Kershaw stared at the ceiling. He realized that all of his enemies had caught up with him, that this was final. For a second he thought of his wife, Mary. He didn't care what happened to her, to himself, or anyone else.

Joos van der Graaf was the same age as his friend, Charlie Averkamp. He was in his early thirties. People were always surprised to see such delicate hands on such a large man. Hands covered with freckles, like his face. His red hair was close-cropped, like a shaving brush. He was a trained conservator, with a degree in art history from the University of Utrecht. He had done postgraduate work in London at the

246

Courtauld Institute and three years conservation and restoration study with the Louvre. It took him thirty minutes to apply the weak solvent solutions and remove the impasto. He didn't dare take the cleaning any further. He would take the canvas back to the lab, where he had the proper equipment and temperature control. In the stuffy atmosphere of Heathrow, the picture might be further damaged, though from what he had seen, whoever had painted on the impasto knew what he was doing. The overpainting was lightly applied and easily removed. None of the paints used would react adversely on the original.

"Your verdict?" Finnegan was speaking.

"It's our Everdingen Rembrandt all right."

"But you got it back." Superintendent Graham had never watched anything so unbelievable. Under the horrid blobs of paint was a most exquisite self-portrait.

"Are you sure this is the original?"

"It's the original, Mr. Graham. When my director sees it, he will make a public announcement. What we got back was a clever copy, but it lacked something."

"Quality?" the superintendent suggested.

"That, and the mark of genius." Mr. Van der Graaf lifted the painting and gently slid it between two sheets of rice paper. He had a small, flat case to carry it in. "As soon as Charlie Averkamp telephoned and gave me the dimensions, I knew that you people were on the right track."

"But it's so small."

"Small but still Rembrandt." Charlie grinned at Cyrus.

"Although I'm an authority, I couldn't believe that Rembrandt ever painted on such a small scale. I arranged to bring Joos over so that he could inspect the canvas on the spot. But first I checked The Hague and learned that they had a self-portrait by Rembrandt they'd only recently acquired and about which I knew nothing. It is eleven-and-three-quarters by eleven-and-three-eighths inches. We're perpetually in your debt, Cyrus. We're indebted to all of you. I suppose we should be thankful that whoever was responsible for this outrage knew enough about chemistry and art not to do any permanent damage."

Sergeant Purvis and Policewoman Maitland were only half watching this exchange. They had their eyes on Mrs. Winterhalter, who had been allowed to sit down. Neither of them liked her color, and when she began to cough, bending forward as though she had cramps in her stomach, Helen Maitland realized that this was probably a more serious attack than usual. The woman could barely breathe. Her features were inflamed. Helen moved to her side.

"Somebody fetch her a glass of water! Please!"

Mrs. Winterhalter had never experienced pains quite as sharp as these. Her chest ached, her heart pounded and thumped, and she felt her eyes clouding. Once more everybody was looking at her, except Kershaw, the damned fool, who was sound asleep and snoring. Serve the bastard right!

She'd made a proper balls of this. No doubt about that. Somebody brought her a glass of water. It was tepid. There was no ice. She coughed again, and this time the attack seemed to help her eyesight. She could see the two Dutchmen shaking hands with the superintendent and nice Mr. Finnegan. They were in a hurry to take their goddamned Rembrandt back to Holland. Good riddance! Mrs. Winterhalter knew this meant that once again Superintendent Graham and his Sergeant Purvis would be turning their attention on her. They had produced a warrant for her arrest. Well, the embassy would soon fix that bit of nonsense! There had been no witnesses.

But there had been! That wino of a janitor! Probably been too pissed to remember clearly what she looked like. God, how he reeked. Stank to high heaven.

That had been downright careless. She should have ta-

248

ken care of him at the time. Wouldn't have been difficult—
just a second to crack his skull.

But of course, Peter had been so right, anticipating this
moment. He knew all along she wouldn't let herself get
caught. Not nice. Not nice at all to know one had been
involved in something as distasteful as wife disposal. And
one never knew. Each State seemed to have its own ideas
about the death penalty. Jesus! She'd swallow that pill,
whatever the consequences.

"You'll have to come with us now, Mrs. Winterhalter."
Sergeant Purvis and the uniformed policeman raised her by
her arms. Mr. Finnegan and the superintendent were
talking together in the far corner. Now they were listening
to the Scandinavian lady. They all looked very serious.

And so they should, arresting her on suspicion of murder
when they couldn't prove a damned thing. Another coughing attack was on its way. Perhaps now was the time to take
the small white pill Peter had given her back in New York.
Was it only a week ago?

They had not taken her handbag. Not yet. She undid the
clasp. The pill was attached with Scotch tape just inside the
little pocket where she kept her car keys.

"Looking for something?" It was that nosy sergeant
again. How she hated him!

"My Kleenex. That's what I'm looking for."

"Let me help you. Take one of mine." It was the policewoman, doing her best to be kind to her.

"I'm O.K., thanks. I've got one."

Mrs. Winterhalter held the pill between her thumb and
forefinger, hidden behind her Kleenex. She was about to
put the pill in her mouth when a sudden spasm of coughing
made her drop it. She saw it roll across the floor. She saw
Mr. Finnegan pick it up and give her a most peculiar look.

This time the pain in her chest was unbearable. Is this a

249

heart attack, she wondered. Am I going to die? Mrs. Winterhalter tried to say something. Somehow she must get word through to Peter. She knew her words had no sound to them, that her head was bursting, and liquid filled her throat.

Mrs. Winterhalter grabbed at the two policemen on either side of her and dropped dead at their feet.

Epilogue

Peter Knowles sat in a comfortable seat in Amtrak's club
bar. He was enjoying himself. It was his first trip across the
U.S. by rail, and he was headed for San Francisco.

It had taken six months in probate to settle his wife's
estate. Larry Grossmith had looked after the funeral arrangements. Her ashes had been delivered the following
week to their Connecticut home, where Peter had scat-
tered them on the lawn. Hadn't he warned her to take care
of her health, to weight-watch? At least the cause of death
was natural. He wondered what had happened to her pill,
for it was not in her handbag when her personal effects were
gone through.

Peter Knowles naturally hadn't gone to her funeral.
Larry had telephoned him and advised him not to, because
Tony Kershaw had squealed. The police knew all about the
sixteen works of art that Tony had stolen and their disposi-
tion. Five had been sold by Messrs. Grossmith and Wur-

litzer; the other eleven had been handled by Peter himself. There was a possibility that if he flew to England, his stay there might be stretched—to as much as ten years. Larry and Morrie were themselves expecting a visit from the police any day now, and when Tony Kershaw was released from the violent ward of the county psychiatric hospital, he would come up for sentencing for theft and forgery. Served him bloody well right. He'd signed Rembrandt's signature!

Mary had written, enclosing the bill for the lad's funeral. Her parents had settled this, and she had had the gall to ask him to reimburse them. The hell he would! If they'd used their noggins, they'd have had Charles buried at public expense. He didn't want to see Mary again, either. All the more so after he had read the postscript to her scrawl, which said that she was willing to wait and take Tony back, to start over again, if he would come. Holy cow! Fancy having her for a sister!

So it was all over? So what! It was time for a change anyway. A pity that the Everdingen Rembrandt had been lost. A client in Uruguay had agreed to pay $750,000 cash, with no questions asked about the picture's provenance.

Peter had enjoyed hearing from Larry Grossmith. He wrote lengthy, informative letters. His descriptions of Cyrus Finnegan and that superintendent delighted him because of their sarcasm and wit. Perhaps Larry would get an opportunity in prison to take a course in creative writing. He was a natural, a real ding-a-ling. Peter was sorry when the letters suddenly stopped coming. He could see a cowboy mounted on a palamino; was this Texas or Colorado? He was again thinking about his wife, and the huge fortune she had left him. That, when added to his profits after taxes and expenses, made him a very wealthy man. It softened the blow of having a wrench thrown into the works by that bloody fool Kershaw. How that man changed through the years! Like Edinburgh and Larry and Morris, he'd been too greedy.

Peter himself had changed also. These days he wore a trim Van Dyck beard. His graying hair was shaped like that of an Elizabethan pageboy.

With money, one doesn't have to make plans for survival. Thus Peter was free to roam the world. He had no idea how long he would stay in San Francisco. He had been told it was a beautiful place, and corrupt. His sort of city. Afterwards, he might try the Far East or Latin America. He would like to take up residence in a country that had no extradition treaty with England or the U.S. But that wasn't a plan, it was just something to look into.

As Mr. John Brown, a gentleman with substantial credit references, he looked forward to a happy future. Peter had the attendant bring him another Bloody Mary. Well named, he thought. He gave the man a dollar tip. Some people have all the luck, and he was one of them. Some people get away with murder. He was one of them, too!

Through the window he noted that the train was now crossing the most arid desert he had ever seen. The train, a shining metal caterpillar dwarfed under a giant dome of blue, the horizon unshifting in the distance. Peter, despite the coolness in the air-conditioned club car, began to sweat. The rhythmic drone of the wheels on track provided a whispered background to his very troubled thoughts.

One thing could be counted on when it came to Scotland Yard, and the F.B.I. too, for that matter: tenacity. They'd never let go. They'd follow leads and track him to the end, and what an end that might be. Certainly violent. He would not allow himself to be taken. Never!

What was happening to him now was respite. Borrowed time. He felt that he could count on Larry and Morrie not to betray him. When they had done their stint in prison, with time off for good behavior, they would re-establish contact with him. Next time around they'd switch form, leave the art market and concentrate on furniture, or china, or even postage stamps. They'd do something. The world would always be full of suckers and easy money.

But could he really count on them? If, on the other hand, Superintendent Graham, or that interfering busybody, Finnegan, came up with a deal or forced, yes forced, a confession out of the lads, then that would alter the situation. It certainly would change it completely. Even so, the police would still have to catch up with him.

And Tony Kershaw? Well, Tony had gone bonkers. Kaput. Off his rocker with terror. He always had been a weakling. Mary was a bit of a weakling herself, always kowtowing to her parents and to others.

Peter toyed with the idea of having a third Bloody Mary. Instead he walked through to the adjacent dining car. And, as he held the menu in his hand, rather like a mirage out there in desert, by some trick of mind and eye a single word momentarily flashed into focus. An extremely unpleasant word. Interpol!

Not a nice thought at all if one looked back across his past. Just as good as giving Superintendent Graham a thousand extra arms and accompanying brains. The workings of Interpol were not always infallible, though, especially if one were artful, and a good dodger, like himself.

And as he concentrated on the menu offerings he thought back, almost sorrowfully, but not quite, to the splendid meals he and Mrs. Winterhalter, the second Mrs. Knowles, had enjoyed together in so many first-class restaurants. What a superb glutton she had been, a masterpiece of avarice and greed. Not like the first Mrs. Knowles, who had been a nibbler. But she also had served her purpose, until she'd mistaken the cyanide for aspirin.

He could picture only too clearly Mrs. Winterhalter's

254

expression as she helped him carry the weighted body and topple it into Lake Michigan. Puffing and quite out of breath she'd been, and scared. From then on, like some minor form of blackmail, he could make her do anything he wanted.

He ordered his lunch with a half bottle of California champagne. "To absent friends!" he toasted silently, downing the entire contents of the glass and refilling it.

As he looked through the window, waiting for the first course to be served, he made a decision. He would get off the train before it arrived at Los Angeles, rent a car, and drive to San Francisco.

It was really rather uncomfortable, this feeling that somebody, Graham or Finnegan, for example, might be watching him; looking over his shoulder, as it were, in mid-desert.

But Peter had no doubt that he would become accustomed to it. He never gave it a second thought.